A

KILLING
Climate

THE COLLECTED MYSTERY STORIES

ERIC WRIGHT
(Photograph by Richard Kuzniak)

A

KILLING
Climate

THE COLLECTED MYSTERY STORIES

ERIC WRIGHT

Crippen & Landru Publishers
Norfolk, Virginia
2003

Cover and dust jacket painting by Barbara Mitchell

Cover and dust jacket design by Deborah Miller

Crippen & Landru logo by Eric D. Greene

ISBN: 1-885941-86-2 (limited edition)
ISBN: 1-885941-87-0 (trade edition)

FIRST EDITION

Crippen & Landru Publishers
P. O. Box 9315
Norfolk, VA 23505
USA

E-mail: info@crippenlandru.com
Web: www.crippenlandru.com

For Peters Sellers
Who provided the first home for many of these stories

Table of Contents

Introduction

Most courses in Creative Writing that I've experienced start by teaching the short story on the assumption that it is the form that is most accessible to the beginner. This is a mistake; short stories are much harder to write than novels. You can begin writing a novel without a clear idea of where it will take you, and even write a chapter or two before you commit yourself. James Thurber once wrote a nice parody of an extreme form of this kind of writing called "Bateman Comes Home," in which nothing happens while a group of characters are sitting on a stoop, talking in dialect, waiting for Bateman. The piece ends, or rather stops, followed by the words, "If you carry on long enough it turns into a novel."

Thurber was making fun of the new gothic novels coming out of the rural South, but there is a truth here about the difference between the novel and the short story; you can't write a short story without having a solid idea of where you are going and how long it will take you because there is nowhere to hide in a short story while you are figuring out what it is about. This, as well as its length, makes it different from the novel, and harder to start, at least. Thus, although I enjoy reading them very much, I have written fewer stories than I have novels. Even if the market were stronger, as it seems to be becoming lately, I do not think I would have written many more than I have.

Most of the stories in this collection are occasional in the sense that they were written on request, on the occasion of someone putting together an anthology, usually. Those in the largest group were written for the Canadian anthology *Cold Blood* which has appeared five times so far. Here I must acknowledge the industry of Peter Sellers who, in creating that anthology, became, though not in the usual sense, very much the father of the Canadian short crime story, for without *Cold Blood* so many Canadian stories would not have been written. Some others of mine were generated at the request of other anthologists in Canada, the U.S., and Britain. The remainder were commissioned by newspapers and magazines, in Canada and Europe, except for a couple that were written for this collection.

It seems to me that the short story can conveniently be thought about as a kind of fiction that has grown out of two roots. The first is usually identified with Chekhov, the sort of story that once might have been a sketch, written to fill a space in a newspaper, a character study, or small observation about the passing scene. With the addition of a narrative element the modern short story arrived, still from Chekhov, today producing the wonderful stories of William Trevor, to name just one master. Commonly this kind of story aims for an epiphany (it is James Joyce's term), sometimes by a discovery at the end, a turning on of the light, as it were, although in the hands of a master, we feel the epiphany almost from the beginning.

The other kind of story has its origin in the anecdote, the story in which the narrative is all, including the surprise ending. Many critics locate the beginnings of this sub-genre in the tales of Boccaccio, but the type is older than that. Nevertheless, whatever literary antiquarians put forward as the earliest examples of this form, it is O. Henry who matters most in the history of the short crime story, while we can appreciate that he was not the only one writing like this. De Maupassant's "La Parure", for example, is a perfect O. Henry story, written before O. Henry got going and probably never read by O. Henry himself.

The O. Henry story does not deal in epiphanies. There is nothing subtle, or profound, or elusive about the core of an O. Henry story, the meaning, which is all in the ending, the famous "twist." This type became ubiquitous in English fiction so that fifty years ago (the last time I looked) handbooks on creative writing were warning students to avoid the O. Henry ending at all costs. The device had created too much formula fiction and the public wanted something else, something more realistic and true to life. So the Chekhovian story came to seem superior, more literary, than its neater cousin. At the same time, it didn't always replace the surprise ending with anything else as strong, and these stories sometimes seem to be returning to their roots in the sketch, rendering them elusive and unsatisfying, one reason why the short story declined in popularity and began to disappear into literary magazines. Lately it is returning, given a boost by the production of tapes to be listened to in cars, although the new anthologists who put these tapes together rarely seem to commission new, original stories.

The first story in this collection, "Licensed Guide", was written ten years ago for an anthology, *Criminal Shorts* of which I was co-editor. The setting is a fishing camp where I worked as a guide in 1957, thirty-five years before the story got written. The framing incident took place in a schoolroom in England in 1942. I had wanted to write about this incident for fifty years and then the two experiences came together in my mind to form this story. While I hope the ending is a sufficient surprise, the thing I most wanted to capture was the world of the fishing guide in late August when the Eden he found in May has turned into the fallen world where the sun has been shining too long, the fisherman have turned into predators, and it is time to leave.

"The Boatman" is my favourite of this collection. The first version was written five years ago and has undergone a number of changes before emerging in its present form. It began as a story requested by *Descant*, a Canadian literary magazine. At the time, I was beginning to shape my memoir, *Always Give a Penny to a Blind Man* of which the substance of this story was to form a chapter, and when *Descant* called, I thought I would see if the story could stand alone, and I rewrote it in the third person, which is how the magazine published it. For the memoir, I returned it to the first person, making some minor changes. The version here is again slightly changed to put it back into a rounded story form.

"One of a Kind" grew out of an incident involving a character I came across in Fort Churchill, an army camp on the Hudson's Bay. In 1951, I spent a vivid year in Canada's near north, and I have often tried to reach back to it for material for stories, but the experience resisted being turned into fiction until recently. "One of a Kind" concerns a cribbage board carved from whalebone by a janitor in a construction camp during the building of the Distant Early Warning line in the fifties. Again, the theft of the board was no more than the plot that allowed me to write about what really interested me, the hostile environment, the atmosphere in the camp when the theft was discovered—so much like the barrack room in *Beau Geste*—, and the unsavoury janitor made passionate by his carving, and destroyed by its loss.

"Twins" was written on a dare. I had some time on my hands and I had always wanted to challenge Father Knox's list of things that you can no longer put into a crime novel. I chose "twins" (Fr. Knox cites male twins, but my example is trickier than that) because as I brooded over the list I recalled an image from a transatlantic steamship crossing, a memory of two Australians, a husband and wife, who were travelling the world. They were small, very fit with similar haircuts and identical clothes—denim jackets, blue jeans, sweatshirts printed with a map of Australia, and trainers. She had wider hips, but otherwise they looked alike from the other end of the boat deck. I wrote the story for Elizabeth Walter, the editor of the Collins Crime Club, who recognised the challenge I was trying to meet. The story has since become a favourite of anthologists who are putting together a text for the high schools, being included in five different collections.

"Two in the Bush" is in the tradition of the comic caper story. Thanks to the quality of writers, like Donald Westlake, comedy is very much a part of the crime fiction scene, although it is still a minor part. This may be because, as Edward G. Robinson is reported to have said, "Dying is easy; comedy is hard." The mode of comedy has much in common with crime fiction; in both, the plot is very important as is the discovery at the end. Northrop Frye, Canada's greatest literary critic, once observed, pithily but inaccurately, that melodrama (for which substitute 'thrillers') is "comedy without humor." He also said that "in the melodrama of the brutal thriller we come as close as it is normally possible for art to come to the pure self-righteousness of the lynching mob." (Against this we have to set the recent revelation in his just-published diaries that all his life an important minor pleasure was the reading of thrillers). But if you put humour back into the thriller, does it then become what Frye called, in the Theory of Modes, Comedy? Probably.

The next three stories grow out of my experiences on the Hudson's Bay, although all of them were written long after I left that world.

"The Duke" is the only story here that was not written on demand. I had come across the camp cook almost immediately after I arrived in Fort Churchill, when as job timekeeper, responsible for the tiny office, I was given the privilege of eating with the foremen. I was very aware of the strange, not-quite-human figure behind the steam table. I became aware that he had finally, perhaps, found a role and a home that would allow him to function with satisfaction in his work and pride in himself. Then along came his tormentor and thus, after forty years, my story. I wrote two-thirds of the story, put it away, then, on a Thanksgiving Sunday during a Bouchercon conference in Toronto recently, Liza Cody and Michael Lewin came to dinner at my house and afterwards asked me to submit a story to *2nd Culprit*, a new anthology they were editing, and I finished "The Duke."

"Kaput" was intended to show the kind of violence that a combination of long winter nights and the monastic life of a construction camp in the north could foster. The central incident of the brawl in the sergeants' mess was something I observed, as was the ferocity of the arctic storm. The serendipitous likeness of 'Kaput' and 'Capote' was waiting for me when I began the story. The rest was a matter of getting people dressed in the right costumes.

The last of the three, "Caves of Ice," was written with this anthology in mind though published first in *Ellery Queen's Mystery Magazine*. The story was created from two elements. I was a very young twenty-two and fresh from England when I landed in Fort Churchill, and I looked and sounded like a classic greenhorn. I was certainly the recipient of some very tall stories, which the locals trotted out for new arrivals from the big city. The idea of building a dock in winter by shaving down the ice until a space was cleared was told to me by an old steam-fitter with a glint in his eye. I did not know then and I don't know now if he was pulling my leg. The small group of sailors doing something mysterious behind the locked doors of a hut on the shore of the Bay was also something I took away with me. Fifty years later it required only the addition of my uncle in the secret service who was a notorious liar to give the story its legs.

"Hephaestus" sprang out of a bad experience in a Caribbean chain resort.

It took me a long time to get "Bedbugs" straight. It is obviously a comic tale, but for a long time I was consumed with trying to shape the events into the plot of a mystery, and when a Swiss newspaper asked me for a story, I responded too quickly. By the time this anthology was projected I had realised what the story really was and I think I finally got it straight. (Like a lot of writers, I have in my desk several stories and a novel that haven't matured yet, and maybe never will. These are separate from the stories I've abandoned because I've realised they are hopeless.)

"Duty Free" is an exercise in ingenuity which I sketched almost as the events happened, a bitter quarrel I observed while I was in the waiting lounge of Heathrow airport. It belongs probably in the sub-plot of a caper novel. The occasion this time was a request from an *In Flight* magazine.

"Jackpot" is another story that took some re-writing. The idea of the story grew out of the guilt I felt as a child when I kept the pennies that had spilled out of a malfunctioning call box. In those days, around 1938, public telephones in England were equipped with two push buttons, "A" and "B". You put in your two pennies, the price of a local call, and if you got the person you hoped for, you pushed button "A" and were connected. (This is the origin of the phrase "The penny dropped" meaning "Now I understood.") If a strange voice answered you could push "B" and get your money back. As children, we used to prowl the streets, pressing "B" buttons, looking for coins that had been left behind. One night, a call box malfunctioned and I got several handfuls of pennies. (It may seem that this is the ur-experience behind "The Boatman," too, but they both, as they say, really happened.)

"The Cure" is my first crime story, written back in 1983. It has its origins in my belief then that I was primarily a humorous writer because the first piece I wrote, a reminiscence, was published in the *The New Yorker*, in 1963. Thus I defined myself early and wrongly because I didn't publish another humorous piece for ten years. But when I was asked for my first short story I instinctively turned to the story of a crime committed in the middle of a comic feud. It is still my daughter's favourite story.

If you are in the habit of staying in the group of tourist hotels around Tavistock Square in London, you will know The President, where I located "The Lady from Prague." The actual lady was looking for business in a hotel near Victoria Station, but The President had the balcony that fitted my story, and nearly everything else. When I met the lady, I had just returned from a conference of crime writers in Prague, a conference which was very much on my mind because while we were there Vaclav Havel was arrested and imprisoned for laying a flower on the spot where a student had set fire to himself in protest against the regime.

"An Irish Jig" is my latest attempt to construct a decent locked-room mystery.

I learned through the writing of "The Lady of Shalott" that the novella is a good form for crime fiction. One single plot carries the tale, there is no need to pad, it can be written over a short enough period of time so that you don't forget the names of your characters, and it can be read at a sitting.

The story here was written out of my disaffection with the Olympics, all the drug-boosted achievements, the shamateurism, the bribes offered by the cities competing for the games, the financial shambles those cities are usually left in, and the idea of including ballroom dancing as a sport next time. I thought that the energy that Toronto was spending on trying to get the games, and the enormous amount more energy and money that would be spent if we were successful, belonged to Toronto's homeless, a growing army in a prosperous city in prosperous times. The two concerns came together, and the novella form seemed just right as a home, and I shall do it again.

I'm grateful for the chance to bring these stories together and the chance to think about them again. People have wondered if these small tales were worth writing and now keeping alive. I refer them to James Thurber's response when accused of wasting his time writing trivia, instead of more important things. "Trivia Mundi," Thurber said (I am quoting from memory), "is as dear and as necessary to me as her elder and more glamorous sister, Gloria."

Now that I've looked at them again, I feel the same way about these stories.

Eric Wright
Toronto, Ontario

Licensed Guide

Our history teacher in grade nine was insane. He was an old man—
"grizzled," I realized, when I discovered the word about that time—
who wanted in his youth to be an athlete and got as far as the training
camp of a professional football team. After he failed to make the cut he
went into teaching—physical education and history.

He spent most of his time on the playing fields and in the gym,
assisting the team coaches and generally getting in the way. He had a
simple mind, and an equally simple code of life. He liked to see strug-
gle, effort, self-discipline, the team spirit, and death in battle (he had a
very distinguished war record, having fought at Ypres with the Princess
Pats.) His history teaching was a record of heroes and gallant failures.
He couldn't stand liars, cheats, or boys who didn't look him square in
the eye. We were terrified of him.

On a day in May, he left the room for a few minutes, first warning
us to be totally silent. We were quiet for thirty seconds, then someone
said, "He's having a quick drag in the can," and old Baker reappeared
in the doorway, his face dark with fury. "Who said that?" he asked. No
one spoke. He was clearly already out of control, looking to kill.

He went round the room. "Was it you?" he asked us, one at a time,
and one at a time we looked him in the eye and answered, "No." All
except Simpson, whose gaze wavered. Baker asked him again and
Simpson denied it a second time, but now he blushed and looked
away. Old Baker hit him so hard that Simpson's head bounced off the
wall. (He told us later that he was deaf for two days afterwards). "I can
always tell," Baker said, looking round the room. "I can always tell."

What has this to do with the drowning of a man in a fishing camp,
fifteen years later? A great deal, apparently, because even now, thirty
years after the drowning, one incident always recalls the other.

They arrived one afternoon, three of them, a man named Baxter and
his wife, and his business partner, Crossley. Three was an awkward
number because we were set up to guide the guests in pairs: it was not

17

possible to put three guests in one boat, and uneconomic to allocate a guide to a single guest. There was nothing else for it, though. Bailey, the camp owner, (Bailey's Circle Lake Lodge—"We fly you in, We fly you out"), assigned them to Henry Goose and me, and the following morning we waited for them on the dock to ask them how they wanted to split up.

"We'll go with Henry," Baxter said after a glance at the two of us. You could see his mind working; the Indian was bound to be the better guide.

I moved to put Crossley's bag in my boat. "No," Baxter said. "*We'll* go with Henry. *You* take *her*."

His wife said nothing, simply leaned against the rail of the dock, smoking, while she waited. I picked up her bag, held the boat steady for her to get in, and checked with Henry where we should start the day's fishing.

"Grassy Narrows," Henry said.

I started the motor and headed across the lake. We would meet up at noon for shore lunch.

It took me half an hour to get to the first spot I wanted to try. As we travelled across the lake to the Narrows, Mrs. Baxter kept her eyes on the landscape without attempting to make any contact with me. She was a handsome woman, lean rather than slim, whose clothes were made for her, as well as being right for a day's fishing.

For the first hour with a new party you tried to assess the kind of guests they were, and then you planned the next three days. There were the familiar, chatty ones who wanted your approval at first. You had to be careful with these because they quickly became bored and could turn on you. Usually knowing very little about fishing, they measured their pleasure in terms of the number and size of fish caught. At first they were delighted to hook a two-pound walleye, but after two days a hundred five-pound fish a day wasn't enough.

At the other extreme, and much to be preferred at the end of summer, were the professional fisherman who knew that fish stopped biting sometimes, and judged you by your skill, not on the day's luck. You had to work hard for these, but they knew what you were doing and appreciated it.

Occasionally a third kind appeared, the rich sportsmen who happened to be fishing in northern Canada en route between shooting mountain sheep in Chile, and hunting caribou in Alaska. These people thought of themselves as "bwana" and treated you accordingly. They talked to each other about you as if you didn't understand English, or just weren't there.

These were three such guests. Alone with me, Mrs. Baxter stayed silent. I tried her with a remark when her line was in the water. "I guess those guys want to fish together," I said.

"It was my idea," she said and turned her back.

This was fine with me. Whatever she wanted I was there to provide. It was late in the season, and by this time I was tired of it; I was burned black, my hands were covered in dozens of little cuts from the spines and gills of fish I had handled, and I had told the same stories to too many guests.

She fished hard all day, stopping only when we met the others for shore lunch. Henry and I got the fire going and cooked some of the fish they had caught while our guests drank beer and compared notes on the fishing and on us, their guides. I didn't have to prick up my ears to hear her say I seemed to know my job. She knew I was listening, but it didn't inhibit her.

In the afternoon we fished for pike and bass, and she very quickly absorbed everything I knew, and by the end of the day could have guided me, needing only to know the name of the prey in order to go after it with the right tackle.

At supper in the guides' dining-room that night, Henry said his experience with the two men had been that of a taxi-driver. "I drove, they fished," he said. "I don't think the other guy spoke to me once."

The next day they switched. Crossley went with Henry, and I guided the Baxters. Baxter was not sure yet that he had the pick of the guides, so he was trying me for a day before he let his wife or Crossley have the guide he didn't want. "I'll try Duck Lake," Henry said. "You go to the falls. I'll meet you there for shore lunch."

That suited me. Meynell Falls was actually a very steep rapids where Meynell Lake emptied into Ebb Lake, creating a big whirlpool where the fish gathered to feed on whatever came down the rapids. The pickerel here were darker for some reason, almost black and gold, and they fought like bass, which made for livelier fishing. The thing was, you couldn't anchor as you usually did for pickerel, because the water was too fast. You kept the motor going at half speed and tried to keep the boat pointed at the falls. You were usually good for a couple of minutes before the current caught the prow and swept you round in a circle to come back for another try. All three people in the boat had to co-operate closely to keep their lines clear of each other as you circled, especially if one of them had a bite.

The Baxters could see the way it was and we did a couple of passes and caught three fish. Then, on the third pass, he threw the anchor over the side without checking with me first. The anchor was only a big piece of rock on the end of a rope tied to the back seat, and the rock was in front of Baxter on the floor of the boat. I didn't see him throw it in because I was turned around to watch to see the lines weren't crossing behind us, but I felt the boat lurch and I heard the rope twang as it went taut. I had my filleting knife handy on the seat beside me because I liked to clean the fish as soon as we caught them, otherwise you had to clean a sackful of fish at the end of the day in the camp fish hut, a stinking shed full of flies. I cut the rope just as the water started to pour over the back of the boat, and we stayed the right way up. I shut down the motor and we drifted while I scooped some of the water out of the boat, not wanting the motor to pull the stern down any further until I had lightened the boat a little. Then I started the motor and pulled over to the shore where we dried out and I ex-plained.

"The anchor and the current pull against each other, so in fast water the current pulls down the back of the boat and we fill up. Can you swim?" I was speaking nearly as hostilely as I felt, but Baxter didn't say anything. Nor did she. I think they saw the whole thing as my problem.

Henry appeared for shore lunch and I waited for Baxter to tell his pal, but he didn't say a word, so I helped Henry cook the lunch and we went fishing again. I said it wasn't worth going back to camp for a new anchor rope, and we would spend the afternoon trolling.

"I'd like to try this spot again," Baxter said, looking back at the rapids as we picked up for home. "Now I know how it works."

The next day Baxter went up north by himself for three days to try the Arctic char fishing at Bailey's other camp. Both men were sched-uled to go, but Crossley pleaded too much sun and said he wanted to stay inside for a couple of days. While Baxter was away I took care of his wife. Best of all she liked to fish for bass, so I paddled the shore of Duck Lake while she cast her lure close to the rocks along the shore-line. She still said almost nothing, indicating what she wanted from me with a word or a gesture, fishing hard until mid-afternoon, then gesturing me to take her home. That suited me.

Baxter came back a day early. The weather up north was bad, and he arrived before supper. Someone told him they thought his wife and I were still out on the lake—my boat wasn't in its usual spot. Baxter decided he was hungry and went up to Crossley's cabin to see if Crossley would join him for an early supper, but his pal was along the shore, watching Bailey's carpenters put the first logs in place for some new cabins. So Baxter ate alone.

I ran into him as he was leaving the dining room. He still had his bag, and I took it off him (the guides were also bellboys if needed) and walked with him up to his cabin. On the path we ran into Crossley and Mrs. Baxter, who were on their way to supper, Crossley having called in to collect her on the way by. I left them all to tell each other the news, and put Baxter's bag inside the door of his cabin.

Two days later, Crossley drowned at Meynell Falls.

It happened like this. On Baxter's second day back, I had Mrs. Baxter to myself again, while Baxter and Crossley went off on their own, without Henry. When we had checked with them after breakfast, the two men hadn't wanted to fish, but Mrs. Baxter was keen so I took her out and Henry accepted the day off and went into town. Then, according to Bailey, about eleven o'clock Baxter had appeared and asked if he and Crossley could use Henry's boat by themselves. Bailey hated to allow this; even experienced guides from another part of the province could get lost around the English River system, and people from New York City were not to be trusted on their own out of sight of the dock, but in the end he agreed if they just puttered around the shore line.

I had a pretty good day. Even without too many words, I knew what Mrs. Baxter wanted now, and I was happy to provide it without a lot of chat. Around three o'clock she pulled in her line for the last time, and I took her back and tied up at the camp dock just after six. Bailey was standing on the dock, looking worried.

"You pass Baxter on the way through the Narrows?" he asked me, before I had even tied up.

Mrs. Baxter took no further notice of us, simply walked up to her cabin.

I shook my head.

"They probably ran out of gas." He dropped a full tank into my boat. "Go look for them, will you? They might have missed the channel out of Meynell when they turned around. I'll send a couple of the other boys after you as they come in."

I plugged in the full tank and headed for Ebb Lake and the falls. I found the boat as soon as I turned into the channel. It was upside down, so low in the water that only the front of the keel was showing, caught between a pair of rocks near the bank. I moved my gas tank to the front of my boat to keep the prow down and nudged closer at half speed. Baxter waved from the other shore. He was soaking wet. I pulled in to take him off and looked round for Crossley.

"He's a goner," Baxter said. His teeth were chattering. "We did all the wrong things. He threw the anchor in and the current took us and we filled up right away, and capsized. I never saw him surface."

I took him back to camp and Bailey sent for the police. Henry's brother, David Goose, found Crossley's body tangled up in some weeds in a little bay not far from the falls.

There wasn't much to investigate: Baxter hadn't even seen it happen. All he knew was that the boat turned over while he was sitting in it after he heard the splash of the anchor, and when he surfaced he was close enough to the shore to save himself, but he lost sight of the boat and never saw Crossley again. A coroner was flown in and he declared it an accidental death.

The Baxters left next day. I saw them on the dock, her leaning against the rail, smoking. She caught my eye and gave me that classic signal, the nearly imperceptible shake of the head, then Bailey hustled them on to the plane that was waiting.

He'd killed Crossley, of course, but I didn't speak up right away and then I knew I never would. The thing that made it certain was his story about the anchor. Henry didn't have an anchor: I'd borrowed his when he went to town because I still didn't have one as good as his. I had found a small rock, but it didn't always hold, so I'd wrapped a rope around it and put it in Henry's boat, just so if Henry came back he could fix himself up with some kind of anchor, but I hadn't tied it to the seat, just kind of tucked it under out of the way. The police were surprised the anchor wasn't still dragging the boat, even when it capsized, but in the end they guessed it came untied, so that was that.

I reckon Baxter threw it in, trying to capsize the boat, and when the rock disappeared, he just found another way to dump the boat.

I also knew *why* he'd killed Crossley.

The day he came back early from fishing for Arctic char, he had gone looking for Crossley in his cabin; then, not finding him, had walked on to his own cabin. With his hand on the door he had heard sounds from within, guessed what he was hearing, and turned around to go back to the dining room. Then, later, on his way back from supper, he had met Crossley and his wife on their way to the dining room, and jumped to his own conclusion.

What Baxter had really heard was his wife, giving voice at last, crying out, before I could shush her.

At the time, I thought Baxter was one of the maids, come to clean the room.

The two incidents are not identical. Even if I'd betrayed Mrs. Baxter, the police couldn't have proved anything, could they? And as for Simpson, once I didn't speak up right away I was stuck. And yet whenever I think of Baxter I think of that old history teacher banging Simpson's head against the wall. I still sometimes dream it all again, and still wake up feeling bad about Simpson.

The Boatman

My eldest sister was the first to find a way to better herself, to get out of our tenement flat which she shared with her nine brothers and sisters, including me.

She went on holiday to Cornwall and met a sailor, an officer in the reserve navy, and married him, and they ran a pub in the country for three or four years until the war came along. "The George", it was called.

Vi's husband was one of the first to go to war, before it even started, and then Vi ran the inn herself, and in the summer of 1939 when it was obvious there was going to be a war she offered to take me for the duration as her personal evacuee. The thing was, she had two guest bedrooms which might have been commandeered by the local billeting officer who had to house the evacuees that were coming down from London, so it was better to have me than some stranger.

The River Loddon runs into the Thames, and where it runs past The George it's wide enough and deep enough to drown in. On one side, between the pub and the river, Vi had a tea garden on a lawn, with iron umbrella tables painted white and those little iron fold-up chairs. In the summer, people could order tea and cakes to be brought out there in the afternoon, and drinks at night when the bar was open.

The river ran for miles in both directions. Vi had a lot of boats that she used to hire out, punts, with cushions, and some skiffs for those who fancied themselves as rowers. The punts had to be paddled because the bottom of the river had too many holes for poling, and mostly it was young couples who hired them for courting. They used to paddle out of sight of the inn and tie the boat to a branch of a tree and spend all the afternoon kissing each other.

I was the boatman. Vi had a gardener, Mr. Foster, a fierce little ginger-haired man in Wellington boots. Vi told me to be polite to him because soon gardeners would be hard to find. When Vi's husband went off to sea, Mr. Foster helped out with the boat-hiring, but he told Vi that was not his trade and she should find someone else. When I came, she got me to do it.

25

I thought it was smashing. We charged a shilling and sixpence the first hour and a shilling an hour after that, and sometimes they would owe three and sixpence or even four and sixpence on a sunny afternoon. I used to write up the time they went out with a piece of chalk on the slateboard inside the boathouse, and the time they came back. They often gave me tips. The change from two florins for three hours was sixpence, and I learned to be slow handing it to them to give them time to tell me to keep it. Sometimes, if they had a nice afternoon kissing, I would get more.

Sixpence bought a lot, all the sweets I could eat, but I had to be careful. Vi sold chocolate and potato crisps in the pub and I didn't want to be seen eating anything that she sold and might have thought I had nicked from the pub. Ice cream was safe, as was licorice, sherbert and the loose sweets sold from large glass jars. Any chocolate I bought I ate on the way home from the sweet shop, in Earley. Probably Vi would have believed me that I had bought it from my tips, but she might have told my mum who would have been more suspicious, so I didn't say anything. Vi also gave me pocket-money for looking after the boats and that and the tips was what she thought I was spending.

So I was as happy as a prince, having this important job, making tons of money, and spending it on sweets and comics which I could buy in Earley, the local village which I used to walk to in the mornings when there weren't many customers. If someone wanted a boat when I wasn't there, Mr. Foster would look after them. Sometimes I went for a row in the small rowboat, which we never let out because I might have to row after a punt that got loose, or look for one that should have come back. Sometimes people got out of their punt farther along the river and walked away so as not to have to pay.

I had my own bedroom with a big sweet-smelling bed, and Vi bought me pyjamas which I'd never had before, none of us had. At home we slept in our shirts. Although Vi was my sister, she was gone from the Buildings, as the tenement was called, before I knew her so she was a bit of a stranger, and I was on my best behaviour all the time. One night the door to my room jammed because it was so old and it was warped out of shape, and I wanted to pee but couldn't get out, so I peed in the copper kettle in the fireplace. The next day I tried to wait until the coast was clear to empty it, but there was always someone about so I left it. I could have told my mum about it, and if it had been one of my other sisters I could have told them, but I was too shy to tell Vi because I didn't know her very well, so I left it there.

The only time the war came near was one afternoon when I was in the apple-scented pavilion, lying in a hollow on a great pile of russet apples, and a German bomber came over and dropped a stick of bombs, four, I think, that went crump, CRUMP, CRUMP!, crump as they straddled the inn and me. I thought God had been watching me and sent the bomber to punish me.

In the meantime the boats were very busy and sometimes I collected a lot of money. Did I ever think of stealing some of it? Did I ever *not* think of stealing any? I was from Colliers Wood by way of Lambeth, and nicking stuff was as natural as breathing, so long as it was absolutely safe. It wasn't morality that kept us honest. You didn't steal because your family—my mother—had done a good job of letting you know the penalties: from being skinned alive by her, then handed over to your father when he came home to finish the job, then off to Borstal prison where you would be fed bread and water and knocked about continually by the jailers, and finally kicked out of the house—"I'm not having thieves in this house!"

But I was still inclined towards stealing, most of us were if it could be done in safety, and the boat money was irresistible. Even if I was caught, my sister wouldn't send me to Borstal. So, from the time I saw the opportunity, I never considered not stealing some of it. And besides, I'd found a need for the money. The tips were all right for sweets, but I had started a stamp collection, and I took the bus into Wokingham as often as I could to buy stamps. The ones I wanted cost more than I could get from tips.

And so I took the next step. Five boats had been hired by a party of young hounds (Vi's word) and each others' sisters. Vi had gone to London, leaving the pub in charge of the woman who helped out on Saturdays. I chalked up the time the five boats moved off, and when they came back, collected the money, walked twice round the garden to make sure Mr. Foster hadn't looked in on his day off, wiped out the record of the fifth boat and put a mere fourteen shillings in the cigarette tin where we kept the day's take, pocketing the three and sixpence, to be hidden later in the actual, real, hollow tree I had discovered on the other bank of the river.

And so it started. The swag grew until there were two or three pounds in a little leather bag I once kept my marbles in, tucked away in the old hollow tree, more money than I had ever handled. Now I had to spend it. Apart from stamps, I wanted a big Meccano set. Vi had bought me a starter set, with enough wheels and tiny girders to make a model hand-cart, but the set came with a leaflet picturing what could be done with a giant set: gantries, windmills, trucks—the possibilities were unlimited. But it was out of the question; I could never have accounted for it. So I had to be satisfied with buying stamps. I already had a little collection, bought in Colliers Wood with half-pence, mostly German inflationary issues, printed in the millions. I knew what I really wanted, not penny blacks or cape triangulars, but those gorgeous ones of the British colonies, the king's head in one corner of a beautiful picture of a giraffe (Kenya, Uganda and Tanganyika), and all the other works of art from Africa, the Caribbean and the South Seas.

Then, in Wokingham, I found a dealer and began to spend my money. One by one I brought them home and fixed them carefully in my stamp album. There was no need to show them to anyone yet; I could do that later, at home, when I saw my mates again. For the time being I could enjoy gloating over the little Stanley Gibbons album I kept in the cardboard suitcase under my bed along with the two lead soldiers, the propelling pencil I found in one of the boats, and the army badges.

And then, one day, the stamp dealer asked me my name, and I thought I'd been caught. "William Brown," I said.

"Where's all the money coming from then, William?" The stamp dealer with a look invited his hovering wife to listen.

"My paper route."

"You're not from around here. You're a Londoner. You don't have a paper route."

I looked out the window, thinking. "That's my Dad," I said and ran.

For three days I lived in fear, but the dealer never appeared at the inn. Nobody set any traps, like they did in the stories I was reading and no one asked me why I rowed over to the old hollow tree every day. No, this was how it happened.

After a few days the habit of stealing some of the boat money came back, but I didn't take as much as I did before because now that I couldn't buy stamps I didn't know what to do with the money. Then, one day, the fair came to the village and my sister gave me a shilling to visit it. It had been a quiet day on the river and all I had in my pocket was a sixpenny tip. Of course, it occurred to me what a good time I could have at the fair with the hoard from the old hollow tree, but Mr. Foster was looking after the boats for the afternoon, and with him watching I couldn't think of an excuse to row across the river before I went to the fair.

Even so, one and six was a lot of money and I was surprised how quickly it disappeared. Two rides, a go on the shooting gallery, and a coconut shy and I only had three pennies left. I stopped by a stall in a round tent where you could roll the big copper pennies down a wooden slot in the hope of landing on a winning square. On the second try my penny rolled into a sixpenny square. The gypsy lady in charge dealt me six pennies and moved on. The booth was large and busy, and the gypsy had to circle around the inside, picking up the losing pennies and paying out the winners. I rolled down another penny and won six more; I did it again, and again, and again, until I was out of breath with excitement. There was a tiny warp in the surface of the table just beyond my wooden chute, and if my penny reached this warp, travelling at the right speed, it fell over into the square. I won about eight times, and then, deliberately, under her eye, put the penny too high in the chute and lost. I left the booth for a while and threw some more balls at the coconuts, but nothing compared with winning pennies.

When I went back, another gypsy had taken over and I won another four shillings before she started to watch me and I had to deliberately lose again. Now I developed a system, winning a couple of times, going for a walk, coming back to win again as soon as my chute was free. Soon, both my pockets were crammed with pennies; the attendant in charge of the tent with the slot machines changed some of them for me into silver, and most of the rest I spent on rides, shooting ranges, and the other games, until I'd had enough, and I walked home with a story to tell.

I arrived back at The George, passing through the Private Bar to get to the living room behind. The barman was behind the counter, talking to a customer. His face was serious. "Your sister wants to see you," he said. "In the back room."

The customer turned round and I nearly swooned when I saw the face of the stamp dealer from Wokingham. I thought it was the end for me. But the man just said, with a sly look, "Who's this, then?"

"Her brother. Staying with her for the duration."

"Has he got a name?"

"Eric."

"Lucky boy, living in a pub." The dealer took a swig. "Interested in stamps, son?"

"Not much."

"I thought you collected them," the barman said, holding up the flap of the counter to let me through.

"Used to. Don't now."

The dealer smiled, picked up his change, winked at me. "Cheerio," he said, and left.

"She's waiting."

I ran through, dizzy with relief at the dealer's strange loyalty, and slipped into the living room where my sister was waiting with the woman who helped out on Saturdays.

"Come here," my sister said. "Turn out your pockets." She said it sort of sadly, kindly.

Now it looked as if the dealer had told on me after all, as was natural. The scene in the bar had been a tease, a cat- and-mouse scene, while all the time the dealer knew what waited for me in the kitchen.

My sister pointed to the kitchen table to show me where to put the money from my pockets.

"Don't have to," I mumbled.

"You want me to tell Mum?"

Threat enough. I emptied both pockets; I still had a dozen pennies, and several of the shillings that I had changed back. It was a pile the size of a fist. My sister looked at the money without saying anything. The face of the woman who helped out on Saturdays was shining.

"Where'd you get it?" my sister said at last.

"Won it."

Headshakes.

"I'll ask you again. Where'd you get it?"

"Won it."

Now she'd used up the threat of telling mum; it wouldn't have been fair to use it twice. She tried to shame me. "Don't tell lies," she said. "Don't *lie*", she said like a school-teacher.

This wasn't fair. *Everybody* from Kennington lied to the authorities. She knew that. She'd lived there once. She had no right to be on the other side.

"I'm not lying. I won it."

The woman who helped out on Saturdays said, "They don't let you win. Only once or twice p'raps. Our Fred lost six bob on that roll-the-penny game." She gleamed at my sister, encouraging her to carry on.

"You took it out of the boat money, didn't you?"

"No. I won it."

And then I saw what she needed. A little brother who stole was one thing, a thief and a liar shown up in front of the woman who helped out on Saturdays was something else. I could feel her wanting me to tell the truth.

"Some of it was tips," I said.

"Not that much." She looked at the pile on the table. "Elsie here watched you all night. You went on all the rides."

"Spent a fortune," the woman said.

So it had been *this* rotten cow. The dealer had kept quiet, after all.

"Some of it probably *was* tips," my sister offered. "Not all of it, though, was it?"

"Not all of it, no."

"Some of it was boat money, wasn't it?"

I nodded, a quarter of an inch.

"Make 'im say," the woman who helped out on Saturdays said. "Go on."

"That's all right, Elsie," Vi said. "Leave us alone now."

"Make 'im say," the woman repeated as she went through the door.

"Don't tell Mum," I said, when we were by ourselves.

She shook her head. "What are we going to do with you, then?" I could feel her yearning across the space between us. We'd never touched each other; you didn't hug in our family. "Will you promise never to take the boat money again?"

"Oh, yeah." Then, suddenly, "I don't want to look after the boats any more."

"You can still look after the boats …"

"I don't want to."

"What do you want to do, then? Help Mr. Foster?"

And then it came. "I want to go home," I said, and as I said it I did, want to go home, back to bread-and-margarine, back to the other liars and thieves on my street, back to a world of crime and punishment I understood. "I want to go home," I said again. "Let me go home."

"P'raps that's best. Don't say I sent you, mind. If I take you up to London and put you on the right tube, can you manage?"

" 'Course I can." We used to ride all day on the tube for a penny, changing trains. She was treating me like a kid. "You don't have to come up to London, even. I can go on the train myself." Then, to be certain, I said again, "Don't tell Mum."

"No, she'd kill you. What'll we say? You got homesick?"

"That'll do. In the morning, then?"

She sniffed and looked down at her hands.

"It's not *your* fault," I said. "I'll just say I got homesick."

She nodded, and sniffed again. "I thought p'raps you might want to stay on here, even when the war's over. We would have sent you to Reading Grammar School," she said.

It was tempting because I was right in the middle of my schoolboy story period, the "Hotspur" stories especially, stories which all took place in schools like Reading Grammar. But the Buildings won. The thing was, I wasn't at home at The George. My sister was nice to me but we weren't friends—there was twenty years between us—and she wasn't trying to be a mother. She was just an old sister I didn't know very well, and though I knew she was trying to get me to better myself, like her, I found it a strain.

She did my washing and ironed it herself, and drove me to Earley station the next afternoon, and I caught the train to Waterloo.

I didn't row across the river first and get the money out of the old hollow tree. If I'd been caught doing that, I think Vi *would* have told my mum. She thought I'd just nicked the odd sixpence or shilling, but the leather bag was nearly full. As far as I know, it's still there, like the pee in the copper kettle.

One of a Kind

None of the plumbers and steamfitters I worked with on the D.E.W. line bothered with Eskimo carving. The most prized art up there was the work of trappers, the carvings made out of bone, especially narwhal tusks. This bone-whittling has no name of its own: the closest to it is scrimshaw, the carvings made by whaling crews.

Billy Benson's cribbage board was generally agreed to be the finest example of bone carving in that part of the north. People in settlements hundreds of miles away had heard of it, and it was not unusual for a bush pilot who stayed overnight at the camp to ask to see it. It was that famous. The base of it was a single piece of bone or tusk about four feet long. The top surface had been polished flat (this alone, Billy said, had taken him all one winter), and the bottom left rounded. To keep it steady, a dozen small bone pegs had been inserted into holes in the base, tiny legs that kept the board level and clear of the surface of the table. Four rows of holes to take the cribbage pegs had been drilled into the top face, and then, surrounding this scoring area, running along both sides of the board and around the ends, a set of smaller holes had been drilled. In these were pegged elaborate scenes of arctic life, all carved out of bone. A full dog team and sled, the dogs no more than half an inch high, formed a centrepiece on one side. Before and after the dog-team, Billy had carved replicas of arctic fox, and beaver, and mink. At one end of the board a tiny bone igloo concealed an Innuit family tucked up for sleep. At the other end, a herd of caribou were being stalked by two polar bears.

Billy would show his board to anyone who was interested, and everyone saw it on Saturday nights, when he took it out to polish or file some detail while the men played poker. He got a lot of offers for the board, many for hundreds of dollars, but there was no question of his selling it. It was his life's work, his accomplishment. Billy had taken up trapping in the thirties when there was no work in the city, and twenty years later his trap line still yielded only a bare subsistence. But he had carved this astonishing board, made his mark, created something. And he was only the best; there were plenty more, men who illuminated the solitary dark winters with carved rings, toothpicks, little knives. Others composed poems, far more than have survived: Robert Service was a product of these scribes, not an original. Our camp sanitation engineer, the one who pumped out the holding tanks, was a former trapper who, when drunk, could reel off a dozen ballads of his own invention.

Billy Benson had abandoned his trap line when the army brought prosperity to the area in the form of a camp to house the warriors along the Distant Early Warning Line. Billy had been hired in the first instance by the army as a cleaner, for wages that were marginal in the city but far more money than he had ever earned on his trap line. Then when the army was properly established with its own servants in place, he was hired by the construction company to clean our dormitory and do odd jobs. At first, with the casual racism of the time and the place, we treated him as a kind of native servant. Billy was white, of course, but he behaved as if he did not expect to be accepted by the plumbers and steamfitters, as if he found himself outclassed. He had a lot of time on his hands and he was keen to accumulate as much of the newly discovered money as he could, so he became the laundryman, too: washing, ironing, even repairing, for very low prices. He also found a hot plate and a coffee pot from somewhere, and made and sold coffee for five cents a cup. He had plenty of customers, especially on Sundays when liquor was unprocurable, and later, when he expanded into chocolate bars which he sold for two cents more than they cost in the camp store, he admitted that he was doubling his wages.

He was an unpleasant character. He didn't wash enough, his fingernails were like claws, long and yellow, and he spoke in a sneering whine. He slept in a kind of filthy nest of old blankets in the little storage room at the end of the bunkhouse where he kept his cleaning materials; he made no attempt to be part of the gang, and no one made any effort to include him.

And then, one Saturday night, he brought out his cribbage board to alter a detail on one of the animals, and his status changed immediately. He had been carving the board for twenty years and the result took everyone's breath away. We immediately became proud of him, bragging about him all over the camp, so that Billy became the camp celebrity and his cribbage board the area's most admired artefact.

Thus, when the board was stolen, the effect on him and on us was huge.

Billy acted as if someone had taken his child; or it had wandered off. He searched, dumbly, again and again, all the places he might have put the board, knowing that he had never moved it away from his bunk. We all joined in the search at first, but then, inevitably, gave up and left him to it. It would have been easier if we had liked him, but our admiration for his skill had not made us warm to him personally. Our pity was mixed with and increased, perhaps, by our guilt that we did not find him more savoury.

The men responded to the theft in the different ways that a community does react to a piece of human villainy. Most were horrified and quietened by the event; a few became noisy and spelled out what they would to the thief, personally, if they caught him. On or two of the young apprentices were frightened, experiencing their first taste of community outrage and fearing the violence that would be visited on any suspect. We all had foot lockers, surplus American army boxes, and one of the apprentices got hold of a huge padlock to keep his secure. We all understood. This was not the city. What the boy wanted to make sure of was that no one planted the cribbage board in his locker. He even stripped his blankets each morning and doubled back his mattress on his metal cot so that it was impossible to hide anything in his gear. He was simply believing what he heard, that anyone caught with the board would be crucified before he was tried.

In the end, there was no search of personal belongings. First they had to sort out the responsible authority: the crime was a civilian one, committed on a civilian, almost certainly by a civilian, but on army property, so the investigation was preceded by a discussion between the lone Mountie in the district and the military police. One problem was that the military police were deeply unpopular with the construction workers, many of whom had served in the war and hated the redcaps. One plumbing sub-foreman, who had spent part of the war in a military prison, hearing that the army might search his belongings, let the world know what he would do to any military policeman he caught near his kit. There were other problems with mounting a search. The Mountie was unable to do the job on his own, and besides, in searching the men's personal belongings he would be making an assumption that the thief was in residence. But everyone on the camp knew about the cribbage board, and most of them had come to see it. Billy had plenty of offers for it from outside the bunkhouse, especially from the American army officers. (One of these kept a shopping list of objects he wanted to take back to Virginia with him, including a polar bearskin, which he got, and a kayak, which he didn't, because the American commander, hearing of the officer's list, and fearing that such booty-hunting would make his unit unpopular, banned the shipment by army plane of any kayak that Captain Miller acquired. Miller had long ago made the largest offer for the cribbage board, and many of us thought that he was quite capable of arranging the theft. We weren't shocked by the whisper that came through that Miller would be happy to buy the board off the thief, although none of us knew about art dealers then.) In the end, the idea of a grand search was abandoned, and the plumbers searched their own bunkhouse. Our foreman, Jack Cotter, suggested it, and he was immediately supported by the sub-foreman who was so hostile to the military police. The rest of us agreed as a way of purging the atmosphere. We didn't find the board, of course.

Billy went into a decline. He immediately stopped selling coffee and candy, and no longer took care of our laundry. He did his cleaning job, but that only took about an hour a day. The rest of the time he lay in his blankets, staring at the wall. If we attempted to communicate, to try to offer some consolation, he simply snarled and turned away. He adopted a single phrase, "Don't need yer" with which he responded to all our overtures.

It might have gone on like this for the whole winter if it had not been for the big February storm, which occurred about two weeks later. It was both typical and extraordinary. It was typical in being that month's blizzard which closed the camp down tight. Not a blizzard with all the connotations of deep soft snow pouring out of a fleecy sky, but a snowstorm like a sandstorm in the desert, tiny projectiles of granular snow pounding against the face, making it impossible to raise one's head, while six feet above there was still blue sky as at the end of a tunnel. And the storm was extraordinary in lasting for three days and almost killing Jack Cotter, the foreman, who was caught out in it without his emergency kit.

Cotter lived in the tiny settlement, originally a fur-trading station, that pre-dated the army camp by two centuries, but suddenly expanded with the spillover from the camp. It was about seven miles away, at the end of the only road. Jack Cotter had brought his wife with him to live in a wooden shack he and his crew had built out of plywood and fibreglass insulation. When a storm came he stayed home if he was there, or found a bed in the dormitory if he was at work, letting his wife know through the army signals office that he wouldn't be home for supper.

The storm began around noon, and by two o'clock the camp was virtually shut down. Cotter called a halt around two o'clock to give the men time to trudge back through the snow to their bunkhouse before dark. (It was the kind of storm that made it unsafe to step outside alone, because of the danger of immediately becoming disoriented, and within a few minutes, exhausted. It was only safe to proceed in groups of two or more, and only possible by creeping along the sides of buildings.)

Cotter also needed to give himself time to drive the seven miles to his home before dark; he was allowing an hour and a half for the fifteen-minute journey. He probably shouldn't have tried it, but he was unhappy about leaving his wife alone all night, and he had chains on his tires, so he felt justified in ignoring the army's order which grounded all personnel except those in vehicles equipped with caterpillar tracks.

Around eight that night, most of the men were in bed, or lying on their bunks reading and playing gin rummy with their immediate neighbours. The door opened and two soldiers led Jack Cotter in and sat him next to the stove. He hadn't suffered any frostbite, but he was very, very cold. He had to be, because he had been trapped in his pickup truck for four hours without gas, or blankets or anything that would have helped to keep him warm, and without the flares that might have brought help sooner. Cotter was tough, though. It wasn't long before he seemed back to normal, and able to tell his tale.

"I was on the road to town," he said. "I ran out of gas."

Outside the storm blew as strongly as ever. It was not a night to run out of fuel.

"You forgot to fill your spare can?" someone asked, incredulous.

"I couldn't find it."

"How come you had no ..." The speaker wanted a phrase like

"emergency kit" but he was so puzzled he lost the words before he spoke them. Cotter was the last man to get caught like that. If you got into trouble in this country he was the man you would most like to have with you. The previous spring, Cotter and three other plumbers had borrowed an aluminum punt from the Catholic mission to go fishing on the Nelson river. They didn't know the river well and got upset at the second rapids. Later, the plumbers gave Cotter credit for saving all their lives, not through any single heroic act, but by knowing how to survive, soaked to the skin in ice-cold water in a spot so mosquito-infested that people had died from insect bites after a night's exposure. Cotter had with him the means to create a fire and the skill to fix up a shelter, and he had kept them talking all night until help arrived. Now he said, "My blanket and tent were gone, so was my gas can. So were the flares. I didn't have no survival kit."

We digested this very slowly. To be caught out in a storm without the survival kit was stupid, and Cotter was anything but that. Reaction number two was that Cotter had been very, very careless, but you didn't have to know Cotter well to reject that one, either. He certainly wasn't drunk; that was always a possibility with Jack Cotter, but though he often took a day off to get drunk, he chose his own time and circumstances to do it.

So for anyone who knew him, neither carelessness nor stupidity nor drunkenness made sense, and we quickly came to realise that Cotter was saying that someone had stolen his survival kit. This was the most difficult of all to digest. In that country, you must carry a spare can of gas at any time, but especially in winter, because if you happen to run out of gas in a storm, you are on your own. The other emergency supplies are carried to enable you to respond to mechanical failure. A wise man carries a thermal blanket to wrap around himself after he has set out the flares that he also carries. Usually Cotter also carried a sleeping bag, chocolate, and a small screw-cap tonic-water bottle of rye whiskey, a bottle which he never opened for pleasure. He could survive for a long time, so long as he stayed in his truck and didn't do anything dumb like trying to walk back to camp.

His wife had raised the alarm when she figured he ought to have come home even after a couple of hours stopover in the beer parlour. The army went looking, found him fairly quickly, and brought him back.

The final realisation, when his story had sunk in, was that in stealing his emergency kit, someone had tried to kill Cotter as surely as if they had slit a hole in an airman's parachute, and whoever it was should, and would, be charged with attempted homicide.

This realisation of a crime a lot more serious than stealing a cribbage board brushed aside any problems with protocol. Now the military and civilian forces teamed up under the command of the Mountie, assisted by some specially-sworn-in constables from the town: the Hudson's Bay factor, the proprietor of the beer parlour, and the woman who ran the O'Kum Inn (which was really her kitchen, opened after her husband had died the previous spring).

They had to wait two days, until the storm was passing, though there wouldn't be much work done until the snow ploughs had carved a trough along the road. While the ploughs were beavering away, the military were ordered and—what amounted to the same thing—the civilians were requested to stay where they were until the camp was searched. The two teams, the army and the mountie's team, went through the camp, starting with the bunkhouses and the barracks, then on through the service buildings, the stores, the kitchens, even the makeshift hockey rink. They never found Cotter's emergency kit, but they did find the cribbage board, carefully wrapped in an old blanket, under the floorboards of the electricians' stores. And that, it turned out, was the thing they were really looking for.

The Mountie was wise for his age and left the cribbage board where it was, reasoning that it would be impossible to prove who had put it there, but if nothing was said it might be possible to catch them taking it away. And so it proved. The police had to wait for two weeks, checking daily to see if the board had been interfered with. Then one day the floor looked disturbed, and the cribbage board was gone. There was a plane out twice a week, on Tuesdays and Thursdays, a DC7 operated by Canadian Pacific, and the next day the Mountie got between the passengers and their luggage and found the board in a brand new suitcase checked in by one of the plumbers who was going to the city on a week's holiday.

Once more the Mountie was quick on his feet. He could have charged the man with theft, which would have involved holding him in the jail, safe from the noisier vigilantes who wanted to hurt him, then a trial, with all its trappings, ending maybe in a small prison sentence. It would be hard to get a city judge to appreciate the significance of that cribbage board. What the Mountie did was confiscate the suitcase and tell the man not to come back, which the man was glad to agree to. Then the Mountie let it be known that the suitcase had been left, unclaimed, with the airline agent, and when they examined it they found the cribbage board. The truth came out quickly enough when the plumber failed to return. I think Jack Cotter took care of making sure that the man couldn't find a job in the city. He had to leave his trade and the city to find work among men who didn't know the story. Not jailed, then, or crucified; branded.

The real mystery was still what had happened to Cotter's emergency kit which the search failed to turn up. The cribbage board thief swore that he had never seen or touched it, and the Mountie seemed very unconcerned about letting him off so lightly, but he knew, as did a few others—Cotter, his wife, the head of the military police—that the plumber was telling the truth, that they would never find any of the things that were missing from Cotter's truck, for they were all in Cotter's bedroom now, where Cotter had stored them.

I know because six months later I had saved the money I needed for a plan I had to travel and broaden my horizons, and the plumbers threw a farewell party for me. That is, they drove me into town and poured beer into me until I fell off my chair and Cotter took me back to his house to sleep on the daybed in his kitchen. I was due to fly out the following day, and in the morning Cotter's wife cooked me some breakfast and he drove me to the airstrip. While I was waiting for Cotter to get ready, I tidied the daybed and put the blankets back in the storage drawer underneath. That is when I found the thermal emergency blanket and Cotter's old sleeping bag. The bag was black, a rare enough colour for a sleeping bag to make it instantly recognisable to a lot of people who knew Cotter, and he told me he planned to leave it behind when the construction was finished.

"So all the time they were looking for it, the stuff was under this bed?" I asked. "Think about it," he admonished me. "That would have meant that I'd drove back without any emergency kit in the worst storm of the winter. No way." He was embarrassed that I had found the stuff, but enjoying himself, too.

"So where was it?"

"In the only place they wouldn't look for something stolen from the truck. In the truck." He grinned. "Here. Want a little juice." He held out a small bottle of what looked like apple juice.

I took a swig on a stomach soured by the previous night's beer and nearly choked on a mouthful of cheap rye whiskey, his domestic emergency supply in case his wife, a crusading teetotaller, found the bottle he had hidden.

"So it was all rigged?" I asked, trying not to throw up.

"Me and the Mountie set it up. Billy Benson was wasting away without his cribbage board. Getting on everyone's nerves. We were pretty sure it was still on camp somewhere. But the Mountie needed a better reason to search real good, so we decided to try and kill me off." He grinned and finished the little bottle of whiskey. "Christ it was cold waiting for those army guys to come and find me. The wind chill was sixty below. All I had to do was stand outside the truck for a couple of minutes to get real cold, the way you saw me."

"How long were you there, by the road?"

"Half an hour. Then the Mountie and the redcaps came and got me."

"And all the time you had a can of gas, a blanket and all the rest in the trucks"

"Sure. Another half hour and I would've used them. You know what they say about the Mounties: some of them couldn't track a wounded elephant through six feet of snow. But that guy was pretty good. Sure, they knew where I was supposed to run out of gas, but it would have been a hell of a thing if they'd missed me, eh?"

It would have been good if the story had ended there, but it's necessary to add that the experience changed Billy Benson, making him difficult to live with afterwards. He never sold coffee or candy again, and gave up being the laundryman for good. He seemed to blame all of us for what happened. Soon, he started to neglect his job, and shortly after that, the company let him go, to everyone's relief. He had become a burden on us all. The word was that he had gone back to his old trap line. The turnover of labour was so great up there that in two months fewer than half of the plumbers had ever met Billy Benson.

In six months he had become a story to be told during a snowstorm.

Twins

"I want to get it right," he said. "After making the mistake in the last book about how long it takes to get from Toronto to Detroit, I want this to be water-tight. So just go along with me until I'm sure that it'll work."

They were standing on the edge of an old mine shaft about ten miles north of Sudbury. The shaft had been sunk in the thirties and to reach it they had to claw their way through dense scrub pine, and pick the locks on two chain link fences that guarded the hole. At least it was too late in the year for mosquitoes. She wondered how he had found this place.

He seemed to hear what was in her mind. "I found it two years ago," he said. "I came up here hunting with Art. Someone told us we might find a bear along at the garbage dump but we missed the road and came to this place."

He was a writer of detective stories. As far as he could, he liked to "walk the course" of his plots until he was sure they would work. She always went along as a primary test that the story was possible. The stories often took them to some pleasant places, so it was like getting a second holiday, but this time she had come because she needed to know what was in his mind. Sudbury in October is not a popular vacation spot. "Tell me again," she said. "How does he get her to come this far? I wouldn't."

"You just did," he pointed out.

"That was research. Unless you make your villain a writer, you're going to have trouble. What is he, by the way?"

"I haven't decided yet. It's not important. I want to make sure this works, then I can flesh it out."

"Yes, but it doesn't work if the reader can't believe she would stumble through a quarter mile of bush in this godforsaken landscape. You've got to find a good reason."

"I'll find one. Let's get the plot straight, shall we?"

"This isn't the way you usually work. Usually you get the characters first then let the plot grow out of them. So you say, anyway."

"Yeah, but this plot is ingenious. I mean, the villain thinks it is, so I want to test it before I spend my time creating his world. Okay?"

"Okay, so now he kills her. Right? And drops the body down there." She kicked a small rock over the edge of the hole and listened hard, but there was no "ploomp" or rattle of the sound of the rock reaching bottom. It must go down hundreds of metres.

"That's right. He throws the gun in after her; he's made sure it's untraceable. Then he drives south to the motel in Parry Sound where they have a reservation. When he gets there, it's dark." He looked at the sky turning pink in the west. "He registers as her."

"Where did you get this idea?"

"From us. People are always saying we look alike, as if we're a couple of gerbils."

"Where does he change his clothes?"

"In the car, on a side road, probably the Pickerel River Road, somewhere quiet. He doesn't actually have to change much: just put on a blonde wig, lipstick, glasses." He looked down at himself to show what he meant. Both of them were dressed in sneakers, blue jeans and heavy bush jackets that came well below the waist. "Then he checks in at the motel, as her, saying 'her' husband is turning the car around or picking up beer or something. The point is the motel people have seen 'her' and believe that he is there, too. An hour later, he goes to the motel office, as himself, to ask for a wakeup call, so now the motel people have seen 'her' and him. Then, around midnight, the fighting starts. The people in the units on either side hear a hell of a row going on, sounds of someone being smacked around, and it goes on so long they complain to the desk, and the night clerk phones over and asks them to pipe down."

"The row is on tape, right?"

"Right. Then early in the morning the row starts again and there's a lot of door-banging and the neighbours see "her" leaving, walking away. At breakfast time, he checks out, leaving a message in case his wife returns. He tells the clerk she walked out on him during the night. She's probably gone to another motel. His message is that he's not going to wait around; he's gone home."

"So he left the motel in the blonde wig, then came back quietly as himself a bit later. Wasn't he taking a chance?"

"Not really. If anyone saw him, he could always say he had tried to follow his wife, but she disappeared. And that's that.

"He goes home and when his wife doesn't appear that day he reports it to the police. But in circumstances like these it looks likely that the wife has simply gone off somewhere. It's a few weeks before he can get the police seriously interested."

"And when they do take it seriously, do they find her?" There was not much light left now. In the east the sky was almost black.

"I don't know. It doesn't matter. A few weeks is as good as six months."

"They'll suspect him. After the row."

"But they won't be able to prove anything. When he leaves the motel after breakfast, he checks in with the Ontario Provincial Police in Parry Sound, in case "she" has checked in with them, and he does the same thing all the way down to Toronto, establishing a solid time trail with no gaps for him to drive back up to Sudbury. Then it's easy to make sure he's covered for the next week in Toronto."

"It might work," she said. "Have you figured out how you are going to solve it? How Porter will, I mean." Gib Porter was the writer's hero.

"Not yet."

"You could start with a hunch. You could find out what time he left Sudbury and why it took him five hours to get to Parry Sound. Did anyone see his car parked along the highway, stuff like that?"

"Why would anyone be suspicious?"

She pondered. "Her father. He never liked the man she married, never trusted him, so he hires Gib Porter." Now it was close to dark. "What about the car? Someone might have seen their car parked along the highway."

"It's rented. Perfectly ordinary rented car. If anyone sees it they won't memorise the licence plate. They'll just assume that it's a couple of hunters. But I haven't seen anyone around, have you?"

"No, I haven't. Who would be wandering around this moonscape?" She had to admit that he seemed to have everything covered. "Yes, it might work." She turned her back on him and walked towards the road. She needed to know one more thing. "In the meantime, old buddy-boy," she said over her shoulder, "We'd better be getting back."

He reached inside his jacket and pulled out the little handgun he had bought in Detroit. "Don't turn round Lucy," he said.

She turned and saw that her last question was answered. It wasn't a game. She said, "It isn't going to work."

"It'll work, all right. It's going to work." He pulled the trigger once, twice, three times.

Everything else went smoothly. His wife had often criticised his plots for being too complicated, but this one worked. Two hours later the night clerk at the Sturgeon Motel in Parry Sound signed in Mrs. Harry Coates, a blonde lady with sun-glasses (though it was quite dark), while her husband unloaded the car. During the night the clerk had to call them twice to ask them to pipe down because they were fighting and arguing so loudly that the guests on either side had called to complain. The rowing ended in the early morning with a lot of door-crashing, then Mrs. Coates came to the desk to check out. She still had sun-glasses on, but now the clerk thought they were probably covering up a black eye. Her husband, she said, had left her, taken a train or bus back to Toronto, maybe even hitch-hiked—she didn't know or care. She left a message for him in case he called. He never did, though.

She drove home and waited for two days for him to return, then she called the police. They made some routine enquiries, but they weren't very interested. The story of the night in the motel was clear, and the guy was almost certainly putting a scare into her by taking off for as long as his money held out, but pretty soon he would use a charge card or something like that, then they would be able to reel him in. They did establish that he had a girl-friend tucked away in a condominium on Sherbourne Street, and they kept an eye on her place but she was as mystified as they were, and he certainly never showed up. Nor did he try to call her.

A month later the police assumed foul play and sent out a serious enquiry, and she began the process of establishing her legal position if he should have disappeared for good. When the first snow fell she knew they wouldn't find him until the spring at the earliest, and then what would they find? A body, with no money in the wallet, and the murder weapon, which she had thrown down the mine shaft after him. (She had thrown *his* gun, from which she had removed the ammunition the night before they started their trip when she realised what he was planning, into the French River on her way to Parry Sound.) And what would they conclude? That he had been picked up hitch-hiking, robbed and killed and dumped into the mine shaft by a local thug. There was still the very slight risk that someone had seen them when they went into the bush that evening, but it was a chance he was prepared to take, so it was pretty small. Since the chance of finding the body in the first place was about ten thousand to one, the further remote chance that someone saw them near the mine shaft was an acceptable risk. All she had to do was nurse her grief for the few weeks while the police made their enquiries. His plan had been perfect, or pretty good. If she had not long known about his girl-friend, tucked away in the condominium, and if she had not come across his fishing tackle box with the loaded gun, the wig, and the make-up kit, packed ready to go, while she was searching for a pair of pliers, she would never have wondered what he was up to. After that it was just a matter of getting hold of a gun herself, and giving him every chance to prove her guess was wrong. The rest went exactly as he had planned.

Two in the Bush

From the day The Boozer became my cell mate and first told me about Clyde Parker, it took us nearly a year to set him up. In the end, though, the long delay turned out to be for the best because when we did catch up with him, the timing, Christmas Eve, was perfect.

Clyde Parker was the owner of a pub on King Street East. The Old Bush was a beer parlor, not a "men only" parlor but not the kind of place that ladies felt comfortable in, either, and as the man said, those that came in left, or they did not remain ladies very long. It had graduated from being one of the worst holes in the east end of the city to being quaint, one of the last unrenovated survivors of the days when drink was as feared as polyunsaturated fat is now. The Old Bush was such a relic that it was discovered a few years ago by a wine columnist who wrote an article about it which brought in a few people who were looking for an authentic experience, but they didn't come back once they'd got it. The regular patrons stared at them. If there was only one or two of these tourists they'd leave them alone, but if six or eight of them came in, someone would give a signal and the pub would go quiet as the regular patrons stared at them. They didn't like that.

A lot of old-timers used the place, and you could generally count on finding a few rounders there on a weeknight. It was The Boozer who put us on to the fact that Clyde Parker, the owner, might be whispering into the ear of the coppers. I say "might" because we weren't sure for a long time, which was why we didn't go for Parker in a heavy way as soon as Boozer had tipped us. We had to give him the benefit of the doubt.

The Boozer had just done a nice little job over in Rosedale. At the time he was paying a window cleaner to let him know of any empties he came across, and one day he reported that the inhabitants of a certain house on Crescent Road had gone on vacation, and access was relatively simple. The Boozer duly dropped by at 3 a.m. with a few copies of *The Globe and Mail* in case anyone was about, let himself in the back door, and helped himself to a sackful of small stuff—silver, jewelry, and such, including a real piece of luck, a twenty-ounce gold bar he found in a desk drawer. The Boozer claimed it was about the cleanest little job he'd ever done. He worked with Toothy Maclean on lookout. Utterly reliable, Toothy was. So when they came for The Boozer, three days later, he had a long think and the only one he could see shopping him was Clyde Parker.

See, the night after the job, The Boozer had called in at the Bush for a few draft ales, and to pay for his beer he off-loaded a few trinkets, cuff links and such, on Old Perry. Old Perry paid him about a tenth of what they were worth, which in itself was about a tenth of what you'd have to pay in a store, but The Boozer was thirsty and he had plenty of goods left. Old Perry made his living by having the money in his pocket when you were thirsty, and we'd all dealt with him. We'd have known years ago if he was a nark. The other alternative, Toothy Maclean, was unthinkable. Then The Boozer remembered that Clyde Parker had been hovering round when he passed the stuff over to Old Perry, so he began to wonder. He confided in me and the two of us did some asking around and we came up with three others who'd been fingered not long after they'd brushed up against Parker. So that's how it was; we didn't have any proof, but we were pretty sure.

The Boozer wanted to send a message to the outside to have Parker done, but I talked him out of it. Not too heavy, I told him, because we might be wrong, and anyway, let's do it ourselves, let's be there when it happens. I was beginning to get an idea, though when The Boozer asked, I said I didn't know yet. We had plenty of time to think about it. I got The Boozer calmed down, but he said if I didn't get a good idea, then he'd torch the Bush as soon as he got out.

I wanted something a bit subtler than that. I wanted to hurt Parker in his pride and his wallet at the same time, I wanted to cost him money and make him look foolish, and, if possible, I wanted him to know who'd done it without him being able to do anything about it. It wouldn't be easy getting past all those pugs that Parker used as waiters.

About three-quarters of the way through our term—me and The Boozer had both of us still a couple of months to do—I got an idea. Or rather, I got the last piece of an idea I'd been putting together for a few months. Ideas are like that with me.

The first part of the idea came from a cell mate I'd had at the beginning of my stretch. He'd got ninety days for impersonating a Salvation Army man. You know, going door to door, soliciting contributions and giving you a blessing with the receipt. What he'd done, he'd got a Salvation Army cap one night from the hostel when no one was watching, and another night he got a pad of receipts off the desk in the office, and with a black raincoat and a shirt and tie he looked the part perfectly. He said he picked up five hundred a night, easy, in a district like Deer Park. A lot of people gave him checks, of course, which he threw away, but he didn't count on them calling the office when the checks didn't go through. (A lot of people *deserve* to be inside). Two months later the coppers were waiting for him. He should have worked it for a week, then stayed off the streets for at least six months, as a Sally Ann collector, I mean. There's plenty of other things he could have been doing. But he got greedy and silly and they caught up with him taking up a collection round the Bunch of Grapes on Kingston Road. So that's where I got a bit of an idea.

I got the second part of my idea at a prison concert. You had to attend, and there was this citizen on the bill, singing a lot of old-fashioned songs. "Sons of Toil and Sorrow" was one. "A Bachelor Gay Am I" was another. In prison, I ask you. Some of the younger cons thought he'd made the songs up himself. And it wasn't just the choice of song. He couldn't sing. He was terrible—loud and embarrassing, hooting and hollering away, the veins sticking out all over his neck as he tried to get near the notes. The others nick-named him Danny Boy, which he said was his signature tune. I thought, you should stick to hymns, buddy, because he reminded me exactly of a carol singer who used to sing with a Salvation Army band when I was a kid.

Then I realized that I had it.

All I needed was a trumpet player and someone on the accordion, and we were all set.

Me and The Boozer were both sprung in October and we moved in together. My wife had visited me once to tell me not to try going home again, ever, and Boozer had no home, so we found this little apartment on Queen Street near the bail and parole unit where we had to appear from time to time.

We were both on welfare, of course, at first; then we both found jobs of the kind that offered no temptation, and that no one else wanted.

The Boozer got taken on at a car wash, and I found a situation in a coal-and-wood yard, filling fifty-pound sacks with coal. Neither of us needed the work. Boozer had gone down protesting his innocence, so he still had his loot stashed away, but he couldn't touch it for a few months because they were watching him. As for me, I was always the saving kind.

Did I tell you what I got shipped for? I sell hot merchandise on the streets. You've seen me, or someone like me, if you've ever gone shopping along the Danforth. I'm the one who jumps out of a car and opens a suitcase full of Ralph Lauren sweatshirts that I am prepared to let go for a third of the price, quick, before the cops come. You buy them because you think they're stolen, which is the impression I'm trying to create, but in point of fact I buy them off a Pakistani jobber on Spadina for five dollars each. I'd pay ten if they weren't seconds and the polo player looked a bit more authentic. I've sold them all— fake Chanel Number 5, fake Gucci, Roots, the lot. Anything to appeal to the crook in you. Sometimes the odd case of warmish goods does come my way, but I prefer to deal in legit rubbish if I can get it.

So there I was, unloading a suitcaseful of shirts that had withstood a warehouse fire, good shirts if a bit smoky, and the fuzz nabbed me for being an accomplice to a dip.

I was working the dim-sum crowd on the corner of Spadina and Dundas on a Sunday morning and I was just heading for my car to load up again, when someone shouted his wallet was gone, and then another shouted, and then another. Before you knew it, two martial-arts experts grabbed me and the cops were called and I got twelve months. I never even saw the dip.

But to get back to my story. First I had to get a couple of musicians. That wasn't easy until I bumped into one in the lineup at the bail and parole unit, a guy I'd known inside, who played in the prison band. He played trumpet, or cornet really, when he wasn't doing time for stealing car radios. He found me a trombone player. Then I had a real piece of luck because right after that I ran into the original authentic terrible hymn singer from the prison concert.

At first he wouldn't hear of it, but I went to work on him and he saw the virtue in what we were planning and promised to think it over. The next time we met, he agreed. I should have known.

We decided we could manage without an accordion player.

Now we had to get some uniforms. All we really needed were the caps. The trumpet player used to be a legit chauffeur and he still had his old black jacket, and he thought he could put his hand on some others. The owner of the limousine fleet kept a bundle of uniforms in his garage storeroom, and Digger Ray assured us that getting access to them would not be a problem. Digger Ray was the trombone player. He was Australian and his specialty was playing the fake sucker in crooked card games, but he'd done a few B and E jobs. Toothy Maclean lifted the caps for us while The Boozer created a disturbance during prayers at the Salvation Army shelter. (He started crying and repenting right in the middle of a prayer and Toothy got all the caps from the office while they were comforting him.)

Now The Boozer had to line up three or four cooperating citizens who would be unknown to Clyde Parker, fellas who didn't use the Old Bush. It wasn't easy, but Boozer came up with three guys who hardly ever drank—not too common among his acquaintance, I can tell you, and once they heard about it they were keen to be included. So we were set. Now I had to go to work. I had the trickiest job of all.

I was the obvious person to approach Clyde Parker because I'd only been in the Bush once, years ago. I hate the place, always have. It's the kind of beer parlor where there's a civil war being fought at every table and the waiters are hired to break up fights, and if you stay until midnight someone will throw up all over your shoes. I like a nice pub, myself.

So Parker didn't know me and when I approached him he was very wary, at first. I went in two or three times until I was sure who he was, then I got talking to him. Had he heard, I asked, of this fake Salvation Army band that was going around the pubs collecting? He hadn't, but if they came near the Old Bush, he'd be ready, he said. He nodded to indicate a couple of his waiters who were lounging against the wall, waiting for orders. I don't know where he finds them, but they look as if he has to chain them up when the pub is closed. No, no, I said, there's a better way than that, and then I told him.

People like Parker are born suspicious, but they are also born greedy and very conceited. They think they are smart. So the plan was designed to make Parker feel smart, which it did, and to make him some money, and when he saw the point, he was in.

It was a lovely night, Christmas Eve. About ten o'clock the sky was black and clear with thousands of stars winking away. It must have been like that the night one of them started to move. I'd've followed it.

Danny Boy had the car and we were to meet at my place. I drove after that. We reached the street behind the Bush at ten-fifteen. Zero hour was ten-thirty. We figured four carols, about fifteen minutes, then the collection during one more, and out of there by eleven.

They waited in the car while I slipped across to the pub and made sure Hooligan was in place. Didn't I mention Hooligan? His real name was Halligan, and renaming him Hooligan tells you something about the level of wit in the Don Jail. He was our ace in the hole, the one Parker didn't know about. Because of him we had to steal another cap, and this time I couldn't get to one nohow. Then Toothy remembered that a buddy of his had a dog that his kids had trained to catch Frisbees. It got very good at picking them out of the air, but the trouble was that when there were no Frisbees to chase, he filled in the time chasing kids and snatching their hats off. He was harmless, but parents complained, and they had to keep him locked up. The kids could get him to snatch anyone's hat by pointing to it and whispering. As I say, Herman never hurt anyone. He could take off your hat from behind clean as a whistle without touching you, just one leap. So we borrowed Herman one night and waited near the Salvation Army shelter and pretty soon out came an officer and set off down Sherbourne Street. A few minutes later Herman lifted his hat. It fit Hooligan pretty good, too.

I checked that Hooligan was in place, and in we went. Parker had arranged a little clear space by the door, though he pretended to be surprised when we walked in. I approached him, very formal-like, and asked his permission to play some carols and pass round the collection plate. He acted up a bit by shaking his head, then he seemed to change his mind. "All right," he said. "Four carols." I looked grateful and swung my arm the way conductors do, and off they went.

A trumpet and a trombone wouldn't amount to much, you would think, but these fellas made them seem just made for the job. Very simple, just the notes, no twiddly bits. They were good. And of course, there was Danny Boy. He was as good as another trumpet. He didn't wait for a cue. Just started right in, head back, veins sticking out. He could be heard right in the back of the room, right in the corners. They started with "O Come, All Ye Faithful," which Danny Boy gave a verse in Latin of, then "Good King Wenceslaus" and "We Three Kings," and finally, one of Danny's shut-eyed ones, "O Holy Night." By then we had them. Danny was terrible, of course, but he was very sincere and you could recognize the tunes. I wouldn't say anyone was crying—this was the Old Bush, after all—but they were quiet. So now we went into "O Little Town of Bethlehem," very soft, *piano* they call it, and Toothy and I began the rounds with the money bags.

This was Parker's signal. We was getting something from nearly everyone, a dollar here, two there, a five, then another. There's a psychology to these things. As soon as someone puts in five dollars, that becomes standard, like the ante in a poker game. People stop fingering their change and open their wallets. After four tables, five was normal. Then Parker spoke. "Gents," he said. "Gents, this is Christmas Eve." He paused, looking sincere. "I want to announce that I will match all contributions made tonight toward this good cause."

"And a free beer all around," someone shouted.

One of the waiters moved to throw him out, but Parker only hesitated for a second. "Never mind the free beer tonight, of all nights," he said, implying that free beer was standard on other nights at the Bush. "Tonight is for the others out there." He waved at the door. "The ones with no beer," he said.

The arrangement was, of course, that Parker would get half, three-quarters, really, including his own money, but free beer could never be recovered.

The next voice, though, nearly took him off balance, I reached a table where The Boozer had planted one of his cronies, and Boozer gave him a wink from the back of the room, and he jumps up and shouts, "Then here's fifty dollars."

Parker looked a bit greasy for a minute, but he caught himself in time to shout, "Good for you."

Then the fever took hold. The biggest single contribution we got was a hundred dollars, but no one gave less than twenty, and every time I came to one of The Boozer's cronies he would whip up the excitement with a fresh fifty. We went round the room with Danny Boy crooning away in the background, and when we were done we went back to the counter and emptied the bags onto the bar. Digger Ray and one of the bartenders counted it and Digger made the announcement. "Two thousand three hundred and twenty-seven." Someone shouted, "Your turn now, Parker."

Parker turned to the barman and held out his hand and received a wad of money which he handed over to Digger. Digger held it up to show it was a lot of money, no need to count it on Christmas Eve, and he swept all the money back into one of the bags and we were ready to go. There was still three minutes on my watch, so I made a little speech, and then, right on time, Hooligan made his entrance.

He was got up like the rest of us—Salvation Army gear, and a little collection box.

We'd rehearsed the next bit carefully.

"Merry Christmas all, and God bless you," Hooligan says, while the crowd started to look a bit puzzled.

Parker looked at me in a panic. The smell of something fishy was now reaching into the farthest corners of the room and I would have given the patrons about ten more seconds. "Holy Jesus," I said to Parker. "It's a real one. What'll we do now? There'll be a riot if they find out."

The two musicians and Danny Boy slid out the door and one of the patrons said, "What the hell's going on?"

"Give him the money," I said. "For God's sake, give him the money."

Parker couldn't speak, but he nodded, and I stepped forward.

"Coals to Newcastle," I said very loud and heartily. "Coals to Newcastle, sending two groups to the same place. But you're just in time, Captain. Here." I handed him the sack of money.

Hooligan's eyes rolled up in holy wonder. "Bless you, gentlemen," he said. "Bless you."

I was praying he wouldn't do anything silly like make the sign of the cross over the room, and I signaled to Toothy that we should be on our way. Then I heard a sound that made my blood run cold. Someone opened the door and "Joy to the World" came flooding through, played by all fifteen members of the Salvation Army's silver band.

Parker, of course, was not surprised. Hooligan was his surprise, and he assumed that the band was backup for him.

Now there was just me and Toothy—Hooligan could look after

himself—so I put my hand on Toothy's shoulder in a brotherly way and we almost got through the door before we were stopped by Sister Anna herself. She looked at Hooligan, puzzled. Hooligan looked at me. Parker looked at us both, and I did the only thing I could. I took the money off Hooligan, put it in the sister's hands, said, "Merry Christmas, Sister," and took Toothy and Hooligan with me through the door.

The car was gone, of course—the motto with us, if a job goes wrong, is "Pull the ladder up, Jack. I'm in." But no one was chasing us, so we threw our caps away and hailed a cab.

We waited until after New Year's, then we got an educated friend of Toothy's to pretend to be a reporter for a news station doing a story on Christmas giving, and the Salvation Army commander told him what had happened. "Someone phoned us, here at the shelter," the commander said. "They told us if we would come to the Old Bush and play a few carols, we would get a major contribution. We gathered it was some kind of surprise, arranged by the proprietor."

We never knew for a long time who had done it; then, about six months after, The Boozer and I were stopped dead in Nathan Phillips Square by the sight of Danny Boy, eyes closed, head back, in the middle of "Abide With Me." He was in full uniform. Behind him was the Salvation Army silver band.

We waited for him to come round with the collecting box. We kept our heads down, and when he drew level I looked up sharply. "Hello, Danny Boy," I said. "How long you been with this mob?"

He looked surprised, but not for long. "I saw the light last Christmas," he said. "Brother." And he moved away, shaking his box. The Salvation Army were just being charitable, of course, welcoming the backslider, never mind that his singing hadn't improved a bit, not to sinners' ears, anyway. You could say that what mattered was that he was in tune with God.

The Boozer wanted to do him right then and there, but I held him off. As I pointed out, it had cost us nothing, but Parker was out a couple of thousand, and the boys in the Old Bush (to whom we'd slipped the story) were still laughing.

Even on a good day, you can't win every race.

The Duke

After half a lifetime of not being very much at home in the world, Duke Luscombe had finally found exactly the right job. He was a cook, trained in Montreal by a catering company to run the kitchen of a construction camp. The training could not have been very extensive: the Duke could cook about twenty different menus, though the same vegetables appeared on most of them, but because some of the items, like steaks and chops, were offered at least once a week, and because there was a roast or a boiled ham every Sunday, some of the menus, like pork tenderloin, appeared only once a month, giving the Duke's repertoire an appearance of being much bigger than it really was. But his skills matched the needs of the men. They wanted soup, and then meat, in some form, every night, and while they were prepared to eat canned fruit for dessert occasionally, most nights they wanted pie, with ice-cream. The soups were shipped in from Montreal, in drums, and the pies were made from dough prepared in Montreal and from huge cans of pie filling. The Duke had printed instructions for the preparation of every meat dish, so the best test of his skill came at breakfast, where his bacon was crisp and his eggs done to order.

By the time I came to the camp the Duke was well established. He had command of a dining-room serving the foremen, of whom there were about twenty, including the timekeepers, the men who recorded the labour and materials used on each contract. Even a kitchen this small called for two cooks, but the Duke did it all with some help from a couple of Ojibwa girls who came in from the Indian camp down by the railway tracks. There had once been another cook before I arrived, but he had only stayed a month. The Duke had complained in headshaking fashion from the day he arrived about the 'goddam useless bum' that Montreal had sent him, and at the end of the month the new man was gone. When the foremen appeared for breakfast one morning the Duke told them he had put his assistant on the train and told him not to stop until he got to Montreal. "He was just under my feet all the time," the Duke said. "Help like that I don't need. And if

59

the Montreal office don't like it, they can find someone else to replace me."

The new man had tried to get the foremen to hear his side of the story when it became obvious that the Duke intended to get rid of him, but the prime concern of the men in the dining-room was that the Duke not be upset. All of them had worked on jobs where one day the cook had been too drunk to make breakfast, or had gone berserk with a knife, and they could tolerate the knowledge of the Duke's unfairness for the sake of their food. No one was surprised when the assistant left. And presumably the Montreal office was happy with the saving in wages.

The Duke got up at five to pick up the Indian girls. Breakfast had to be ready by seven for a workcrew who started at seven-thirty. Lunch was soup, cold cuts with some kind of vegetables, and pie. Around three, the Duke began on the supper which had to be ready at five-thirty. He closed the dining-room at seven-thirty and ate his own sup-per—usually a steak—and the girls helped themselves to what was left over from the night's menu. He waited, then, until they had cleaned up the kitchen, and drove them back to town. The Duke took respon-sibility for more than their transportation. While they worked in his kitchen they might as well have been in a convent. There were very few women around that far north and inevitably, since all the foremen had pickup trucks, someone would have offered them a ride home, but the Duke watched closely for any suggestion of that and cut it off immediately. One of the men said that he got the impression that the chief sin that the short-lived assistant had committed was nothing to do with the work, but that he had cast his eye on one of the girls, and perhaps even made a suggestive remark to the Duke.

When he returned from driving the girls to their camp, the Duke went to the beer parlour, drank two beers, and went to bed by ten. On Sundays, he cooked a big meal at noon, usually a roast, or—a special-ity of the catering company—a New England Boiled Dinner, the only place I have ever seen it on a menu, then, at five, laid out a cold supper of platters of boiled eggs, cold meats, pickles and canned salmon, which the girls served while he looked on, dressed in his best clothes, thus proclaiming that he was not there to work, although there was no question of absenting himself while anyone was in the dining-room. He worked six fourteen-hour days, and on Sundays he worked for six hours and watched for three. On Sunday afternoons, before the supper buffet was set out, he joined in the poker game that had been going since Friday night, dropping out when he had won or lost $10, about a day's pay at that time. He usually lost, and seemed in this way to be paying his dues. Apart from the weekly poker game, he relaxed by sitting at the foremen's table in the beer parlour, listening to the talk and contributing only confirmatory remarks; he went to the army cinema two days a week, and spent a lot of time looking after his clothes. He was not a dandy, but he prided himself on his ironing, even doing a shirt for one of us for a special reason, to have a clean one when we went to Winnipeg, for example. The Duke never went to town: we understood he preferred to save up his leave and take it in one lump when the contract was finished, but I believe that more important was his distaste for having anyone in his kitchen.

He had no friends. He referred occasionally to a sister in Montreal to whom he sent money to spend on her children, but he never seemed to hear from her. He avoided intimacy, seeming to require only as much companionship as he found at the foremen's table. At first I thought him simply intellectually disadvantaged, as they say now. His obsessive behaviour was something I had come across before when a simple person has been given a responsibility that exactly suits his capabilities—running a dishwasher, say—and blossoms in pride and then becomes fiercely protective of the area he has learned to control. Then I realised that this was an arid understanding of him, and I decided then that he was by nature a monk, a monk who had found his work and his monastery. He burned with a low flame in all other areas; as far as we knew he was uninterested in sexual matters except to understand that his girls had to be protected. In his spare time he read—westerns, hundreds of them, again and again as if the West was the paradise it seems to a ten-year-old, and yet, I think, he had already found his Eden in the place where the rest of us saved up to escape. He was a happy man.

Until Paddy Vernon came along.

Vernon was a plumbing foreman who took over in the middle of the job from a man who refused to come back off leave. He was a gregarious

fellow who made it clear immediately that he was used to being re-
garded as the life of the party. Always joking, he was, mostly practical.
I didn't know so clearly then that teasing is a form of cruelty. Vernon
was a born tease, and anyone could see right away that the Duke was
a natural butt for someone like Paddy Vernon.

The Duke was very vulnerable, of course. He took pride not in
being a chef, but in being able to do his job exactly as he had been
taught. If anyone complained, he would taste a morsel of whatever
they found fault with, nod and say, "That's the way it's supposed to
taste. Take your complaint to Montreal." Very occasionally, he would
acknowledge a problem for which he was responsible. Then he would
shake his head. "That's not the way it's supposed to taste," he would
say, not apologetically, but in a puzzled way, and offer to cook something else to make up. For the rest of the meal he would try to think his
way back over the course of the preparation until he found the point,
where, say, too much salt had been added, questioning the Indian
girls, solving the puzzle then and reporting back to the diner, who had
by now lost interest, "I'd put the salt in, but there was a power failure
this morning, remember, when the digger cut the cable, so when the
light came back on I saw the salt still out—I always put it away right
after I use it—and I must have thought I hadn't put it in yet. That was
what it was."

Such an error was rare, and always caused by an outside factor. By
never allowing anyone into his kitchen space, the Duke kept such
factors to a minimum. After the departure of the sole assistant cook, no
one was ever allowed into the kitchen area except the two Indian girls
to stand behind the steam table and serve. When the place was cleaned
up after a meal, the Duke snapped the locks—he kept locks on all the
cupboards including the walk-in freezer. It was obsessive behaviour, of
course: he guarded his territory with the passion of a man who had
never owned a territory before.

In the way of such things, we affected a pride in him, gave him an
'interesting' status. "Old Duke doesn't allow anyone behind that counter," we would tell the surprised newcomer who had found his way
barred wordlessly by the Duke. We did the same thing with the secret
that everyone felt must lie at the centre of his life. The Duke gave us no
context in which to understand him, no past, no family history, no

existence outside the camp, and the men used to wonder what he was concealing. On the whole the reasons men went that far north to work were easy to find. For most, in those days, it was money, because the skilled tradesmen could earn three times what they earned in town, and keep most of it. Alcoholism was another big reason; the north was the last stop for men who had used up their welcome in town. There were several men on the run from alimony payments, a handful of romantics were in love with the idea of The North, and there was at least one with a broken heart. The Duke fit none of these categories: he wasn't saving to go back home, or on the run. He *was* home, but not seeing this we assumed he had an interesting secret. "People don't come up to a place like this to cook without some good reason," Tiny Williams, the general superintendent said, and we nodded solemnly until the Duke began to acquire a touch of Conradian mystery which satisfied our need to mythicise him by failing to answer our questions. Personally, even at the time I was sceptical of this enlargement of the Duke's mysteriousness, seeing it as springing more from his customers' desire to make him interesting than from anything in him, but I knew better than to say so.

Paddy Vernon didn't. He was looking for a target as soon as he arrived. He began with a young timekeeper from Newfoundland, telling him tall stories to test his credulity in front of the other foremen. He also constructed an elaborate running joke at the boy's expense, pretending the boy was meeting civilisation for the first time, though there can be nothing in Newfoundland as barren as that construction camp. "Pass me the marmalade, Hector," he would say. "That's the orange stuff in the jar there." It was mild and feeble stuff, and Hector accepted it mildly as the proper due of the youngest man in the room, and it only lasted until Vernon saw that his real target had to be the Duke.

He started with a string of jokes about camp cooks—the manure-in-the-pumpkin pie joke was typical. The Duke listened carefully, not to the words, it seemed to me, but to the cadences of Vernon's sentences. I think he had no sense of humour whatever, but he had watched and listened to men making jokes, and laughing at them, and learned to chime in with a smile to avoid being noticed. If the joke was genuinely funny, enough to catch the other listeners by surprise, then the Duke would come in late with his response, as if he had just seen it. Usually, though, he could time his laugh to respond to the climax he could feel in the rhythm of the speaker's words. "Ha!" he would bark, once, loudly, then, "You want beans?" or more eggs, or toast.

Vernon made me nervous when he started to tease the Duke, because none of us was sure then what lay behind the cook's facade, what sensitive area might not explode into violence, a not uncommon occurrence in that place. Fights happened for trivial reasons. But Vernon found the Duke irresistible and pretty soon he had progressed from jokes about cooks to more active horseplay. Very early the two men had a small confrontation over territory. Vernon wandered behind the steam table for the first time to help himself to some corn, but as he dipped his spoon into the well, the Duke pushed the lid across to close off the reservoir, trapping Vernon's spoon against the edge. Vernon looked up, genuinely surprised, as the Duke pointed to the notice prohibiting non-authorised personnel (everyone except the Duke and his girls) behind the counter. He lifted the lid of the well so that Vernon could retrieve the spoon, and Vernon looked around at us to see if we found it as ridiculous as he was beginning to, but so sacred was the Duke's area by now that I think we were shocked to find Vernon in it, and waited for him to come away. Vernon saw that it was something he didn't understand, and decided to try it for laughs. He read the notice again, jumped back in alarm, and made a business of running out of the Duke's area before he could be caught, one hand behind him to protect him from being spanked. Some of the men smiled politely, but Vernon was left looking foolish by the lack of a real supporting laugh. I could see he didn't like that.

So he tried to find a space on the edge of the Duke's territory where he could mock the very idea of a territory sacred to the cook. He would keep his eye on the Duke, and when the cook disappeared for a few minutes, as he did occasionally to fetch supplies, Vernon would race round the counter and help himself to something he didn't want, then run back before, or as, the Duke reappeared. The point, of course, was to get almost caught by the Duke.

The Duke appeared to understand what Vernon was up to, and rather neatly, I thought, turned the joke against Vernon. Now and again he would return immediately, before the door had swung closed, making Vernon hurl himself across the end of the counter to get back without being 'caught'. "Ha!" the Duke said, thus turning Vernon's tease into a kind of "What's the time Mr. Wolf" game for grown-ups, and Vernon had to try something else. Once he took our breath away by locking the Duke in his own freezer, a large walk-in locker by the exit where the cook kept all the meat and fresh (frozen) milk, and bread. It was hardly necessary for eight months of the year; for part of that time it was probably warmer in the freezer than it was outside, but its main function was security. It was one of the Duke's two lockable storage areas; the other held all the canned goods. They were locked, not simply because the Duke was responsible for the inventory but because they were his. We had a little hot-plate in the bunkhouse, a frypan, a kettle and a coffee-pot, and we could make ourselves a fried egg sandwich late at night, during the poker game. The Duke supplied us with everything we needed; we only had to ask. But we did have to ask, because he would hand over the key to the stores to no one. The Duke fetched what we wanted.

One day at suppertime, Paddy Vernon asked if for once he could have a little fresh milk in his coffee. Normally the fresh (frozen) milk was kept for special purposes because it was expensive to ship and bulky to store, and we regularly drank Carnation in our coffee. But this time the Duke looked at the ceiling for advice, nodded, unlocked the freezer and disappeared inside. Vernon was over the counter in one jump and had the door slammed in a second. The idea, I guess, was to wait until the cook was good and chilly, then let him out, but the Duke was out before Vernon got back to his chair. There's a safety lock on those doors; you can't get locked in accidentally, and once more the joke was on Vernon as the Duke shouted "Ha!" and went back to work.

After that Vernon seemed more or less to give up on the Duke, concentrating on leaving two-dollar bills in the urinals to see who would pick them up, that kind of thing. I say 'seemed' because in fact he was working on a major joke.

All the elements are now in place; you can write the rest of the story yourself. You must know what comes next. Inevitably Paddy Vernon will have to construct a practical joke involving the Duke's territory, and the heart of that territory, the freezer. Inevitably, too, given the safety mechanism of the freezer door, Paddy Vernon will have the bright idea of getting inside the freezer to surprise the hell out of the Duke when he opens the door. How Vernon does it is irrelevant. Say he goes to town and gets hold of some duplicate freezer keys from a pal in Winnipeg. Anything will do. Now you have to think of a way to give Vernon an audience when he leaps out on the Duke. Make it Sunday at suppertime when the Duke will not have had to use the freezer for an hour or two. Then set up one of the men to suggest to the Duke that he check his freezer because there was a power failure that afternoon. Will that do?

The important thing is to get all the men assembled in the dining room, waiting for the Duke to arrive and open the door.

Make the Duke disappear after lunch, forgoing the poker game. At this point, you will have to put in the information that one of the timekeepers who prefers the Duke to Vernon has tipped off the cook. Probably the boy from Newfoundland. At any rate, at suppertime after they have waited long enough, the timekeeper tells them that the Duke knows about the joke and is probably not coming. But why hasn't Vernon already let himself out? Because, someone points out, there is a three-inch nail threaded through the flange of the handle making it impossible to turn. Is Vernon dead, if not of cold, then of suffocation? Is this going to be the Duke's revenge? I don't think it will do. He's only been inside a couple of hours at most and there's plenty of air for that long.

Someone pulls out the nail, but the door is still locked, so they smash the lock and the door swings slowly open and a frozen, much chastened Vernon stumbles out. Or better, he faints. Yes, because then he has to be taken to the camp hospital, giving time to discover that the Duke left on the afternoon train. This seems excessive behaviour. Was the violation of his territory that important?

Such seems to be the case until Vernon recovers and leads them back to the freezer where he spent two hours in the company of that other cook who had been there for three months.

Leave the rest to the reader.

Kaput

"Loneliness was bad," he said. "It could do terrible things to people. But there was worse. I knew two fellas up here once—they worked a trapline near Mile 42—well, I tell you, they got to hate each other those two, like one of them marriages where the husband and wife is exchanging notes all the time, not speaking. These two got like that. They couldn't agree on anything after a while. Never mind, though, they had to stick it out to the spring. What they did to avoid arguments, they had a deck of cards, d'ye see, and they cut'em to see who was to do the chores. They cut for everything. It worked out pretty well for a while. One of them would have a run of luck and he would have a nice time watching the other work, then it would swing back. Some of the chores was worse than others, of course, like going out to see why the dogs are restless in forty below in a snowstorm that fills your tracks behind you. That's a bad one, because maybe you've got to scare off a pack of wolves, or a bear. Still, that's how they worked it. Then one of them got cute. He picked up a book somewhere, probably from the mission or the Hudson's Bay store, on how to be a conjuror. There was a bit in it on how to do card tricks and one of them showed you how to cut any card you wanted. This fella took the book and hid it and practised when his partner was away on the trapline and he got so he could cut any card he wanted. Pretty soon his partner was doing all the dirty hard jobs and he was doing the easy ones, like making the coffee in the morning. His partner never tumbled to it, just waited for his luck to turn. Then he found the book when the other fella was away.

He didn't say anything at first, just waited. Then one night they thought they had a bear outside, so they cut the cards and the poor fella lost again. What he did then was interesting. He took his gun and got dressed like he was going after the bear and went out the cabin and started to holler. His partner came out with his own gun and the fella who was being cheated shot him as he stood in the door. Then he fired off three or four rounds of his partner's gun, laid him on the floor of the

67

cabin with his gun in his hands, closed the place up, harnessed up the dogs and three days later turned himself in at the Mountie post. He told the mounties he'd shot his partner in self defence. Said his partner had gone crazy and suddenly started shooting at him while he was out seeing to the dogs. Lucky, he said, he had his gun with him so there was only one thing to do. The mounties accepted that. They had no choice. It happens." Duncan Bane swallowed his beer in a long smooth slide and I signaled the beer-parlour waiter for more. I figured we had a while to go before I got what I wanted.

I was in Churchill, Manitoba, collecting material for what I hoped would be an oral history of the near north. My idea was to find some of the really old people who were still around who had been there in the thirties, the old trappers, the missionaries, perhaps the odd Hudson's Bay factor who had decided to stay after retirement. I started in Flin Flon, then moved on to The Pas and now I was in a beer parlour in one of the oldest settlements on the Hudson's Bay. So far I hadn't had much luck. Churchill is a grain port for a few weeks a year, a year-round railhead for the twice-weekly train, and, as I was finding out, a tourist town. Duncan Bane was the chief tourist attraction.

I was staying at the hotel above the beer-parlour and the waiter, hearing of my mission, had insisted that Duncan Bane was the man I should talk to. Bane was a retired trapper who had come up north as a young man during the depression. Now in his eighties, he spent his days in the beer-parlour at his own table in the corner. I introduced myself to him, bought him some beer and he started to talk. He had been talking now for half an hour and none of it was any use to me. My experience of this kind of thing is that sometimes you have to wait a long time to get what you want.

I was beginning to think, though, that Duncan Bane was a waste of time. He was certainly dressed for the part: old work pants, held up by suspenders, a much-washed check shirt, and best of all, a huge tangle of beard beneath a blue-veined bald head. He made his living, or his beer money, sitting in the parlor telling stories for tourists, and probably allowing them to take his picture, for a consideration. So far he had told me three stories. The one about the two trappers and the deck of cards I had heard years ago in Winnipeg, then again twice on this trip, in Fun Flon and Cranberry Portage. Bane told it well from long practice. First he'd told me the story of the miner who had struck gold in the north and gone to Winnipeg, hired three whores, then, to acclimatise them, filled the hotel suite with two feet of corn flakes so that he would teach them how to walk on snow-shoes. This has always been one of my favourite stories. Bane claimed to have known the miner. His next story had concerned the pregnant eskimo woman who had been left to die by her band, but who had appeared out of the blizzard two months later with a healthy baby dressed in the skins of animals she had trapped, and whose flesh she had survived on, as well as devising needles and thread from the bones and sinews to sew the skins for clothing. This one goes back to Samuel Hearne's diaries, where Wordsworth probably heard of it to write his version. Bane claimed to have met the mountie who took her in when she appeared at his post.

Nevertheless, he had been a trapper, and he had lived in the north for fifty years, and I figured that once he had run through his party pieces I might still get something. He seemed to be winding down now, and I signalled the waiter for more beer.

"How did you find out what really happened between those two partners?" I asked, quasi-sceptically. It was an obvious question and if I didn't challenge him a little bit he might get bored.

"He told me," Bane said. "On his death-bed," and looked expansively around the room.

I decided that acting as if I believed him was wrong. There was something about the way he made his last ridiculous statement that implied the further comment, "And if you believe that you'll believe anything."

"Now you're bull-shitting me," I said, laughing, choosing a level of gullibility that could be a challenge to him.

His mouth opened, his eyes widened and he looked around the room again, in mock protest. Then he laughed. "You're a smart one," he said. "That's a story that was told to me. I can't testify to it."

"And the others?"

"Oh, no," he protested. "Them are true enough."

Now what. I needed something personal, that he might not have polished into a story. "What did you do for entertainment?" I asked. "Did you work alone?"

"I did, yes. About once a month I'd find me way to the mission and have a drink or two with the priest, or up to the post and the same thing with the factor there. Once a year I went into town."

"Winnipeg?"

"That's right. I'd have a whoop and a holler and get me oil changed and a couple of teeth pulled. That was enough for me. People talk about being bushed if they stay up here too long at a time. I been bushed for fifty years. I'm bushed now, I suppose, but I couldn't live in town now, me."

Now I was getting somewhere. "What about Christmas?" I prodded.

"How d'ye mean?"

"Didn't you get lonely at Christmas even?"

"Only once. In the city. I'd broke me hand setting one of me traps and I couldn't get it straight, so I went into town to the hospital. They wrapped it in plaster, but so I could use it, and one of the furriers I deal with made me a good mitt which would go over it. I was all set to come back when I noticed it was the twenty-third, two days before Christmas, so I stayed where I was to celebrate. Well, let me tell you, I've never been so down in me life. Christmas in the Winnipeg Hotel. The city was deserted—and an empty city is a lot lonelier than a cabin, where you can hear your dogs outside and the crack of the lights in the sky at night. After that, come Christmas, if I didn't go to the mission, I'd save meself a mickey of rye for the day. I wouldn't do any work, just sit in me cabin until the whiskey was gone, then go to bed."

"Did you drink much, by yourself, at other times?"

"Never." Now he was serious. "Never. I've seen it kill a few, not the drink but what it can bring. Fella gets to drinking and falls asleep outside. He don't last long. I've seen a few of them, whites and Indians. Matter of fact, there was one up at the fort here, one Christmas Eve. Call that waiter and I'll tell you about it."

Not quite what I wanted, but it sounded better than his tales for tourists. He was more relaxed now—I calculated that he must be on his eighth beer—and he had stopped orating. The waiter loaded us up, and Bane started in.

"Back in the early fifties, it was, there was a big military base there then, Army, Navy, Air force, even a couple of sailors. There was Americans as well as Canadians. I think they were supposed to stop the Russians when they came over the top of the world. They was training in arctic warfare, learning how to survive and fight at forty below. I don't think they ever got to the fighting bit; they was just learning that it took them twenty-three hours out of every twenty-four just to take care of surviving which only left them one hour for fighting.

"There were hundreds of them and I worked with them for a while. They hired me to show them the country and I used to go out with them in their caterpillars when they were mapping the area. I got to know some of them pretty good, one especially, a big sergeant from somewhere down in the south. He wanted a polar bear skin real bad to take back and I got him one. You wasn't supposed to shoot polar bears but one of them attacked me one day and I had to kill it in self-defence." He stuck his tongue in his cheek and gave me a grotesque, owlish look to make sure I understood. "So Sergeant Vivaldi was very grateful and he insisted I come up to the sergeants' mess on Christmas Eve, to the dance, and stay over a couple of days." He shook some salt into his beer and took a swallow. "I didn't want to go but he insisted and so did some of the others so I went and it was quite a night I can tell you. They made a bit of a pet of me, found me a coat and tie—you had to wear coat and tie in the mess—and they give me a nice room. I used my team to come as far as the mission where I staked my dogs out, and they fetched me the rest of the way in a caterpillar.

"The American sergeants was the hosts for Christmas Eve. The different units used to compete in showing each other a good time on the holidays which they celebrated all of, Canadian and American. So the Canadians was the hosts on our Labour Day and the Americans on theirs and on Sadie Hawkins' Day. They'd divided up Christmas so the Americans got Christmas Eve and the Canadians looked after New Year's Eve. As I say, it was quite a night. The mess was all decorated like a night club. 'White Nights' Lounge' they called it, with fancy lights and balloons and such, and a bottle of champagne on every table, free. I don't like the stuff meself, but there it was, one for every table. And they had a band. The Yanks had flown up a band from Washington just for the night and they were really letting her rip. I hadn't danced, me, for twenty years and I wasn't planning to try even if I could've done their dances, but Sergeant Vivaldi kept getting the girls to ask me—I could see what he was up to and I didn't mind, but I couldn't do those dances. The girls? There were some, a few wives and secretaries and such. There was enough if they shared themselves around. There was a Mrs. Caruso at our table, her husband was a sergeant away in Washington and she was sharing herself around a bit but I'll come to that. So I told Vivaldi to stop it. I'd only ever danced the polka, none of this jitterbugging stuff, so I told him, but the next thing you know he's over talking to the band and I'm up there dancing a polka with a girl named Lucy from St. Boniface. French girl. Round we went, all by ourselves with the crowd clapping and a big cheer at the end. I reckon it was the champagne. I don't like it, but nothing else would have got me up. Afterwards I recited a poem through the microphone which I'd made up when I was alone in me cabin, and that got a big hand."

This was what I wanted. "Can you remember it? Could you recite it now?"

"Sure I can, I'll do it for ye later. Let me get on with me story. The band got louder and louder and at one point the trombone player took off his shoes and played the instrument with his bare foot. That was the kind of evening it was. Then, about midnight, they served lunch."

"Supper?"

"We always call it lunch in this part of the world. Where are you from? Anyway, they served the food. Now here is where it started. Some of the civilians had asked the Americans if they could lend a hand. They was responsible for the lunch. So now, about midnight the lights dimmed and there was a roll of drums and then a strange thing happened. The door to the kitchen opened and out came the camp barber, running, pushing one of them steel trolleys they use in hotel kitchens, loaded with plates of spaghetti. After him came another fella with a trolley, and after him came a fella called Figge, all of them running. Figge crashed into the other two, upsetting them, and started fighting with the barber, rolling over and over in the spaghetti which was all over the floor. Well, the band was pretty tanked up by now and they started to play galloping music and we got up on the tables to watch and cheer. But of course, Sergeant Vivaldi wasn't about to let his evening be spoilt—it wasn't being spoilt, we was having a fine time—but him and three or four others separated Figge and the barber, and some others cleaned up the floor and then we lined up in the kitchen for our spaghetti just as they always did on Saturday night. We heard afterwards that the fight had started in the kitchen. That fella Figge was a nasty piece of work, he'd been by the table earlier during the dancing and he'd had a few. He asked our girls, but they wouldn't dance with him and the last time he came by he shouted to Vivaldi that he couldn't keep it all to himself."

"All what?"

"He used a word suggesting the female gender as only a fella like Figge would use in mixed company. Even I knew that. Anyway, it had been Figge's idea that the civilians should dress up as waiters and they was supposed to all enter together and form a ring on the floor, in the dark, and when the lights went up there they would be, with their trollies of spaghetti. Sean the barber thought it was a bad idea. He thought they would all bump into each other and they was still arguing when they heard the roll of drums, and Sean the barber took off before the lights was dimmed or any of the others was ready. We saw what happened next. Figge was so mad his little show was being spoiled he smashed into the barber on purpose.

"That wasn't the end of it, either. A little while later they had to separate Johnson, the plumbing foreman, and the barber, and then Figge and Johnson were at each other. It was like a brush fire. But that's what it can get like up here. There was bad blood there between Figge and Johnson because Figge had won Johnson's parka in a poker game one night. That was a beautiful coat that Johnson had brought with him from his last job on the Gaspé peninsula. Made of summer caribou hide—the winter hides are no good for clothing—and it was Johnson's pride, but he was losing heavy and finally he bet his coat against the pot and lost. Figge should have took that coat and put it away, but he liked to dress up in it sometimes just to make Johnson feel bad. Fact is, just about all of the civilians had had a falling out with each other at one time or another over the winter, but I mention the coat because it was the cause of what happened later. Let's have another beer."

When the waiter came, he took two glasses and swallowed one in a gulp. He continued. "The dance went on until one o'clock or thereabouts and then it happened. Everyone went to bed; I had a room in the mess, but most of the construction fellas was staying in their own camp, a couple of hundred yards away, far enough on a night like that.

Did I tell you? Outside it was like walking around the inside of a milk bottle. They went off home in twos and threes and when I went to bed there were only two parkas and a pair of mukluks left in the cloakroom. Mukluks. Boots. Take note of that. It's a clue."

"A what?"

"A clue. I won't say any more. The next morning was Christmas and I wasn't feeling up to much, nobody was, I reckon, but I went down to the mess for a cup of coffee and when I walked in I thought the war had started. The place was full of people all talking at once. Eventually somebody broke off to tell me what had happened. Johnson, the construction foreman had been found in the snow the night before, beaten up, unconscious, and now he was in the camp hospital. The word was he wasn't expected to live. His sub-foreman, his close pal, Claud Dupuis, had gone looking for him because he'd said goodnight to Johnson and had a last drink himself, but when he got home Johnson wasn't there. They shared a room, ye see. Dupuis went back to the mess to look for him but it was all quiet by now so he raised the alarm and they—the construction fellas—went to look for him in case he'd fallen asleep in the snow. They found him soon enough, he hadn't gone far, but he was a bit of a mess. As I say, unconscious, nearly frozen, and lots of blood about.

"They were all talking and jumping to conclusions in the mess but there wasn't anyone could say he knew anything. Dupuis had seen him set off, at least. Johnson had told Dupuis he was going home and Dupuis had one last drink and followed him.

"Now, there was a captain in the Canadian army in charge of security and he took over. It was a military camp but they had never sorted out whether a civilian crime should be investigated by the military or the Mounties, the corporal in town, but since no one could get to town in the storm, Captain Blood—I forget his real name—he took charge. And take charge he did. When he interviewed me late in the day he'd set up what he called an investigations room in the office behind the bar, and he had drawn a map of the area where it had happened with a cross where they found Johnson. All this in coloured crayon on a big sheet of paper pinned to the wall. On another sheet he had a sort of time chart of the before and after all broken up into quarter hours, and on another sheet he had the names of all the people in the mess that night, mostly in black with the fellas who had to walk to the construction camp in red. They was the chief suspects. It looked like a hell of an operation and that was when I realised that poor old Johnson was going to die. Captain Blood was having a fine time, himself, you could see that. It was like the war room of the Pentagon.

"Lots of the names was already crossed off, and after he'd done me, he crossed me off, too. Most of the people he had questioned could account for each other so he'd crossed them off. They'd gone home in twos and threes, and they could testify to each other. I couldn't, of course, I'd just gone to bed, so he asked me for me keys and give them to a sergeant to search my room while he kept me there. Looking for clothes with blood on them he was, though he didn't say. When the sergeant came back, the captain crossed my name off his list as if he'd accomplished something, and I left. There was a few names not crossed off yet. Sean Brady, the barber, was one, so was Figge, and two or three others.

"Christmas dinner that day wasn't very jolly, I can tell you. Everyone had an idea who had pounded Johnson, most of them different, and we got a lot of talk about what would happen to him when they caught him, if ever. Claud Dupuis didn't say much, but you could see he'd want a hand in anything that was done to the man who had assaulted his friend.

"Johnson died the next day. The sergeant hospital orderly was telling us at supper that he croaked a couple of words, then gave up. As the orderly heard it, all he said was 'Kaput', and we all knew what that meant. I did, anyway, and I saw Claud Dupuis look up sharp."

"It means finished," I said.

Bane took a long swallow. "Ah. That's what they all thought. Let's just say it's another clue. I'll explain in a minute. The storm was letting up a bit and the next morning I got permission from Captain Blood to go to town to see after my dogs. One of the Americans took me in on a caterpillar, and while I was there I had a chat with the French priest at the mission to confirm an idea I'd had, and when I came back I told the captain what I'd found out. He got very excited about it and organised search parties to go over every inch of the area. They found what he was looking for under a building pushed out of sight, and the captain took Figge in and he and the Mountie corporal questioned him for the rest of the day."

"Why Figge?" I asked, as I was supposed to. "What did they find?"

"What did they find?" he asked, with an air that made me want to pour my beer over him. "What d'ye think they found?"

"I don't know. What?"

"Figge's parka. Or rather, Johnson's parka. The caribou one that Figge had won off Johnson. Covered in blood."

"So Figge did it?"

"Looks like it, don't it?"

"How did you know? What did you hear from the priest?"

"I'll tell you that at the end if you haven't figured it out. Now the next surprise everyone got, after they got over their relief that it was Figge, was that the accountant for the construction company, Spenser, was involved somehow. He spent three hours with the captain and the Mountie, and after he came out he started to pack his clothes, ready to leave, and Figge was released. They didn't let Figge loose, of course. Claud Dupuis would have killed him, just on the chance that they were right in the first place, so they took him into town and locked him up in the little Mountie jail for his own protection. Did you figure out why yet?"

"No."

The old man looked pleased. "It came out later that Figge could prove he was in the billiard room all night, on one of the couches, because the accountant was there too, for a lot of the time, certainly when Johnson was attacked."

"With Figge?"

"No, no. With Mrs. Caruso, the American lady whose husband was away in Washington. The accountant had to give him an alibi because Figge was a nasty piece of work.

"Now Captain Blood gets an idea. First he figured that it was Figge because of the parka, but now he figures that it must have been someone wearing Figge's parka who had it in for Johnson and Figge. I thought that was pretty smart of him. Now he wanted laboratory tests done on the clothes of all those on his list because those caribou parkas shed a bit, and it should have left some hair. The Defense Research Board had a few botanists and biologists up there—one of them come to me one day and asked if he could get a blood sample from one of my dogs and I said sure take as much as you like and the fella advanced on my lead dog with a needle in his hand before I caught him back. I was just teasing him. Another ten feet and he would have got his sample, all right, and so would they. These scientists had a bit of a laboratory but what Captain Blood wanted would have taken them six months, I reckon. Still, they started in. Meanwhile the Mountie started questioning us all again to find out who had it in for Johnson and Figge, the two of them, and they came up with a name. You know who?"

"Sean Brady, the barber."

"Well done. I could have told them that's who they'd come up with."

"Why didn't you?"

"Because by now I could see they was sucking up swamp-water, and I had my own ideas which I wanted to confirm for meself. I'd had enough of being associated with Captain Blood rushing off half-cocked. So they settled on Sean, as I knew they would, and they went through his room with a magnifying glass, and checked him for bruises, all the time the laboratory was trying to find caribou hairs on his best suit. I knew they wouldn't find anything, but as for Sean Brady, he would have done it if he'd had the guts, so I didn't mind if they gave him a bit of a going over. They didn't find anything but I told them they'd better keep Brady under protective custody, too, because Dupuis was looking to batter anyone to avenge his friend. While they were interviewing Brady I walked over to the hospital to pay my last respects to Johnson, and I offered the matron to take his things back to Dupuis who was packing them all up in a box to send to his wife. Poor old Dupuis was in a hell of a state, so I stayed and had a long talk with him and calmed him down, and the next day he left on the train. And that was it. They never did figure out who was impersonating Figge. I did, though."

"Claud Dupuis, his friend."

"How did you figure that out?" One side of his mouth had dropped, in wonder, apparently, so that you could see his right bottom canine.

"I was just guessing," I said, though it was more than that. Everybody was accounted for except Dupuis. "I don't know how you figured it out but I think I know why Dupuis did it."

"Why is that?"

"It's the story of the two trappers. Dupuis and Johnson had been sharing a room for six months. They hated each other, and Dupuis hated Figge, like everyone else. So he put on Figge's parka and went after Johnson, killing two birds with one stone."

The old man stared at me, forgetting even to drink. He looked stunned. "What are you talking about? Did you know these fellas? No? Well, I did. They were blood brothers, let me tell you."

I have never seen a man so angry. The vein running down the centre of his skull looked ready to burst. In some way I had attacked the heart of his story and he needed to dispose of me before he could continue.

"This is not the goddam story of the two trappers," he spat out. "What I'm telling you is true. Do you understand me? I knew them fellas." He waited to see if I had been dealt with.

I made conciliatory gestures. "So tell me. How did you figure it out?"

He still said nothing for a long while, then he collected himself and took a swallow of beer. "Let's start with 'kaput'," he said. "You don't speak French? I thought we was all supposed to be bilingual these days. I do, and Ojibway, and Eskimo. You have to up here. Did I tell you Johnson was French? It wasn't 'kaput' he said. I knew he wouldn't be speaking German and the look on Dupuis' face triggered me off, so I went to town and had a word with the priest, like I said, and sure enough the word is 'capote'. French. It means a special kind of parka, like Johnson's. So I thought it was Figge, meself, then, but when Figge come up with his alibi, I sorted it all out. As you say, only one fella was not quite accounted for, and when Captain Blood wanted to test everyone's clothes, he gave me an idea. Of course, the two parkas and the pair of mukluks in the cloakroom helped."

"Why?"

"Where was the other pair of boots? You couldn't go out in weather like that in dancing shoes. Somebody had his boots on but not his parka."

"Dupuis? Took Figge's parka and went after Johnson?"

"That's what an outsider might think, who didn't know these fellas." Once more he stared me down before he continued. "Not me, though. What I did realise right away is why Dupuis looked so strange when he heard the word 'kaput'. He knew what Johnson had really said and if he'd been innocent he'd have jumped in quick. But it was no surprise to him and he didn't know how to react."

"So why did he go after Johnson?"

"You haven't figured it out? He didn't. There was no way he would have gone after Johnson." He looked at me fiercely. "No way. He went after Figge."

"But Figge was in the billiard room, listening to …"

"So he was, but Dupuis didn't know that. When he saw a fella going through the door wearing Figge's coat he decided to settle a score, for himself and for his friend. Johnson had stolen back his own coat. They was all pretty drunk, remember. Dupuis beat up Johnson before he got a good look at him."

"Why didn't he leave it at that? He could still discover him a bit later, and watch the whole camp look for someone who had it in for Figge. Besides, he didn't know that Figge had an alibi. It could have looked like a fight between Johnson and Figge over the coat. Why didn't he leave it?"

"Because of the blood. I told you there was a lot of blood on his parka. They wasn't all that drunk, the others. Someone would have noticed. So he swapped parkas on Johnson and hid Figge's parka where it could be found. Then he slipped back and got Johnson's regular parka out of the cloakroom, where Johnson had left it when he decided to steal back his capote. So now Johnson was wearing an ordinary parka with blood on it and Dupuis wasn't."

"You couldn't prove it."

"That's why I went to pay my last respects to Johnson in the hospital. When they left me alone with him, I found his suit, covered with caribou hair. Then I looked in his parka. It was an army surplus parka; the Canadian army had sold them to a lot of the construction workers so it was pretty well identical to a lot of others, and that's why everyone put his name in them on a little white tag they put in for the purpose. Johnson's had been torn out."

"Why didn't you tell the police?"

"Because of the way Captain Blood was talking. He was wanting to charge someone with attempted murder or manslaughter but that wasn't the way it was. Dupuis wasn't a murderer. He just wanted to loosen a few of Figge's teeth. It was a mistake. I felt sorry for him, so I told him what I knew, told him there being no name tag wouldn't signify because the police would have ways of proving it was his coat. So he left.

He didn't have to. I wouldn't have said anything. Like I said, it was a misunderstanding. You take my point? He killed his friend by mistake." I saw now why my easy comparison of his story with the tale of the two trappers was making him so angry.

"I did tell the Mountie, though," he said suddenly. "I waited a year, then I told him. You know what he said?"

"What?"

"He said considering I'd had a year all to myself in the cabin he'd have thought I could make up a better story than that. He didn't want to be bothered, ye see, and besides, Dupuis had taken all the evidence with him. Now catch that waiter before I die of thirst."

"What about the poem?"

"Are you staying at the hotel? Meet me here tomorrow, then, and I'll tell it to you. I'm all talked out now. There's the waiter now. QUICK, before he looks away."

I left him then, but I did come back next day to record his poem. I waited for an hour but he never appeared. The waiter told me to hang on, Duncan Bane was always there, he said, but I had a feeling that Bane would just as soon not talk to me any more. Perhaps he couldn't remember his poem and didn't want to say so. I didn't mind. I had got what I wanted. All I had to do was skim off the stories.

Caves of Ice

When I was about fifteen, I became aware that my grandfather was a liar. Dealing with such knowledge was as much a part of the process of growing up as was learning some years before that my parents were sexual beings. One of the signs that I had moved successfully into a new stage was that my mother could refer to Grandad's way with the truth in front of me, though she still waited until my young sister was out of hearing. She called his anecdotes "Grandad's stories," avoiding the harshness of "lies", but it had the same effect of making me aware that I had grown past him.

So I knew early not to believe in the truth of his anecdotes, but a wise schoolmate helped me not to dismiss the old man entirely, therefore. "They're still terrific stories," he pointed out, and I grew up a little more, as I turned the old man from a source of knowledge into a liar, and then (with my buddy's help) almost immediately into a storyteller, another source of knowledge. I discounted the facts but continued to enjoy the fictions, long after he and I silently understood that it was pleasure not truth that held me now. Once he realised that I was on to him, I think he began to be less concerned about veracity himself, occupying himself more with the aesthetics of his stories, with finding the satisfying shapes.

At about the same time he acknowledged my maturity by investing the male characters in his stories with their manliness. He was always the chief hero in the stories, of course, and now, without sinking into lubricious detail, he invited me to understand that his heroes lived a full life. "When I woke up I was alone," he would say, and wink. "That certainly wasn't how I remembered going to bed." He might have been bragging, but that would not have been consistent with the other aspects of his stories for he often told tales that reflected comically or pathetically on him—it was not his aim to impress me with his former self but to capture me through the quality of the tale. He simply decided that now I was moving into a man's world, he would expand the stories by giving his characters another dimension. At the same time his characters began to swear, more or less as I was beginning to do with my buddies.

By the time I was seventeen he was telling me stories about the war. He was a counter-intelligence officer during the war, and in spite of the fact that I was now treating his stories as works of art, admiring their craftsmanship, the phrase "intelligence officer" seemed enough of a guarantee that the experiences he was embroidering really did take place in some form, even if he was not at the cutting edge of the action, one of those parachuted into Serbia to find out which side the partisans were on, say.

He made no secret of the fact that he had had a good war, and he never tried to construct tales of derring-do, concentrating on the marvellous as it occurred in his day-to-day activities. "Did I ever tell you," he would begin, "How I smoked out the Italian prisoner-of-war who cooked our spaghetti when we were dug in outside Lucca, uncovered the fact that he was the Duke of Albinoni, decked out as a private soldier, a man the partisans were looking for to string up alongside Mussolini? I got him attached to my unit to keep him out of their reach." I guessed that many of these stories were too good to be invented. They simply hadn't happened to him, but to one of his companions-in-arms, and he had absorbed them into his own history. The same was true of his accounts of his amorous adventures.

After the war he stayed in the army (he had never had it so good before the war), still in "Intelligence" and now spending most of his time on courses to keep his training up to date. And then, in 1952, he was sent up to the Near Arctic, to a station on the Hudson's Bay where the Canadian and American governments were building the Distant Early Warning line, the defence shield to protect North America from attack from the north if the cold war heated up. His job was to create a security presence, as he called it. Out of this experience came one of his best stories. Here it is, in an approximation of his own words:

In July of 1952 I was posted to the Near Arctic, a combined forces base on about parallel 59. I wasn't best pleased I can tell you because at the time I was attached to the embassy in Washington, D.C., liaising with the C.I.A. Now Washington is a very nice town to liaise in, what with pay and the special allowances. I had to pick up the check occasionally when I met with my opposite number in the C.I.A. and he always insisted on the most discrete and expensive restaurants to meet in and I persuaded my superiors in Ottawa to accept that he made the rules on his turf. Sometimes we made a foursome with a couple of carefully vetted dollies, one of his, and a Canadian version of Miss Moneypenny. Actually when I didn't have to worry quite so much about security, I was squiring around a plump little chicken who worked for the ambassador's staff on the social side. She reminded me of someone in the movies, Vera-Ellen, only about fifteen pounds heavier, and I've never minded that. From the look on your face I suppose Vera-Ellen was before your time, but the point is, I liked Washington, and the idea of being shipped back to my own northland didn't appeal a bit.

At that time the station at Nelson was only half built, or rather, it had been completed once, in the forties, and found to be inadequate, and now so many new buildings were being added that virtually an entirely new complex was going up, using the old buildings for storage and as dormitories for the construction workers involved in the new work. A camp of tar-paper shacks heated by oil stoves was being replaced by a modern complex of connected buildings—mess halls, sleeping quarters, offices, all heated by radiators supplied from a central heating plant.

There were about five hundred service men on the base, American and Canadian, mostly infantrymen and support staff, though a large minority were American airmen. The permanent civilians fell into two groups: the service group—the barber, the cinema manager, the woman who ran the coffee shop and the woman who operated the Eaton's catalogue office, for example—and the people, mainly scientists and technicians, who worked for the Defence Research Board, doing classified work to do with extreme cold. (In one way or another, everyone on the base was involved in trying to figure out how the cold affected the army's ability to function, because if the Russians did come "over the top," they would likely be troops with much more experience of the climate than we had, and thus they would choose the season which would give them the greatest advantage.) Apart from these, there were the temporary civilians, the construction workers.

Outside the camp, about seven kilometres away, was the town of Nelson, no more than a village, a handful of buildings grouped around the original Hudson's Bay trading post, which had itself expanded to serve the camp personnel looking for something to buy on their day off. A diner had opened in town, catering mainly to people who wanted a change from the meals in dining halls. A taxi appeared, sledded in across the ice, to carry people back and forth the seven miles between town and camp, and, inevitably, a couple of ladies appeared and took rooms in the hotel, selling magazine subscriptions. I understand they were deluged with customers until the mountie put them on the plane back to Winnipeg. I didn't buy any magazines myself—I had already fixed myself up with plenty to read by the time these ladies appeared, but I couldn't see what harm they were doing. But it was Canada, and therefore illegal, of course.

My first job was to assess the security needs of the base. The Americans had their own security officer and he and I met and agreed that there was not a lot for us to do. We were not made aware of any specific secret activity that required a security focus. Obviously the army was testing its equipment to see how it performed under these conditions, how long it took to start an engine at thirty degrees below freezing, for example, and how big a battery was required (I'm not mechanical myself so I am just giving made-up examples) and their conclusions were recorded and filed. I inspected our filing cabinets to make sure they were hard to break into, and Hector, my American colleague, did the same. The only genuinely sensitive area was the Defence Research Board laboratory, a small warehouse-like building surrounded by a high steel mesh fence, guarded from the inside by their own security personnel who issued their own passes to anyone granted access. They told me the laboratory was outside my jurisdiction, and I was not eligible for a pass. I queried this with Ottawa and was told to accept it. I then put it in writing that I did not wish to be held responsible for any breakdown in the D.R.B. security. Rule No. I, my boy: Cover your rear end.

This was the general picture, then, and you might ask why I was sent up there at all, or why someone in Intelligence wasn't already in place; in other words, why send me up *at that point?* The reason was that somewhere on the base, or nearby, a hostile agent had recently opened for business, someone collecting and sending information, probably to a spy ship in the North Atlantic, for onward transmission to Moscow.

Ottawa had intercepted his transmissions and I was shown a sample when I was in Ottawa getting briefed. The material I saw was so ordinary that I wondered at first why he had bothered to send it, consisting as it did of a stream of more or less disconnected comments and notes about the agent's daily encounters. "I talked to a couple of American officers just arrived today. They'd been transferred from a base near Butte, Montana ... three Dakotas landed today, up from Washington, one of the pilots said ... more Van Doos arrived—they were in the beer parlour celebrating their reunion; apparently they'd been split up lately into small groups and posted all over the country, but now they are being brought together ..." (The Van Doos are the Royal 22nd regiment, of course. Frenchmen. From Quebec.) My superior in Ottawa put together several transmissions as a sample, and told me to study it, see if it told me anything.

I could make nothing of it. So trivial was the information that I could only assume that it was in code, and I'm not qualified to deal with that.

"We wondered if it was a new version of the wheelbarrow story," my superior said. "We tried hard at first to penetrate through to the underlying text, break the code, but there isn't one. The real information is in all this inconsequential stuff. If you put it together you get a picture of what is going on in Nelson. These three officers transferred from Butte, for example. They had been in Butte working with a civilian factory on manufacturing survival clothing. They'd come to Nelson to field test it. The Van Doos had been brought together for a field exercise to test the support required for arctic warfare. See, they have far too many N.C.O. quartermaster types with them. And so on. In other words everyone he is reporting on is doing exactly what everyone knows they are doing, trying to prepare to fight a war in the arctic. What he's telling them is that nothing else is going on."

"The wheelbarrow story?" I asked.

"The story of the construction worker who wheeled a barrowload of rubbish—bits of pipe, broken taps and so on past the security gate of the construction site every night. The contractors had the guards sift through this rubbish, and sometimes they took anything semi-valuable away from him—copper scrap, for instance—but they knew he was stealing something else they couldn't find. Every night the guy walked away with a barrow full of bits and pieces, until one day he told them he was quitting, and the guards asked him, as a favour, to tell them what he was stealing. The answer, of course, was wheelbarrows. So this stream of low-grade information that our man is sending is not covering up anything else—it is the thing they want to know."

"You mean that by putting together all this data they get a picture of what's happening?"

"Well, no. What they could get from the data was a picture of what *wasn't* happening. By thoroughly analysing all their agents' information they could be sure that nothing was going on. They didn't uncover anything striking, but that was valuable knowledge, do you see? It enabled them to make their own plans without having to worry about us."

"No news is good news?" I said.

"That's it."

"Then why send me up there, now that you know?"

"We want the agent, of course. We don't like the idea of someone up there with a transmitter, keeping Uncle Joe in touch. Especially if nothing much is happening. Much better that he should be in the dark. So we're sending you in to find him. You won't find him if he's any good, of course, but just sending you up there will send a message that we're on to him."

"You don't think I have a chance?"

"You might stumble across him, I suppose."

I said, "How covert should my operation be?"

"The point of it is that it be known what you are. We want him to know that security is being tightened."

"Why?"

"Sometimes, if you get close to the burrow, the rabbit bolts. Make sure you keep tabs on anyone leaving the camp."

"How many ways out are there?"

"Air: civilian plane twice a week. Land: all winter when it's frozen and you have some dogs, or a tractor. Sea: during the six-week summer if you can find a boat."

Even then I think I smelled a rat, but hindsight can be tricky. You don't like to feel you've been taken for an absolute horse's arse, a certain amount of pride is involved, so I made the decision then to try to find this beggar if I could. I assumed that this would be totally consistent with what they wanted from me: they just didn't think I could do it. (I should say at this point that I was not instrumental in catching the beggar: this is not that kind of story).

As far as our own boys were concerned, Hector, the American, and I agreed that there was little room in our ranks for a spy. In the first place, the base had quite a high classification so all the troops of both jurisdictions had been screened before being posted up there. And because the only real way in for the military was by air, by military transport, no one could have brought in a transmitter—they were big in those days—without being noticed, and on the chance that someone had found a way, bringing one in piece by piece, say, there was no possibility they could have operated it in a barrack room. So the search was limited to N.C.O.'s and officers, all those with separate rooms. The first chance we could we accompanied the duty officer on his routine inspection, and found nothing. We also did a tour of the married quarters with him and came up with nothing there, either. So we were down to the civilians, as we had expected.

The civvies were a purely Canadian problem. First I went to town to liaise with the RCMP who are responsible for national security, and the constable showed me what he had done. He had a nominal roll of all the construction workers by trade and company. Within days of each man's arrival at Nelson, Constable Duthie interviewed them and card-indexed them. Before I arrived he was not looking for security risks, primarily, but for those with criminal records. Nelson was a frontier town and all kinds of people came there to pause on the way downhill. Twice Duthie had arrested men who were wanted in the city for major crimes (he had been warned they might be arriving). He never worried about non-payment of alimony and such-like offences, reckoning them to be no danger to the state or other individuals. He was most keen to find the ones previously convicted of violent assault before they infected the camp. In my time I think he sent six men south without arresting them—the security angle gave him the power— and he missed one who within a week of arriving got into a knife fight and laid open the face of a steam-fitter from his chin to his eyebrow. The man had a long list of similar assaults and Constable Duthie blamed himself for not catching him when he arrived.

No one could get on the base without a security pass, and if he was a civilian the pass had to be counter-signed by Duthie, which meant that Duthie had a complete list, with, in each case, a copy of the small interview he had undertaken—not an interrogation, really, just a primary impression.

I went through Duthie's list methodically, interviewing again every civilian against whom there was the slightest question, which meant every civilian not born in Canada. Then I boiled that list down to those who had arrived since the end of the war, because I agreed with Duthie that this surely must be the group most likely to contain one of Uncle Joe's boys.

No one I interviewed offered any reason why I should take any special note of them.

But I had made my presence felt, and after a month I could think of nothing else to do. Equipment existed which would enable me to trace the signals being transmitted by the enemy, but when I asked Ottawa about supplying it they said it wasn't a matter of sending up a piece of equipment but of a whole team necessary to operate it over a twenty-four hour shift, and the appearance of such a team would certainly be noticed by the agent, causing him to shut down until the team was withdrawn.

Of course, the construction workers came and went and I interviewed the new arrivals, but none of them made my antennae quiver. It would have been pretty boring if I had not met Isabel, a schoolteacher: there was a small school on the base run by the Canadian military but staffed by civilians. My first marriage having failed while I was in Italy, I was very much open to suggestions in the romance department, and Isabel and I soon became an item, as they say nowadays.

(Here my grandfather's voice dropped and he winked, and I tried to look knowing.)

During the mornings I was generally able to keep busy. I was put on the list of those whose signature was required when the military was posted on or off the base, along with the pay office and the quartermaster's stores, and the army always generates a certain amount of routine paperwork, weekly reports, and so on. But the afternoons dragged until I worked out a routine of calling on people who would welcome a chat,

Hector, for instance, and the boys in the fire hall. A couple of times a week I got a truck from the transport pool to visit Constable Duthie in town. I had coffee with someone or other most afternoons. Often I called in on the barber, a very nice Polish chap who fought with Paderewski and had been taken prisoner by the Russians but got away to the West and wound up in a Displaced Persons camp, and so immigrated to Canada and made his way to Nelson. I didn't get my hair cut every two days, of course, though he did trim it once a week, but the thing was the barbershop was the equivalent of the village general store, full of interesting and occasionally scandalous gossip about the neighbours and their doings. Figaro himself (as we nicknamed him) had a great curiosity about everyone and everything around the camp and speculated endlessly with me about the meaning of the comings and goings of his customers.

And then, sometime before Christmas, the navy arrived.

It seemed a curious unit from the start. Two petty officers and two leading seamen comprised the entire roster of enlisted men. As well, they brought six civilians who were skilled tradesmen, two carpenters, a plumber/steamfitter, an electrician, and two others who I suspected were armourers. Then, over the ice by tractor-trailer came the materials to construct a kind of blank windowless shed with big doors on each end which they put together on the beach, extending it slightly over the ice, like a boathouse. Finally, over the ice came a crate about twenty feet long and six feet square, completely sealed. This crate they slid into the waiting shed, closing the doors tight. The next day a pile of lumber from the dismantled packing case—for that's what it was—was burned on the beach. Finally a steel mesh fence was erected around the whole structure complete with a tiny guardhouse, which the four sailors then proceeded to man in shifts, one at a time, sending their civilians home.

I thought at the time that their efforts at deception were a bit rudimentary. Given the location of the "boathouse" and the size and shape of the mysterious crate, it seemed obvious that what they were doing must have something to do with operating a vessel under the ice, and because midget or two-man submarines had already proved themselves during the war, that seemed the most likely possibility, finding out how a midget submarine behaves under the ice. We couldn't confirm this because the sailors formed a compact group in the mess, the three who weren't on guard duty always eating together, occasionally playing billiards, but never responding to casual queries about their mission. Actually, that's not quite true. They made no secret of the fact that their work was secret, "classified," which ended enquiries but not specu-lation and gossip, and to add to the mystery, from time to time an officer would appear, someone below field rank, usually a very young lieutenant. This officer would spend a day or two in the boathouse and then fly back to Ottawa. While he was there, special permission was granted by the regimental sergeant-major, the senior N.C.O., for him to take his meals with his own N.C.O.'s, in the sergeants' mess. Did you know that no officer can enter the sergeants' mess without the permission of the senior N.C.O. present?

As I thought, and said to Hector, they were managing things rather clumsily. It seemed to me that it would have been cleverer to create a false mission, to say they were conducting a study, for example, on the pressure exerted on a ship's hull by ice of different thicknesses. Every-one else seemed to be studying ice, and surely the navy had its own questions. Instead they seemed to be going out of their way to suggest that what they were up to was much more arcane than studying ice.

About now I was called to Ottawa again to discuss the whole secu-rity situation, specifically, it turned out, the vulnerability of the navy's operation to penetration. I was let in on the fact that what the navy was doing was very delicate and extremely important, but not told exactly what, and I came away absolutely certain now that it involved operating two-men submarines under the ice. Later, I could not recall a concrete remark that I could attribute my understanding to, but an understanding I certainly had. The point of my meeting my O/C, though, was to instruct me to mount a more intense search for the agent.

When I returned to base, I undertook to call a meeting of myself, Hector and Constable Duthie, to create a united thrust to root out this beggar. At the same time the navy doubled its own guard. A second perimeter fence was erected around the navy compound, with a sec-ond gatehouse the army was asked to man. Now regularly, new naval officers, occasionally one of field rank, flew in for the day, visited the boathouse, whispered with the navy N.C.O.'s for an hour or two in the corner of the mess, then departed without fuss. And now a sign appeared on the outer fence, 'Extreme Danger, Stay Away'.

And then, early in October, we had a bonfire. Did I tell you we used to celebrate every holiday of both countries—Queen Victoria's Birthday, July Fourth, both Thanksgivings—the lot? On this night there was to be a bonfire and fireworks put on by the Americans, mainly for the kids, but afterwards there was to be a dance in the sergeants' mess to which officers were invited. It looked like being the party of the year.

The day before the party I was called to a meeting in the navy building. I had never visited the boathouse before, and when I arrived, more curious about what was inside the shed than I was about the topic of the meeting which was pretty sure to be some kind of review of security precautions, I found Hector and Constable Duthie present. The room was tiny, only half the interior of the shed, which had been divided into two equal compartments. The door to the other compartment was shut tight. Two navy men were present and the five of us made a pretty full room.

"Thank you for coming. I won't keep you long," the senior petty officer said. "Let me get to the point of the meeting: we have information that someone will try to breach our security tomorrow night."

"Break in? During the fireworks?"

"Precisely. They see it as an ideal opportunity."

"Who passed on this information?" I asked.

"Ottawa," he said. "Now, we have no idea if the information is good or bad. We—I mean Ottawa—don't think it's necessary to inform anyone not involved with security. We don't want it known that we are on to him, we might be wrong, and besides we just want to … defuse him. So, with your agreement, we'll meet here tomorrow night. We'll arrive separately at fifteen-minute intervals after sunset. Wear your parkas as you arrive, just in case; they make a pretty good disguise. And be prepared for a dull couple of hours until he shows up, because we can't have any light showing."

"How will we know he's coming?" I asked. I was referring to the lack of windows.

The sailor pointed to a hole, a knot-hole, in the wall behind him. "There's one on each wall," he said. "We can see out but he can't see in. That's why we can't show a light. If he gets alarmed, he will scuttle off before we've laid hands on him. We want him actually inside the door before we jump. If there are more than one, both should be inside before we move."

"Three?" I asked.

"We are taking precautions against two, sir; we think three very unlikely."

"And our job?"

"Grab him, of course. There will be five of us, two of my people and you three. Enough even to grab two men."

"Will you be armed?"

"In a space this confined it would be dangerous to wave guns about. We have to smother him."

"Any idea who he is?"

"Not the slightest."

The next night we assembled one by one and took our places round the tiny room. The Chief Petty Officer watched through his peephole, and when the first firework exploded he switched off the lights, we manned the other peepholes, and waited. It was a curious feeling, as if we were in a seance, awaiting a spirit manifestation ("a spook" joked Hector, when I mentioned it. You know that in the trade that's what we call spies? Hector was sort of punning, you see).

It seemed safe to chat quietly and we swapped stories of our pasts. The Junior Petty Officer had, typically, grown up in Regina, two thousand miles from the sea; Constable Duthie came from a long line of mounties in Prince Albert; Hector was in the middle of his story, about growing up in Sioux Falls, South Dakota, when the quarry appeared, or rather the chief sailor saw him, silently cutting a hole in the outer perimeter fence. A few minutes later he had breached the second fence. "It isn't designed to be a major barrier," the sailor said. "It's symbolic. More to attract than repel. I didn't think we'd made it that easy, though. I'm surprised he hasn't caught on. Here he comes now. He's all alone."

"Can you tell who he is, or where he's from?" Hector whispered.

"His parka isn't military issue. He's a civilian."

"A construction worker?"

"He's below the sight line of this hole. Now."

There was the sound of metal scraping metal as he tried the lock, then a heavier, meatier scrunching as he inserted a bar into the jamb and forced open the door.

We held our breath until he switched on his flashlight, and the sailor flicked on our switch and we saw who it was.

"Drop the light, Figaro," the sailor said.

The barber put down his flashlight. "Why aren't you all at the party?" he asked.

"We were waiting for you. I think he's yours, Constable."

Duthie nodded, then turned to me. "Put him in your lock-up for the night, would you? I'll go over to the barber shop, see what I can find." He held out his hand to the barber. "Give me the keys."

"The transmitter is in the seat of the customer chair," the barber said. "You can slide it out. No need to break anything. You might as well leave the shop intact for the next barber."

It all seemed anti-climactic—no shoot-out, no chase, and although the barber was a surprise, I had expected more. Then I remembered. "There's something I'd like to know," I said. "What was the barber after? What *is* in the back of this shed? Are you going to tell us?"

The sailors looked at each other. The senior petty officer said, "That seems fair. Lieutenant, you are bound by the Official Secrets Act while you are in Canada, not so?"

Hector said, "Not by yours, but I'm bound by our version of it to reveal nothing except to my superior officer in Washington."

"I think you will find your superior is already in the picture. Okay. Put Figaro away and come back. I'll show you."

We locked the barber up in the guardhouse and returned to the navy compound. The sailor opened the door to the back compartment. It was bitterly cold. At the end, where the shed extended out over the now frozen water, there was a chamber about six feet square carved out of the ice. The walls of the chamber went down to the sea-bed. Inside the chamber a double row of posts rested on the sea-bed about twelve inches apart, topped with two twelve-inch planks and decked over with one-by-fours.

"What the hell is it?" Hector asked.

"In the spring, when the ice melts, it will be a dock."

"But it's only three feet wide."

"This is a model to test the technique. The real dock will be as wide as we decide. Probably fifty feet square."

"How did you do it?"

"To put it simply, a few weeks ago, when the ice was a foot thick, we cut and shaved off eleven-and-a-half inches. Then, as the thin part collected a foot of ice under it, we cut down again, and so on; it didn't take long before we were building inside a solid wall of ice."

It took us some time to think it through. I said, "And that's what this is all about? *This* is what you've been guarding? *This*? We all thought you were testing little submarines, or some such. Something secret and complicated. All the time you were building a damn ice palace."

"Give it it's proper name: 'Investigating Techniques of Undersurface Construction in Sub-Freezing Temperatures'."

"But there's nothing to it. What's so secret?"

"It's a simple idea, granted, but so is the wheel, and the plough, or the fore-and-aft sail. All simple ideas. But this one we'd like to keep to ourselves for as long as we can. Now I have to remind you again of the Official Secrets Act; you can't talk about this to anyone outside this building."

Then two weeks later they were gone, first dismantling the boat-house and flooding the ice palace by chiselling a hole in one wall. There was a snowstorm the day they left, and in two days you could see no trace of the operation. The dock was invisible through the ice, and in the spring it had floated away before anyone noticed it. That was something they apparently hadn't considered, that the posts would have to be anchored to the sea-bed, and *that* told me that they had probably abandoned the project, and I'm ashamed to say it was some time before the truth dawned on me."

I said, "What was that?"

"It wasn't an ice palace, or any kind of study of under-ice construction techniques. The whole thing was just a bloody mousetrap, and the ice palace was the cheese, designed to trap Figaro. I mean the *idea* that there was something going on was the real trap. They didn't need to build anything, in fact; they just built that ice palace to amuse themselves while they waited for Figraro. That must be true, but I was never able to confirm it because I was posted back to Washington shortly afterwards." There he ended.

It's a good story, I think, and Grandad told it well, as he always did. But I have been wary of telling it myself. First I want to find someone who has lived and worked in the north, an engineer from Toktoyuktuk, say, and ask him if the thing is possible, building an ice chamber like that, shaving the ice and all that. Then I'll know whether it was the sailors' creation or Grandad's, which one invented it to pass the time on a winter's night.

Hephaestus

On the fourth day, Clayton was sitting with Jensen in the bar by the pool. They were watching the video of the day's picnic, an amateurish, incoherent production which was being received with huge enjoyment by the crowd in the bar, most of whom had been on the picnic. Everybody on the screen looked slightly drunk, and the games involved a lot of "mooning" as the celebrants competed to expose their bottoms to the camera. Occasionally the scene was cut off abruptly and the audience howled with glee as they remembered what the camera could not show.

Jensen said, "You should have gone, Fred. I wonder if they set up a shrine to Dionysius?" He was a man in his early forties with a round, moon-like face and very large horn-rimmed glasses, who smiled constantly. Clayton had met him and his wife on the first day and stayed with them ever since because, like him, the Jensens had not come for the organised fun but for whatever else the club in its surroundings had to offer.

When Clayton arrived at the vacation club and was greeted by the combination of summer camp and college pep rally by which the management made everyone feel instantly at home—group shenanigans which involved learning the club song, with gestures, and singing it every night to the setting sun—he made some effort to keep his distance, refusing to wear a coloured ribbon to show what team he was on for the week, taking no part in Olympics Day, and so on. The effort worked; by the second day the Jolly Organisors, as the camp staff were called, began to leave him alone.

Jensen made no effort at all. One look at the amusement on his balloon of a face, one remark—"Ask the Leader if I may be excused compulsory games if I attend the torch-light rally later, will you?"— and they never bothered him again. Thereafter the three of them watched the high jinks on the beach, did not participate in the show put on by the jolly guests (the holidaying patrons), and avoided the disco altogether. By the third day there was an imaginary circle around the three of them, carved out by Jensen's stream of commentary, vicious and funny, on the activities of the other people. The Jolly Organisors were trained to be cheery above all, and they would shrug at Jensen's response to their overtures, smile and walk away, but they were not stupid, and occasionally one of them showed clearly enough that whatever their public face, they were very much aware of Jensen's contempt for them and their club.

One incident in particular made Clayton nearly want to apologise for Jensen. One of the Jolly Organisors was a man who called himself Kiki. Most of his duties consisted of clowning around, wearing outlandish costumes and pretending to flash the girls on the beach. One day Clayton and the Jensens were helping themselves to the lunch buffet, part of which was a huge metal pot with a label, "Lobster Salad." Beside it an assistant chef waited, inviting the guests to help themselves, but when they lifted the lid there was Kiki's head grinning at them like a decapitated lunatic. Kiki had a powerful grin and the surprise created a lot of hilarity.

Jensen saw the joke from another part of the dining-room, then filled up his plate with macaroni salad and approached the pot looking innocent. When he lifted the lid and saw Kiki, he reacted in dismay and dumped his macaroni salad all over Kiki's head. Everyone else thought this was hilarious, but Clayton caught the assistant chef's eye as he cleaned off Kiki's head with a wash-cloth, caught it and was held by it long enough to wish he was not such a well-known Jensenite. But in the end, Clayton laughed with Jensen, preferring to make a circle with Jensen and his wife than be outside on his own.

Why had the Jensens come? For the tennis, Jensen told Clayton. The club's major daytime activity was tennis, and Cynthia was an avid player, like Clayton. And like Clayton, the Jensens were curious about what these places were really like. Tennis was both a reason and an excuse.

Cynthia Jensen was at least ten years younger than her husband, an attractive blonde made slightly too thin by the amount of exercise she took and by her devotion to fruit juice as a substitute for food. While she played tennis, Jensen went for walks with his camera—he had several including a video camera—and sometimes he submerged himself in the pool.

Clayton joined them for brunch after the morning's tennis and they idled away the rest of the day together until it was time for the five o'clock tennis session. They stuck together for meals; Jensen assumed Clayton was of their party from the start, and spoke as if the three of them were on Mars, trying to make sense of the natives. Once, when the Jensens were out on a boat excursion, Clayton fell in with three psychologists from New York City but Jensen wanted no part of any larger group. He needed Clayton as someone to enjoy his misanthropy, a larger audience would have recoiled from him, perhaps even defanged him. Once he was accepted by the Jensens, Clayton understood that he was assumed to share Jensen's every attitude, and he let it happen. Jensen was very funny, and he suited Clayton for a week, as did his wife. All of them were getting what they came for.

Cynthia and Clayton were not in the same tennis group. The players were graded from one to six, according to ability, and Cynthia was a three, whereas Clayton was a four. They played at the same time, learning the same skills but at different levels. On the first night Clayton went to the disco, but once he had met the Jensens he never bothered again. (Jensen said, "I only go to discos to exercise my wife, and that isn't necessary here.") Cynthia said very little. She played tennis, read bestsellers, and smiled at the stream of entertaining malice that flowed from her husband. Clayton speculated to himself about their relationship, but he gained no real clue, for Jensen discouraged chat about personal matters. It suited him to treat Clayton as a fellow observer of the mating games being played around them, but he never introduced a personal note.

Inevitably they talked about the reputation of the club and whether it was living up to it. Cynthia and Clayton were up early for tennis, and they could confirm that at dawn not a few souls were making their way back to their cabins. Jensen was a very close observer of the way partnerships shifted between one day and the next. He made a particular study of one couple from the mid-west who prowled along the shore, hand in hand, scanning the beach as though looking for a lost child. On the third day they found another couple and were hardly seen again.

And then on the fourth day, the world changed. Clayton hadn't played tennis that afternoon, and he and Jensen were awaiting the arrival of Cynthia after her game. After they had watched the video of the daily picnic, Jensen said, "Cynthia is having an affair, if that is the word for it."

Clayton waited for the joke but none came. "When?" he asked eventually after he had got his breath back. "When? She's either playing tennis or with us."

"When she is assumed to be playing tennis, she is, in fact, fornicating."

"Who with?"

"I can't tell yet. One of the tennis pros, I would think."

"The pros spend all their time on the court. There's no way."

Jensen shook his head. "They get time off. Perhaps she is fornicating with all of them, one at a time, on their days off." His voice, his demeanour, were unchanged. He might have been discussing anybody. "Haven't you noticed? When she is supposed to be playing tennis, she's not always there."

"She isn't in my group."

"Right. You wouldn't notice. This morning I followed her down to the court where she was supposed to be playing. She wasn't there. The pro of the day, the rat-faced boy with the yellow hair, said he hadn't seen her since the first day. Every day when I thought she was serving and volleying, she was, in fact, playing the two-backed beast."

"How do you know?"

"What else could she possibly be doing?"

Cynthia appeared on the other side of the pool and waved.

"What are you going to do?" Clayton asked.

"I don't know yet. This picnic has given me an idea, though."

He stopped talking as his wife approached. When she sat down, sweaty, with a small blister on her thumb, Clayton glanced at Jensen to see if he doubted that at least on this occasion she had been playing tennis.

"Have a good game, dear?" Jensen asked.

"The best since I arrived. I need a drink."

"Why don't you play with Fred here occasionally?"

"We're not in the same group." She stood up and walked over to the bar.

Clayton had to act, to warn her about her husband. He followed her to the bar on the pretext of getting another drink for himself. "Your husband thinks you are having an affair," he said. There was no time to introduce the subject gently.

She looked at him as if he had made a joke. "Does he, indeed? Does he say who with?"

"He suspects a tennis pro."

That was all they had time for, but he had done his duty and the rest was up to her. They walked back to Jensen and she sat down and reached over to push back a bit of hair that was sticking out over Jensen's ear.

The rest of the evening passed like all the others. When Cynthia had changed, they ate dinner, watched a series of comic sketches put on by the Jolly Organisors, and went to bed.

The next morning Clayton got up a little earlier than usual and stood among the trees to watch the Jensens' door. Cynthia appeared in tennis clothes, and started off towards the courts. Shortly afterwards, Jensen came out with a video camera slung over his shoulder, but instead of following his wife, he struck off along a path that led over the hill to a village around the other side of the cliffs, leaving Clayton wondering what he was up to.

After lunch the three of them sat by the pool, drinking coffee. Cynthia finished her coffee and picked up her beach bag, and Clayton got ready to join them in a walk down to the beach. Jensen put a hand on his arm "You go ahead, Cynthia," he said. "I want to tell Fred a dirty joke I heard this morning."

She wrinkled her nose in mock disgust and walked off. Jensen turned to Clayton. "I've thought of a way to get my revenge on Cynthia," he said. The sun sparkled on his glasses. "The video we were watching the other day gave me the idea. Do you remember the story of Hephaestus?"

Jensen was a money broker of some kind, but he had been educated in the classics and enjoyed stuffing his conversation with literary allusions. One day as they were watching the parachute skiers climb the sky, he compared them to Icarus, wondering which one would get too near the sun, hoping he would be there when it happened.

Clayton said, "Who was Hephaestus?"

"You may known him as Vulcan."

"The god of blow-outs?"

For a moment all of Jensen's contempt was focused on Clayton. "The smith god," he said. "He made fabulous armour for the other gods. He was married to Aphrodite. Now Aphrodite was unfaithful to him with Ares, the god of war—a lecher and a braggart, by the way—and Helios the sun-god saw them at it and told Hephaestus. Hephaestus then fashioned a very strong, very thin net which he hung over his bed. The next time Aphrodite and Ares were copulating, Hephaestus dropped the net, catching them in the middle of their act and binding them so they could not move. Then Hephaestus invited all the other gods over to laugh. How they laughed."

"What has all this to do with Cynthia?"

"Let's go for a little walk. I'll show you."

He took them along the path that Clayton had seen him take that morning, away from the tennis courts, over the hill, and then through some scrub until they reached the cliff edge. They had gone through two hundred and seventy degrees and were now on the other side of the tennis courts looking down on the beach. Jensen stopped. "Look down there," he commanded.

Clayton saw an indentation in the cliff-face like a huge mine-shaft with an crack opening on one side towards the beach. A patch of sand at the bottom of the shaft was nearly enclosed by the cliff face. As they watched, a couple came along and climbed over the rocks by the entrance to the shaft and lay down on the patch of sand. The shadows at the bottom of the shaft were too deep for the two men to see who they were but after a while it became obvious what they were doing. It was a perfect love nest.

"So what has this to do with Cynthia?" Clayton asked again.

"I overheard some people talking about this place I put two and two together and it seemed possible that Cynthia knew about it."

"So?"

"Hephaestus." Jensen tapped his camera. "My net."

"You're going to take pictures of Cynthia making love? Do you know it's her?"

"It's her all right. Look through this." He handed Clayton his camera. Through the view-finder, the same scene was visible, perfectly framed by the circle of rock.

"You still can't see who it is. It's too dark."

"Not in the morning. Helios comes up there ..." he pointed to the sea "... and sends a powerful shaft of light into the cave about eight o'clock, when my Aphrodite and her Ares are locked in each other's arms."

"Who is he, this Ares?"

"I thought I would save that as a surprise. Their heads were still in shadow so I didn't see myself, but it will be clear on the screen I'm sure."

Then Clayton realised. "You are going to record them and show it on the camp video?"

"I've already done the recording." He patted his camera.

"Christ!" Clayton lunged for the camera and Jensen twisted to stay out of reach, and stumbled, grabbing for Clayton's trousers as he fell, like Icarus, to the rocks below.

As Clayton stood staring down, two Jolly Organisors came out of the bushes, Kiki and the rat-faced tennis pro.

"I'll take the camera," Kiki said. "Now tell us what happened."

Clayton told them: Jensen and he were taking a walk and Jensen was taking a picture then stepped back too far. "It was an accident," he said.

The Jolly Organisors looked at each other. "This could get complicated," Kiki said. "Okay, you were up here taking pictures, and he stepped back to get you in focus, right?" Kiki looked at Clayton and continued to speak slowly. "That's what happened. Okay? Danny and I were walking along here. We saw it all. You were twenty feet away from him. Right, Danny?"

Danny nodded and turned away.

Kiki walked to the edge of the cliff. "He was *here* and you were *here*. Okay?"

Clayton said, "It wasn't my fault."

Kiki said, "How could it be? You were twenty feet apart." He waited until he was sure that Clayton understood.

"What were you doing here?" Clayton asked.

Kiki said, "See that guy?" He pointed to a figure high above the sea, dangling from a parachute. "Danny here was up there this morning and he thought he saw a Peeping Tom, taking pictures down the tunnel of love. That's the local name for it. So when we noticed you two heading this way with a video camera, we decided to take a look."

Down below the beach was filling up with people trying to look at the body. Faces were turned up to look at them.

"You were *here* and he was *there*. Okay?"

"He was spying on his wife, taking pictures of her."

"Let's go down now," Kiki said, cutting him off. "Look shocked now, and shut up."

"What are you going to do with the pictures?" Clayton pointed to the video camera.

"That depends." Kiki said. "Keep them safe, anyway. Eh, Danny?"

"Let's go down," Danny said. He turned to Clayton, "And like Kiki said. Shut up. Okay?"

Bedbugs

"They simply appeared one afternoon and said that there had been an accident, and asked me to call the police."

The proprietor of the inn, acting as his own desk clerk, swivelled the register and pointed to the place for my signature.

We were on holiday, three of us, my wife and I and an old school friend of hers, touring Corsica, staying the night in a hotel in Bastia. So far we had been lucky with the weather. We landed in England, stayed for a week in the Cotswolds with some friends, and then flew to Marseilles where we picked up a car and drove up to Cadenet to spend a few days with an old school friend while we looked at Provence. After Corsica we would take the ferry to Italy and Tuscany, where some more friends owned a villa near Lucca. Travelling like this can be more expensive than staying in hotels, by the time you have bought gifts for the hosts and treated them in the best local restaurants, but it's a pleasant way to structure a tour.

On this part of the trip, across Corsica from south-west to north-east, we were staying in hotels for the first time, and some problems had occurred. My wife had booked the hotels and the ferries through an agency in Britain, and wires had become crossed. Somehow the message had been conveyed that we did not need two rooms, so every night so far I had to explain that we needed a reassignment of rooms from the family room my wife had inadvertently requested to a single and a double. I tried to make a joke of it on the first night but I was stretching my French too far (not difficult: in a bar in Nice once I ordered a ham sandwich pret-a-porter, and the face of the innkeeper remained opaque as he explained to me that I had ordered a sandwich ready-to wear). My wife said there was no need to make a song and dance about it, just tell the desk clerk to change the rooms, but it seemed to me that making myself agreeable to the man at the desk could only help us to have a pleasant stay. Fortunately the season was over and the hotels were half empty so we had no serious difficulty once they were clear what we wanted.

The composition of our party reminded this innkeeper of a story about an Englishman who had been killed in a fall the year before. In Corsica the tourists ritually talk about the hazards of the mountain roads the way the English discuss the weather. I think I had introduced the topic.

He continued, "They had stopped to take photographs at a place about ten kilometres back where the road curves around a disused stone cottage—you saw the place?—Yes. You parked there to take pictures—wonderful views. Yes, that was their idea also. They set out down the cliff with their cameras to find separate vantage points and soon lost sight of each other. After a few minutes, both women heard a shout. They scrambled back up to the car and saw the man's body lying on a ledge about a hundred feet below. His neck was broken: he must have died immediately.

"Are we ready?" my wife called from the elevator door, meaning, "Get a move on, for God's sake."

It had been a long day and we were all a bit tired. So far our little trio had worked well as a travelling party. When my wife first suggested the trip I had been wary. I've had more experience than the other two and I could remember trips all the way back to the time I went youth-hostelling with a couple of pals at the age of sixteen: three can be a bad number. A group of three is always in danger of breaking up as two gang up, innocently at first, on one; I've seen it happen brutally, with adolescents, and thickly camouflaged but with the same dynamic operating among three men in their sixties at a Club Med tennis camp. By the third day two of them were obviously getting up early to dodge the third. It suited me at the time because my wife didn't play tennis so I was happy to have a competent partner free for the week.

We had no such problems, of course, because I anticipated them and watched for the tiniest friction between the two women that could turn into a major irritant, and got between them, so to speak, to smooth it over. But I caught a whiff now of what might have been as I chatted to the innkeeper while the two women waited to be released to their rooms and their baths.

"As I say," our host continued, "These ladies were English, so they stayed very calm, answering all the gendarme's questions, refusing the doctor's sedative, but taking a little whiskey, and afterwards, boiled eggs in their rooms. One of them—let's call her, without prejudice—'the other woman', not the wife, had blotches on her face and neck which our booby of a doctor diagnosed as 'suppressed hysteria', a phrase I think he had found in a magazine." He swung the register back to inspect my signature, and looked up at the board to choose our rooms. "One double and one single?" He continued talking. "The police were happy to leave it there. The death of a foreign tourist is very little trouble for the authorities if they can label it 'accidental'. But I was suspicious. I know that place. I don't believe that all three of them could have lost sight of each other entirely. Think about it. You were there. Don't you agree?"

I heard or felt a movement behind my shoulder. The women had come closer and were now standing behind me. My wife was tapping her foot. "Are we set?" she asked. "I'm hot, tired and thirsty, and so is Cynthia."

"*Bloody* tired," Cynthia agreed.

I put my hand out and squeezed Cynthia's arm and nodded to the innkeeper to continue.

"The police ordered an autopsy, but what good was that? No one had been shot, or stabbed. Just a little push. But I let the police have their way.

"The next morning the women received a fax. Wonderful invention, the fax! The entire world reads your mail! It was from a London travel agent, and it enclosed a second message from a hotel down the coast, a hotel about which the women had complained, apparently. The message said, simply, "Impossible. This is a three-star hotel. We have never had bedbugs."

He laughed. "Now the police had to pay attention. The women had said nothing about bedbugs to them, allowing this idiot doctor his diagnosis. Why? They knew what those blotches were."

"Perhaps they were ashamed," I said. "Perhaps, being English, unfamiliar with bedbugs, they were afraid they indicated something about their personal cleanliness."

The women behind me stirred. "Dear God," my wife said. They moved back towards the elevator.

The proprietor said, "The ladies look restless. Perhaps I should finish this story later?"

"No, no. Let's hear it all. They won't mind." I waved and smiled towards the elevator to reassure them, and turned back to the inn-keeper. "Keep going."

"Where was I? Yes, perhaps that is why she made the suspicious error of not telling the police about the bedbugs. But then the results from the autopsy arrived. The body of the husband also was bitten by bedbugs." He paused, savouring the drama. "Now the police ques-tioned the two women again, and got an ingenious explanation. They said that the night before the accident the man had become restless and sat out on the balcony to smoke and read. The other woman, not his wife, you understand, seeing his light from her room, called out to him suggesting they change beds, that she would sleep with the wife and he could have her bed so he could read without disturbing any-body. That, possibly, is when the husband was bitten, the women said."

I said, "Presumably the wife knew about the bites?"

"Why?"

"That is why she pushed him down the cliff. I assume that is where this is going? Unless the other woman pushed him." I smiled and waved at the women, who did not respond.

"It is a question of timing, I think. If the wife had not noticed the bites on her husband, or perhaps if they did not become evident until the next morning, then she might have believed they came from the single bed, quite innocently. The two women were certainly very sup-portive of each other here at the hotel." He raised his eyebrows comi-cally. "But the story is not over. Next we learned that the innkeeper in Calvi was so angry he had called in the health officials to inspect his hotel to give him a clean sheet." He laughed and raised his eyebrows. "A clean sheet," he said again. "Which they did. No bedbugs. Now this is serious evidence. You cannot trust an innkeeper on the subject of bedbugs, even me," he added unseriously. "But the health authori-ties would not perjure themselves."

"There is nothing in it, then. Just an accident."

"On the contrary, proof positive. Where did the bedbugs come from?"

My wife appeared beside me with her hand out. "The keys," she said, "Both of them. Join us at your leisure but can I have the keys, please."

She was demanding, not requesting, and the innkeeper hastily gave her both keys and sped up his story as she returned to the elevator.

"I will tell you. I made a few phone calls to my friends in Calvi to try to confirm my suspicions. Although I could not find the actual hotel, I am sure of what happened. At the age of these people, they often require a rest. Not all together at the same time: Sometimes one of them, sometimes two. In the afternoon, the wife says she is tired, and returns to the hotel to rest. The husband and the other woman walk along the beach. They find a no-star hotel, for an hour. All the rest follows. Those no-star hotels are full of bugs."

"Did you tell the police?"

"They refused to listen to me. You see, they could never prove who actually did it: either one, or even both. By now the women had gone back to England, and they would be expensive to bring back. And this island is largely supported by tourists. What we don't need is a sensational murder story involving hotels with bedbugs, incompetent doctors, and stupid police."

"So officially it was an accident."

"That is the official version, yes."

"But the wife pushed him off the cliff when she saw the bites, right?"

"Perhaps. But consider. A question of timing. Suppose, as I said, that the bites on the husband had not yet appeared in the morning, or he had been able to conceal them from his wife: and suppose when they did appear he had told the other woman but not his wife; and consider how important their thirty year friendship might have been to the two women ..."

"Why are you telling me all this?" I asked.

"It's what innkeepers do," he laughed. "Entertain the guests with tales. Enjoy your stay."

"The innkeeper's wrong," my wife said, later, as she was luxuriating, at last, in her bath, a gin and tonic resting on the soap dish. "I don't know which one did it, or if both of them did, but I think I know why. Nothing to do with bedbugs, or thirty-year friendships. Or sex."

Duty Free

It was impossible for an observer to mistake what was going on. The middle-aged couple in the corner of the airport lounge were involved in a marital fight, all the more savage for being conducted in near whispers. It was evidently the end of the holiday; their nerves were raw, and they needed a rest. Probably they had under-estimated the amount of energy their trip needed, and now they just wanted to get home. But the plane was delayed, a delay which, when added to the requirement to arrive early for security reasons and to the long journey to the airport, would mean they had spent six or seven hours preparing for the flight, and there was still the flight itself, another seven or eight hours.

"I don't think a bottle of duty-free will make the slightest difference," she said. "They've got scotches here you don't ever see at home. I think it's bloody ridiculous." She spoke to the air in front of her.

"Bloody ridiculous or not," he said, addressing himself to the window, "When we get there I want to go home and go to bed. I want to walk out of the gate at the other end and go home. I don't want them asking me if that's the only duty-free I've got, and turning out my bags to prove it."

"Everybody buys duty-free," she said, lifting up her foot and addressing the heel of her shoe. "Everybody. They're more likely to wonder why you haven't got one, and make us turn everything out."

"Will you shut up!" It was still only a whisper, but his voice was filled with fury. "It's bad enough that you have to use that great sodding bag as a carry-on. I told you once, I'll tell you again, I want to get out, get home. I've had enough. Besides, George will be waiting for us. I'll ask him to buy you a bleeding bottle of scotch, shall I? Now shut it!"

He lifted his own small carry-on bag off his lap and tried to sort out his clothing. He was wearing a shirt, tie and pullover under a heavy tweed jacket, and he was carrying a raincoat in case the weather in London was bad. He changed his paperback over from his raincoat to his jacket pocket, then left it out entirely as he tried to think through the garments he would stow in the overhead locker.

"Sit still," she said. "You're driving me crackers."

He put the raincoat, the book and his bag on his chair, touched her elbow and pointed to them, instructing her to guard his possessions, and went in search of a place where he could have a last cigarette; but before he had gone five steps their flight was called and he had to scurry back and load up to get in line. She watched him drop his paperback twice, shaking her head. "I was wrong," she said. "If you had duty-free to carry, too, we'd never get on that plane."

The first three hours of the flight passed in the usual routine of drinks, food, and more drinks, then the film came on and the plane settled down. It was not full, but she had booked them in non-smoking seats, so once the trays were removed he went back to look for an empty seat in the smoking section.

Watching him come down the aisle was a man in a check shirt with the air of someone looking for a chat. As he drew level with the row, the man nodded to him and indicated the empty seat beside him and he sat down. "Give me five," the man said, as soon as he had lit up.

"Do what?"

"Give me five," the man repeated holding out his hand at a forty-five degree angle, face up.

Gingerly Henry placed his palm on the outstretched hand and slid it across.

"Wayne." the man said.

"Henry."

"How ya doin', Henry?"

"Very well, thanks."

They smoked in silence for a while, then the stewardess announced that the duty-free shop was open.

Wayne said, "I already got my share. You?" When Henry did not respond, he said, "I noticed in the lounge. You don't have any duty-free. You buying any?"

"No."

Wayne twisted in his seat. "Not even your allowance?"

"No."

"Would you do me a favour? Would you walk a bottle of cognac through for me? I don't want to declare it and pay thirty bucks or whatever, but if you don't have any you could carry it through for me."

"No. Sorry. I'm in a hurry. I don't want to chance being stopped. I've had a very tiring day and I want to get home."

"Why would they stop you? One bottle of booze?"

Henry waved his hand to push the suggestion away. "It's too much to carry. Sorry." He got up from his seat quickly, nearly forgetting he was smoking, stubbed out his cigarette and went back to his wife.

"That was quick," she said.

"Man back there wanted me to carry through a bottle of duty-free. He's got a bottle over his allowance."

"And I suppose you said yes."

"No, I didn't."

After a minute, she said, "How did he know you don't already have your allowance?"

"He's been watching us. In the lounge and here."

"Watching us? Why?"

He thought about it. "Not so much us as everybody, looking to see who might not have duty-free."

"You sure?"

"Why would he pick me out?"

After that he tried to sleep, but an hour later he was still thinking about Wayne and his duty-free. As the breakfast appeared he said, "I've been thinking. I'll take his bottle through for him."

"Just like that? Why the change?"

"I've been thinking."

"Sorry to be so … offhand last night, Wayne," he said. "I was a bit on edge. I'll take the bottle through for you."

"That's my boy. I'll get it from the locker."

"Hang on. Give it to me when we get off the plane. Did you check any bags?"

"One."

"We have two. So we'll both have to wait for the luggage to come down. We could wait by the carousels and go out together. Then I won't be able to run off with your bottle."

Wayne laughed. "You wouldn't get very far."

They stood together waiting for the bags to come round.

"Here's the cognac," Wayne said, holding out the bag from the duty-free shop. "Wait for me by the gate."

"Hang on until I've got my bags."

When all the luggage was assembled, Henry gave his wife her bags to carry and organised his own. He put his raincoat on his shoulder to leave his hands free but when he bent to pick up his bag, the raincoat slid down his arm and he had to start again. He rolled the coat into a tighter bundle and put it back on his shoulder and this time bent his knees so that it wouldn't slide down.

"Here," Wayne said, again, handing him the duty-free bag. Henry extended his fingers under the handle of his carry-on bag so that Wayne could hook the plastic liquor bag over them, but in leaning ever-so-slightly sideways, he caused the raincoat to slide down again and smother his hand. He put his raincoat back on his shoulder and hooked the plastic bag over his wrist, but as he curled his fingers around the handle of the carry-on bag the plastic bag slipped across the back of his hand, crushing his fingers against the handle of the case.

"Bloody hell," his wife said. "I'll see you outside," and marched off through the gate.

Now Henry got himself loaded up with everything except his over-night bag. He bent to include the handle of the overnight bag within the fingers that were already curled around the liquor bag and one of the plastic handles slipped free and the bag opened and the bottle of cognac slid out on to the floor. "This isn't going to work," he said, looking appealingly at Wayne.

Most of the other passengers had gone now. Wayne looked around the baggage area, worried and impatient. "Gimme that little sucker," he said, picking up Henry's overnight bag.

Gratefully Henry let him pick it up. "Now we'll manage," Henry said.

One of the two customs officers who were watching from behind the glass, said, "That was as good as the old sticky-hand routine," and tried to explain the vaudeville act involving three men on a scaffold trying to get unstuck from each other as they were putting a poster on a wall.

"I think they're up to something. I think we should have a look at that duty-free bag," the other officer said. He was a very new recruit to the service; this was his first week on the job and he was looking for major smugglers on every plane.

"What do you think's going on?" His older colleague was amused.

"The duty-free belongs to the bloke in the check shirt, but he's very keen to have the other one carry it through for him."

"Right. He's got extra, the other one's got none, so the bloke in the check shirt is getting him to carry it through. Nothing illegal about that. Well, there is, but it's not worth bothering about."

"I don't know." The young man shook his head. "What makes a better donkey"—using the technical term he had just learned—"than some poor unsuspecting tourist, doing someone a favour."

"You're barmy, son. All right then, just to prove it, let's stop them. You take the little man with the duty-free, I'll hold the other one up. Right? Then when you find out it's just whiskey, tip me the wink and we'll let them through. Just have a look at his duty-free, all right? Nearly time for coffee." He smiled, for he had just realised what was going on.

As Henry reached the exit, the young officer took him to one side.

"How much duty-free do you have, sir? May I see?" He took the box out of the bag, broke the seal and lifted out the bottle of cognac. He stared at it thoughtfully, then put it back, aware of his colleague's eyes on his neck. "Right you are, sir. Thank you."

While he was watching his young colleague, the older officer was checking Wayne's bags. He passed a hand through the big suitcase, then asked Wayne to open the carry-on bag. "It's not mine," Wayne said. He pointed to Henry, "It's his. Henry!"

Henry had already started to walk through the gate after his wife. He came back to where the customs officer was waiting with his bag, sending his wife on to wait for him.

"Would you mind opening this, sir?" the officer asked.

Reluctantly Henry produced a key and opened the leather club bag. The customs officer lifted out his toilet articles one by one until the bag was empty. Then he checked the bag itself until he was sure there were no false compartments. Finally he began to unscrew Henry's talcum powder, then changed his mind, shrugged, and put everything back and chalked the bags. He looked up at Wayne and jerked his thumb at Henry. "You know, don't you, that if this bloke walks off with that duty-free, you wouldn't be able to do much about it."

Seeing the officer was entertaining himself, Wayne smiled. "When I get my cognac," he said. "He'll get his bag."

The officer walked over to his colleague. "Did you taste it?" he asked.

The young man looked startled. "It was sealed."

"An old trick. Probably hash oil. You should have tasted it." He grinned. "I was wrong, too. Come on, let's get a coffee."

Outside in the concourse, Wayne said, "Thanks, pal. That could have been tricky. Those guys were watching. They knew it was my liquor, but they couldn't be bothered." He handed over the carry-on bag and picked up the cognac.

Henry said, "I wondered there for a minute, if you'd got me to carry the crown jewels through. Your duty-free was the only thing they were interested in."

"And your bag. They get a bit keen sometimes." Wayne winked and walked off.

George, who had been waiting some distance away with Henry's wife, came forward now and bustled them out to the waiting car. He buckled on his seat-belt and started the car. "Let's have a look at it before we go," he said.

The wife lifted her carry-on bag on to her lap and opened it up to show George.

"Christ," George said. "Must be worth a quarter of a million. Easy. Let's get out of here."

When they were well on their way, Henry's wife said, "See, you could've brought a bottle of your own through. What a performance you made of carrying a couple of bags. Not exactly inconspicuous, were you, but it didn't make any difference."

Henry said, "You don't understand anything, do you?"

Jackpot

When Fred Dawson's wife proposed a week in the Carribean sun before the Canadian winter set in, she was surprised at his immediate agreement. Dawson had always balked at do-nothing holidays. He liked travelling, enjoyed sitting in foreign cafes, talking to strangers, riding on ferries; but lying on a beach, trying to avoid skin-cancer, surrounded by women of his own age (fifty-seven) wearing nose-guards, was something he found ignominious and boring. This time, though, he said yes, as long as they chose a beach that did not have to be heavily guarded to keep out the poverty-stricken natives. Two motives lay behind his condition: he was a genuine liberal who felt uncomfortable when he could not avoid seeing how the underprivileged lived; and he was timid, afraid that he was an obvious target for a hungry beggar with a knife. So he agreed to go on condition that he chose the island they would go to.

For Dawson had another agenda. A holiday in the Carribean was an opportunity to satisfy a dream that had been growing for twenty years. At his age he was reconciled to the setting aside of most of his early ambitions: he accepted that he would never now try sky-diving, or ride a racehorse in a steeplechase, or jig in a disco, or fornicate in an airplane. But if he chose the right island, he would, finally, be able to visit a casino.

Dawson was a gambler who lived in Toronto where the opportunities for gambling were limited. He visited the race track occasionally, but his family and other interests competed for his time on weekends, and he was not so addicted that he would seriously upset the pattern of his life or his bank balance in order to bet. Sociologists tell us that a man who "needs" one drink a day before dinner is an alcoholic, and by this criterion Dawson should have signed up with Gamblers Anonymous. He liked always to be awaiting the outcome of a small bet. For him off-track betting would have been ideal but Ontario politicians preferred to open casinos, the nearest a hundred miles away from Dawson's home.

So Dawson bought tickets to all the lotteries that were available and played poker on Friday nights with a group of bookkeepers and customs clerks where the maximum raise was two dollars except for the last hand when it was five. Dawson did not repine: he could satisfy his needs, more or less, and he was wary of Toronto becoming the Atlantic City of Canada in case he couldn't control himself. But he did want to visit a casino before he got too old to travel, and without the expense of flying down to Vegas. A week, he thought, was probably just enough time for him to get settled in, find out where the casino was, circle the idea conversationally for a few days with his wife, then make the plunge, probably on the Friday before they returned.

He spent most of an afternoon in a travel agent's office where he was able to read his way through all the brochures, and he narrowed his choice down to three islands, all of which boasted casinos. He suspected there were others but none of the publicity he read made much fuss about the availability of any form of gambling, from which he surmised that casinos were like the kind of night-life in pre-Castro Cuba; anyone interested knew all about them, and the resorts could safely rely on word of mouth. So he raised the subject casually with his Friday night poker group, and sure enough got a firm recommendation which he passed on to his wife without telling her where the recommendation came from. He did mention, as an afterthought, that he would like to drop in on a casino for an hour, and she received this cheerfully enough. His gambling had been the smallest of hobbies within the family, no more expensive or time-consuming than if he had been a member of an amateur string quartet, and beyond forgetting occasionally to leave his Fridays clear, she hardly thought about it. It was enough for her to be going on vacation. For his part, Dawson was as excited as he had been twenty years before when he had visited an English racecourse and learned how to bet with the bookmakers on the course.

They arrived on Saturday and spent the weekend establishing themselves in their room and on the beach. Dawson was more gregarious than usual, hoping by chatting up the other guests to meet someone who knew casino etiquette (was a tie required, as at Monte Carlo? Did you have to keep your hand on your wallet? Did you pay to go in?) and on Sunday evening, at the bar by the pool, he struck up a conversation with an amiable-looking piston-ring manufacturer from Wilmington, North Carolina, who raised the subject himself. He had just come back from the casino after "dropping a couple of hundred" and Dawson was easily able to find out much of what he needed to know. He couldn't conceal his interest, or his ignorance, sufficiently to fool the manufacturer who recognised a fellow addict and offered to take him along the next night and show him the ropes. Dawson backed off: Monday was too soon because it involved the risk that if everything went well Dawson would go back on Tuesday and on every evening after that. He also wanted to go alone, as he went to the races, not wanting to discuss his betting with anyone else, and he therefore stuck to his intention of going on Friday, the night before they were to return, and told his wife so in order that she wouldn't make any social arrangements with any of the other guests. Friday, they agreed, was his night.

When the day came, Dawson had made all his decisions. Minimum stakes, of course, and only blackjack and the fruit machines. He planned to lose two hundred dollars (if he won that much he would quit) but he had another two hundred in his sock just in case, held in place by a rubber band. He left his wallet and his credit cards in his room so that the worst that could happen to him would be that his pocket might be picked of the two hundred, and he could afford that. He had made similar arrangements on the one and only time he had spent an hour with a Paris prostitute, guessing what she might charge, doubling it just in case, then putting an equivalent sum in his shoe in case, he was wildly out in his calculations. He did underestimate the price that time, but still emerged from her room without having had to take off his shoes. Now he added ten dollars for the cab fare home and made his way to the hotel lobby. The rest was easy.

He was stunned by the casino at first. The intensity of light was intimidating, but he allowed himself to be carried through the doors by the continual surge of arriving gamblers, catching his breath inside the door. The scene went far beyond what he had imagined: literally hundreds of fruit machines glittered in rows as in a giant showroom, shining, spinning, spewing out coins; dozens of blackjack tables; half a dozen dice games ringed with shouting players; at least four roulette wheels; and in a corner, a group of baccarat players pursued their passion in silent devotion.

When he was used to the hubbub, Dawson began to circle the room, watching. He was appalled and excited by the twenty-five dollar minimum of the first blackjack tables he came to—a poor run of luck would wipe him out in five minutes—but he was getting most of what he came for just by watching, and he changed the limit of his loss to four hundred, all he had. It was going to be worth it. Then he came across a blackjack table with a five dollar limit and sat down to play.

In five minutes he had lost fifty dollars, and he played automatically for a couple of hands while he tried to calculate how best to maximise his pleasure. Losing the money was only slightly less exciting than winning, but he worried about using himself up too fast. If he carried on at the present rate he would only last about half an a hour, and now he wanted to stay until at least midnight. There were the slot machines to be tried, and now, just possibly, a go at roulette after all. Already, watching was no longer satisfying enough. Having written off the four hundred to clear his emotions, he now allowed his mind to play with the possibility that tonight was his night, that he might make a killing. It didn't matter if he didn't, but it would be terrific if he did.

While he was sorting himself out, his luck turned and ten minutes later he had won back his fifty and seventy-five more. He moved to a table with a twenty-five dollar stake and lost fifty on the first hand and paused to calm down. He needed a drink but was not sure how to go about ordering one. Waitresses appeared regularly to take orders; money changed hands but not always, and he couldn't tell if the drinks were free, and the bills dropped on the tray were tips, or if some of the players were running a tab, so he left the table and made his way to one of the bars. He bought a roll of silver dollars and fed some slot machines along the way, but got nothing back, and still by the time he was seated at the bar with a drink in front of him he was seven dollars ahead. This is the life, he thought, but the thrill of being inside a casino had subsided and been replaced by the desire to make a killing.

Another man appeared on the stool beside him, a good-looking, carefully groomed man in a dark grey suit with a slightly metallic lustre, like a television actor playing a banker—and nodded to him. "How're you making out?" he asked.

"I'm ahead," Dawson said. "Some," he added. He had meant to say "a few dollars" but "some" sounded more appropriate, more idiomatic.

The banker looked pleased for him, and ordered them both a drink. "This your first time?" he asked. "On the island, I mean."

Dawson nodded.

"Pretty nice casino," the man said. "Better than Atlantic City."

Dawson nodded. "Quieter," he said.

"That's it," the man responded with enthusiasm. "Quieter. That's exactly right."

They sipped their beer in silence for a few minutes, two old gamblers taking five. Then the man said, "I think you're the guy I've been looking for. You want to make some money?"

What Dawson wanted to do then was disappear and be translated back to the safe world of North Toronto, away from shark-suited strangers offering to cut him in on some no doubt illegal operation. What he wanted to do was say, "No thank you" and go through the door.

He forced himself to respond. "What are you talking about? How am I the guy you're looking for?"

"I need a partner. All you have to do is play a slot machine. When it pays off, pick up the money and meet me back here for the split."

Dawson looked round the bar, hoping to see someone he knew, but there were only two other drinkers, neither within earshot.

"Okay?" the banker asked.

"Okay what? I don't know what you're talking about. Why me?"

"Keep your voice down. You looked like a guy who'd stay cool, but I could be wrong. I'll spell it out. One of those machines is going to pay off with a small jackpot soon. A thousand dollars. How do I know? Let's just say I've captured the circuitry." Here the man took out a small black box from an inside pocket. It was about the size of a compact disc container with a set of buttons on one side, numbered from one to ten. "I can punch up the jackpot any time I want. But I need a partner to collect." He put the box away as an attendant came through the door. "They see me out there with this thing, I'm a dead man. Not literally." He smiled reassuringly. "They don't do that here. But I can operate this thing remote. I've been working on it a long time."

Dawson swallowed his beer. "Say it again. I go out there, operate one of the slot machines, and you make it pay off. Then I give you half. Right?"

"That's right."

"How much? How much will it be?"

"It'll pay off a thousand; five hundred each. Just enough not to be too conspicuous. You cash in and meet me here."

"What are you? The Wizard?"

The banker laughed. "I'm just a guy who has figured out how to beat a machine, that's all."

"Christ," Dawson said. "Jesus Christ." Then, "How will you know if it's me working the machine?"

"We'll time it. I can make that baby pay off on the second I want. You got a good watch?" He looked at Dawson's wrist. "Take this." He unstrapped a watch from his own wrist, an old-fashioned model with a sweep second hand. "Now we're synchronized. Let's make it you'll be on the machine at nine twenty-seven exactly. Get there at nine twenty-two, play a few coins slowly until the time."

"What if someone else is playing it?"

"Its a risk but it's not a popular machine and five minutes should be enough."

Dawson looked at his new timepiece. "Where will you be?"

"You don't need to know that. Out of sight. That's why we have to get the timing right. I won't be able to watch you."

"Then I come back here …"

"No. The attendant will give you a voucher. You cash that in for the thousand, then you come back here and give me five. You can have anything over."

"You do this every night?"

"You don't have to know that, either. Let's just leave it that this is my living. Are you on?"

Dawson sipped his beer, making it last. He was deeply frightened and just as deeply excited. Every instinct but one told him to stay away from this shark-suited stranger lest he wind up contributing to the pollution in the bay, but the remaining instinct, greed, kept him examining the proposition. All he had to do was play one of the machines, pick up his winnings (if any; he still didn't really believe this) cash in, and pay this man his half. "Which machine is it?"

The banker explained. "There's a row of dollar machines on the right of the front door. My machine is the third one from the end. It's a straight fruit machine—cherries, oranges, you know. The machines either side of it use playing cards as symbols. Okay?"

Dawson said, "One more beer first."

"Make it nine forty-seven, then. Exactly." The man slid off his stool and disappeared.

At nine-seventeen Dawson looked around the gambling hall, getting his bearings. Five minutes later he was standing near the rigged machine, sweating. An old man was feeding the machine a handful of dollars, and then, as if on cue, at nine twenty-three he cursed the machine and walked away. Dawson positioned himself in front of the machine and put in his first dollar. Playing slowly, he put in six dollars, and then, as the second hand swept up to the deadline, he put in the crucial coin and stepped back.

He was prepared for one of two things. He had kept in mind the possibility that the man in the bar was a joker who was now laughing at his expense with some pals (but a joker who gave away wrist watches?) And he worried that if it worked, a thousand dollars would spill all over the floor of the casino.

What actually happened, of course, was that lights flashed, a bell rang, and one of the attendants hurried over and checked the win. He spoke into his cell phone, nodded, and gave Dawson a note for a thousand and fifty-seven dollars. "Congratulations, sir. The cashier over by the door will pay you off."

Above the ceiling, three men were watching Dawson on a row of screens that monitored the casino. As Dawson put the winning dollar into the fruit machine, the banker pressed a button on the console in front of him and the fruit machine lit up. As Dawson hesitated, the banker urged him on as if he were watching a horse race. "Come over to the bar," he shouted, unheard through the ceiling. "Over to the bar. I'm waiting for my money. We had a deal. Ah, there he goes, Joe."

"Run for it, dummy," Joe shouted. "There's the door. Go, go, go, go!"

The third man said, "This some kind of bet?"

"We're looking for an honest man," said the banker, and explained the arrangement he had made with Dawson. "Joe says the door is right there. No one is going to go all the way back to the bar to pay me off, when in three steps he could be gone. *I* say that there must be one honest guy, even in a casino. So far I'm down three, and we're playing double or nothing. What's the guy doing? He's hesitating. Maybe I'm in with a chance."

The old man who had been playing the fruit machine before Dawson came in the door. "What's he doing?" he asked.

"He's hesitating," the banker said. "Remember what your mother taught you!" he shouted at the screen.

Dawson looked at the slip in his hand and tried to make sense of his emotions. Greed, honesty, desire not to look a fool if it was all a joke, fear, all chased each other around as if on a wheel of fortune. He waited to see where the wheel would stop. Fear was the one to dispose of first: surely an organisation as sophisticated as a casino knew all about guys like the banker, and were using him in some way. As bait, perhaps. Probably when he took the banker back his money, they would move in and teach both Dawson and the banker a lesson? The way to avoid that was not to go back to the banker. There was the door. All he had to do was slide into the night. But, again, surely a character as smooth as the banker had associates out there, on the edge of the light, just to make sure that didn't happen? So cash the slip and … and … and … what? Dawson's brain was squeaking as he tried to find the answer. And then he realised, having now taken several steps down the slippery slope, he had one last chance to return to the narrow path, the one he should never have strayed from. There didn't seem any alternative. He called over the attendant.

"Now what," the banker asked. He watched the attendant take a cell-phone from his pocket and waited for his own phone to ring. "Yes," he said. "What's the problem?"

"Man here says someone tried to involve him in some kind of scam." The attendant kept Dawson away with an outstretched arm and spoke quietly. "He says someone has captured the circuitry of one of the machines, whatever the hell that means, and he can make it pay off when he wants. Shall I alert security? He says the guy is in the west bar, looks very well-dressed, like a mobster. I think *this* guy's nuts. He says he's not entitled to his winnings, wants to give them back."

"Of course he's nuts," the banker said. "No, don't alert security. They won't find anyone in the bar." He looked for advice from the other two, but they were in hysterics. "Better play along with the guy. Tell him to keep the money. Tell him we want him to have it as a reward. Tell him we've been looking for the guy in the bar for a long time."

The banker put the phone down and turned to the others. "See? We found one."

"Too good to be true," Joe said, "But here's your money. Double or nothing?"

The banker shook his head. "I'd be pressing my luck."

The Cure

When Bythell decided to rob his old friend, Sligo, his motive was to teach Sligo a lesson, unsettle him a bit. He had suffered from Sligo for twenty years, seventeen of them as his next-door neighbour. When Sligo moved away, Bythell thought, "Peace at last," but their wives were friends and Bythell's wife found Sligo a good sort so he continued to see nearly as much of Sligo as ever. (Sometimes, though, when Bythell raged about him in the bedroom after the two couples had spent an evening together, his wife would say, "For God's sake. Don't see him if he bothers you so much.")

Just why Sligo bothered Bythell was hard for Bythell to explain, because it had its roots in a relationship between the two men that was apparent only to Bythell. It was an attitude that Sligo took to Bythell, an assumption of a mentorial relationship on Sligo's part which Bythell found irritating from the very early days when he otherwise welcomed Sligo's friendship. When Bythell first moved into his house and began repairing the little stone wall that edged his front yard, Sligo appeared from next door and took over. "You haven't had too much experience of this kind of thing, have you," he said with a chuckle. It was true, Bythell had no experience at all of dry-stone-walling, but he had borrowed a book from the library and he was looking forward to finding out if he could do it. That incident set the pattern. When Sligo saw how incompetent Bythell was, he never let him alone. Whenever Bythell appeared in his back yard with a two-by-four and a hammer Sligo was over the fence in a moment, ready to straighten him out.

Sligo's protection and advice spread from house repairs into every corner of Bythell's life. Bythell had no garage, so Sligo cleaned out the rubbish in his own two-car garage and told Bythell to park there in future. He visited the St. Lawrence Market and brought back food on Bythell's behalf, specials he knew Bythell should have at those prices. When there was a sale of wine at the liquor store he bought extra for Bythell, and Bythell ground his teeth and thanked him. Sligo tasted the soup on Bythell's stove and added salt, talked man-to-man with Bythell's children, rearranged the logs by Bythell's fire and dispensed advice like a relative by marriage.

The quality of Sligo's advice and help was as mixed as the next man's. He was far from infallible, but he rarely admitted doubt in the first place or error when something went wrong, finding, when pressed, some fault in the way Bythell had executed the advice. When some question or problem cropped up concerning an area outside his experience he would (or so it seemed to Bythell) bluff and fake an answer, or claim to know the expert in the field whom he would consult next day. Perhaps the worst of it was that Bythell's wife would often forget how much he resented Sligo. When Bythell had a problem, as often as not she would say, "Why don't you ask Sligo? He might know."

And Bythell knew that Sligo lied to preserve his role. For example he told Bythell how much he paid to get his house painted, a real bargain, but the painter, whom Bythell hired also, told him the true figure was twice as much, and when Bythell faced Sligo with this in front of their wives, Sligo said that the painter had exaggerated so that he could overcharge Bythell. Bythell looked hard at Sligo's wife during this exchange, but she didn't blink an eyelash, so she was in on it, too. There were lots of other things like this, but Bythell could not remember them all.

It was no comfort to Bythell that his own wife reported back to him that Sligo thought Bythell was a dear, sweet guy, all the more so for being so unworldly. Bythell was a civil servant and Sligo was a jobber of some kind; he lived in the real world, as he told Bythell, unlike Bythell who never had to worry about his cash-flow.

Bythell was aware, mainly from concerned remarks of his wife, that he was taking Sligo too much to heart and he took the chance to talk about Sligo to a psychological counsellor. The counsellor listened until it was nearly time for their appointment to end, then said. "You have a poor opinion of yourself, Mr Bythell. It shows up in every area. Your friend knows this—sub-consciously, of course—and he sees your uncertainty and translates it into a call for help. He wants to look after you."

"But what about when he's wrong and lies about it?" Bythell cried.

"Are you sure he's wrong? If so, perhaps he has his own needs. You never tell people who depend on you that you are fallible. That would seem to be letting them down."

"So what do I do? Avoid him?"

"I don't think so. That would be a defeat. Besides I take it the initiative in this relationship comes from him?"

"Entirely."

"Obviously he loves you. He must be made to respect you as well as love you."

"How? How do I do that?"

"Perhaps by finding some area where *you* are the mentor, the elder, so to speak. And insisting firmly on your role." The counsellor gave a little peek at the clock on the wall.

"I've found a dozen: gardening, fly-fishing, good hotels in Paris—you name it, I've taught *him*."

"And what happens?"

"A month or a year later, he explains them back to me. He never gives me credit for having told him about them in the first place."

Now the counsellor openly consulted his watch. "Mr. Bythell, I have to speak bluntly," he said. "You sound what we would call paranoid."

"I know that for Christ's sake. That's why I'm talking to you."

"Well, we've got you to recognise your problem, at least. Let's have another go at it next week."

But Bythell never went back. He continued to suffer and dream of an absolute facer that Sligo would not be able to dodge.

When the opportunity finally came, Bythell did not recognise it at first. At the time he was considering simply finding an excuse to pick a quarrel with Sligo (after twenty years!) so that he could cut him off, even though that would be an acknowledged defeat. But when he tried, the result was only a wretched evening and a mystified wife who wondered what had got into him and made immediate arrangements to get together with the Sligos again (with apologies) to get their relationship back on its old footing. Then one evening Bythell went into a fit of rage on a matter as small as whether one should lock one's doors.

Like most people, Bythell kept his house locked when he was out of it and had even installed a small alarm system to warn the neighbours if anybody broke in. Sligo never locked his house up, or his car, never had, never would. "If they are going to break in," he said, "They come ready. Then not only do they steal your goods, but they break your door down with it. Same with a car. Any good car-thief can open a car easy as pie, but if you leave everything unlocked, he might think you are coming back right away."

"How about amateurs?" Bythell asked, getting sucked in again, but not wanting to be proved wrong in such an obvious case.

"Amateurs won't touch an unlocked house, either," Sligo said, authoritatively. "If you lock it, they just use axes instead of a crow-bar. As for cars, amateurs only steal cars with the keys in. They just take them for joy-riding. You always get it back."

Bythell knew this was wrong, and he began to reply, but Sligo had already gone on to something else. "What's the humidity in here," he was saying when Bythell had got his thoughts together. "You need a gauge. I'll bring over our old one."

Shortly after that Bythell was robbed. The thieves cut the power supply to bypass the alarm, got the door open with a bit of plastic which they left behind, took his television set, his camera and his trombone, and, finding the spare car-keys on a hook in the kitchen, drove off in his Rabbit. They were never caught. When Bythell saw the mess the thieves had made he felt as if he had been personally violated.

"See," Sligo said.

Bythell saw all right and began to plan. Sligo was going to have to be robbed, and in such a way that there could be no doubt that the failure to lock his doors was crucial. Bythell set aside, for the moment, the question of whether the robbery would be a joke, to make a point, or whether the robbery would be real. Either way the heist would have to be fairly big and take place in daytime, committed by thieves who evidently acted in the knowledge that they would be able to enter and leave in a natural way. Bythell day-dreamed for a month before the perfect idea fell into his lap. A colleague of his came to the office one morning with the news that his neighbour had been robbed the day before. Thieves using a regular furniture truck had backed up to the man's front door and simply removed the contents of the house in about three hours. No one had questioned them, and when the police went around banging on doors, none of the neighbours could remember what the men looked like—"Kind of guys who move furniture," one neighbour said—or what the name of the company was, or even the colour of the truck.

Now Bythell just had to wait for the next occasion when Sligo was away with his wife, for Sligo left his house unlocked when he went on holiday, too. In the meantime he had to find a furniture removal truck and four thieves. (He had decided on a real robbery, because he realised that if he made the thing the basis of a practical joke, he would not be making his point since Sligo could afterwards claim that just because Bythell was able to move in and out of his house in no way invalidated his position. The point was that an outsider would not know it was unlocked.)

The first problem was to get in touch with some thieves. He had heard the phrase "consorting with known criminals" as something thieves on probation must not do and he reasoned that there must be places where criminals consort, pubs, probably, that they favoured, where they planned the next job. Bythell's scheme to find out about these haunts was to ask for an interview with the public relations department of the police. The inspector was polite, but wary. "A writer, eh, Mr. Bissell," he said. "Not one of those exposé type guys, eh?"

Bythell assured him that the hero of his novel would be a clever policeman, and the inspector listened to his problem. Where did thieves gather in Toronto? He called a sergeant in. "Mr Bissell here is looking for local colour," he explained. "He wants to know where our clients hang out when they are not working. Are there any particular pubs, like?"

The sergeant considered. "Not that I know of, Mr. Bissell," he said. "We wouldn't allow it. If you find any, let us know, would you?"

The inspector smiled and showed Bythell the door.

Next Bythell asked a number of taxi-drivers to take him to the sleaziest pubs they knew of, where he spent several evenings drinking beer and watching nude ladies jousting in imaginary combat. Nowhere did he find what he was seeking. He considered spending a night in the Don jail. Surely there he would find what he wanted? But the only offence he could think of that would get him a night in jail but not the possibility of three months was a refusal to pay parking tickets, and that would probably take a year or more to bring to a climax.

Ruminating on the difficulty of getting into bad company, he was presented one day with an alternative solution. There was a knock on his door and a smiling young man introduced himself as a surveyor commissioned to mark out the property next door for his neighbour who was selling his house. It would be necessary, the youth said, to enter Bythell's garden, and he was introducing himself so that Bythell wouldn't get alarmed and call the police.

Bythell took the surveyor's card and went out to the street and examined the man's car, which had no identifying sign except a CJRT sticker in the window. Bythell switched his plan.

He designed a card, "Royce Dunlop—Surveyor," ordered a hundred from a cheap printer, threw away ninety-eight and put the remaining two in his wallet. The rest of the plan required the absence of Sligo.

In the three months that Bythell waited for Sligo to go on holiday, the two couples dined together twice and each time afterwards Bythell's wife commented on how well the evening had gone. Sligo chose the restaurant the first time, and the food was horrible. The second time Bythell chose, consulting widely beforehand, even to knowing the name of the restaurant's house wine, and they had a splendid meal, and he never felt a thing when Sligo explained why. "This is a Florentine restaurant," Sligo said. "Much better than Milanese."

Then Sligo announced they were going to Bermuda for a week, and Bythell made his move. He chose the Wednesday to avoid any garbage collections on Sligo's street, wanting to eliminate even that much extra activity that might bring the neighbours to their doors. Early in the morning he drove out to a car rental agency on Eglinton West and picked up the station wagon he had ordered the night before, using his own name. It was the one risk he could not avoid, for he was unable, short of stealing someone's wallet, to think of a way of getting a false driver's license.

He parked outside Sligo's house at ten o'clock, tucked one of his cards under the windscreen wiper and walked boldly up to the door. Sligo's front door was at the side of the house, obscured from the street, and there was little chance that Bythell would be seen as he opened the door and stepped inside, the first absolutely criminal offence. So far so good. Sweating slightly, he sat down in the kitchen and took off his coat, leaving his gloves on, and ran over his mental list: an antique coffee-pot, a Kreighoff painting, some silver tableware, and a gold watch on Sligo's desk. On reflection he decided against the painting, and prepared to assemble the loot. As soon as it was piled on the kitchen table he was done for if anyone should walk in. Bythell walked the house like an insomniac, peering out of all the windows at the quiet street, leaping up in the air when the phone rang, then, finally, in a single sweep, he locked the front door, collected the goods together, and looked around for something to carry them in. Here his nerve cracked. A knock at the door had him lying on the floor, then, as he heard the departing footsteps, peeking through the front window to see the meter-reader from Consumers' Gas leave and move to the next house. He was incapable, he knew now, of walking to the car with a bag full of silver, and he tried to tell himself that perhaps he had gone far enough to make his point. The place had clearly been robbed, and the thief disturbed before he could get away with the loot. Wasn't that enough? But Bythell didn't trust Sligo; he might say nothing, lie silently, and then Bythell would have wasted his time. The solution when it came to him was simple, and nearly risk-free. It took him fifteen minutes to set up, and when he was finished he unlocked the front door, drove back to the agency, and returned home in his own car.

His wife said, "Where were you? I phoned the office and they said you'd phoned in sick."

Bythell chuckled. "Caught me, did you. Dear? I spent the day in the arms of my mistress."

"No, where *were* you?"

"I took the day off," Bythell said. "I was driving to work and I said to myself, 'I need a mental health day,' so I kept on driving and took the ferry over to the Island."

"That's not like you," she said. "Male menopause?"

"Could be," he said. "You'd better keep your eye on me."

When Sligo came back he had a tale to tell and he came over to Bythell's house on the first evening to tell it. "They emptied out all the drawers, the closets, all over the floor," he said. "They got Doris's silver, the coffee-pot, and my gold watch. Everything worth taking except the Kreighoff. They probably thought that was cut out from a magazine."

"That's terrible," Bythell's wife said. "Losing all that."

"No sweat," Sligo said. "It's all insured. I'll probably make money on it."

"But if the insurance company knows the house wasn't locked, surely they won't pay up?" Bythell said. It was an integral part of his new plan. He intended to let Sligo suffer for a few weeks and then arrange for the loot to reappear.

"I'm not that dumb," Sligo laughed. "Before I called the cops I locked the whole house up and kicked in the back door."

"I see," Bythell said, the room dancing in front of his eyes.

"Oh, sure." Sligo said. "I wasn't born yesterday."

Bythell raged silently. Then a lovely thought occurred to him, the realisation that Sligo had delivered himself into his hands. For now, whenever he chose, he could pick up the phone and, anonymously, of course, tell the police and the insurance company that they had been defrauded, that in the basement of Sligo's house they would find a wood-box, and under the layer of scrap wood left over from Sligo's last remodelling, they would find some silver, a coffee-pot, and a gold watch. There was no rush. It was only June, and Sligo was unlikely to need firewood before October. At some point during the summer Sligo would become intolerable, and then Bythell would phone.

It was a glorious summer. Bythell's wife remarked on how much more relaxed the two men were with each other. No longer did Bythell grind his teeth at Sligo's patronage—he seemed not to notice it. Often, when Sligo started to give Bythell advice, Bythell just laughed and told Sligo he was full of it. Sometimes he cut through Sligo's monologues, changing the subject as more important or more interesting subjects occurred to him.

As the summer wore on, Bythell realised that calling the insurance company would accomplish him nothing. They *might* assume that Sligo had defrauded them and Sligo might go to prison, which, now that Bythell's sharp need for revenge had faded, was more than he wanted. And, too, they might believe in Sligo's innocence and search for an insider who knew Sligo's domestic habits and where he kept his wood. Bythell knew that even if Sligo or the police failed to guess the culprit, his own wife would.

But if he did *not* phone what would happen? Sligo would find the loot, with two possible results. He might keep his mouth shut and try to sell it later, but the coffee-pot and the silver were listed with the Fraud Squad, so it would be very risky. He was more likely to announce the find, which would bring the police in asking the same questions and pointing the same finger at him as if Bythell had made his anonymous call. And Bythell had heard that the forensic laboratory could identify him from a single speck of dandruff, never mind fingerprints.

Now, as October approached with a rush, Bythell grew more and more frightened. In the end he was obliged to improvise, and one dark and rainy night, when his wife was at a movie and he knew that the Sligos were out, he drove over to their house. He tried the door and found it locked, but he had no time to savour his little triumph. He moved round to the back of the house and waited for the noise of a passing car, then kicked the door in. Down in the basement he packed the stuff into green garbage bags and made a run for it, looking like a cartoon burglar making off with the swag. He drove down to Harbourfront (it was still pouring rain), parked by the yacht basin, dropped the stuff into the harbour, and drove home, beside himself with fear.

When Sligo came home that night, he phoned Bythell after he had finished with the police. "They didn't take anything," he said, "But the police think those guys have got me staked out. Now I'll really have to lock up tight. I was wondering if I could come by tomorrow night and find out about locks and alarms and stuff. You know all about that, don't you?"

"Sure," Bythell said comfortingly. "Sure. I've got information, bro- chures, on all that kind of thing. Come round and we'll go over what you need."

"Who was that?" Bythell's wife asked as he crept into bed.

"Sligo," Bythell said. "He wants some advice." He kissed his wife and arranged himself for sleep. "I think I can help him," he said.

The Lady From Prague

I saw her almost as soon as she spotted me, though she may have been watching me through the glass. She came hurrying through the big double doors, apparently on her way to the lobby, but half a dozen times in her progress she glanced slightly sideways to where I was sitting in the corner by the tiny bar.

It was a big room, created out of some left-over space when the building was converted into a tourist hotel, and the natural route from door to door was down the centre, but there was a kind of runway round the perimeter, one step up from the main area and separated from it by a low rail. When the lounge was full, it made for an easier throughway from door to door, but in the present deserted state of the room it was an unnatural path to take.

She circled the room rapidly, stopping before the exit door, then she turned and stepped down to pause in front of my chair. My antennae were quivering long before she spoke.

There were only two other people in the lounge, a middle-aged, cautious-looking couple drinking coffee on the far side of the room. I had noticed them by the desk when I collected my key and summed them up as a couple taking a cheap three-day break, probably from up north, Leeds, perhaps. The hotel was about half full of people like them; the other half were mainly European tourists. There are many such hotels in the Bayswater area, cheap tourist accommodation, cheaper still if you buy a package from an airline. This one had been converted from a former residence for single middle-class business ladies, and the lounge must have been where they held the weekly dances. I found it a pleasant place to read a paper or to have a snack before bedtime, because it was nearly always empty. The bar was no more than a cupboard tended by an East Indian lady who served coffee and pastries from her own stock, but she would bring you anything from the restaurant if you asked her.

The woman was about forty, I guessed, dark, attractive, slightly dishevelled as if she had just run for a bus. She was carrying a small, new-looking attache case which she put down on the floor beside the armchair facing mine, well inside my "space" when there were thirty other chairs to choose from. "Can I please?" she asked in a very thick accent, pointing to the case. Then she started towards the door, fumbling in her pockets, pantomiming someone preparing to make a phone call.

Now I had to make my first decision, rather sooner than I had expected. I should say now that I write detective stories, and I am always on the lookout for incidents I can turn into plots. When you travel alone things happen to you, and I have had my share of entanglements in other people's lives. I welcome them, always ready, of course, to disentangle myself from the maniacs or the plain boring.

There was the woman on the ferry crossing over to Calais twenty years ago, for instance. I had chatted to her enough on the crossing to find out she was making her first excursion to Paris for which she had saved for a year, so that when she twisted her ankle badly as she was going ashore, I ended up spending two very pleasant days with her in a Calais hotel room while she recovered, even borrowing a wheelchair from the hotel to take her for walks about the town. We talked steadily and freely in the way one does on board ship, not expecting ever to see each other again, and on the evening of the second day she told me a story of her discovery that her father was illegitimate and that her real grandfather was a Norwegian ship's captain whom she intended to track down one day, a story that I used almost intact twenty years later.

Then there was the girl on the railway platform in Copenhagen whom I watched from the train taking passionate and grief-laden leave of her man, and then saw, a few hours later, obviously deeply in love with another man in the dining car. The only way I have been able to make sense of that is by assuming the existence of twins, and the world doesn't need another "twins" story. But I'll find a way to use it some day.

And just to round off these examples let me cite the case of the middle-aged lady with the row of flat curls on her forehead and the spectacularly bad teeth whose opening remark to me in the ship's bar on our first night out was, "My husband and I live like brother and sister." I never followed it up, but it made a good opening to a story in which a character does follow it up and finds that the remark is much more complicated than he thinks.

All these incidents and many more have provided the fuel that stokes my word processor. My point is that it is important not to be careful, or nothing happens. You can always disentangle yourself when it becomes clear that the encounter is getting sticky in one form or another. In London one must be wary of unattended baggage.

As she circled the room, and until she put her case down, I was already slotting her into a Hitchcock-like encounter, but the attache case changed things. I had a second to decide (she had already turned away), but a great deal can be thought, if not actually framed in sentences, in a second. The first possibility was that in a very short time, unless I moved quickly, I would be found littered around the room in unidentifiable fragments. But the room was empty apart from the couple from Leeds and surely neither the room nor I was significant enough of itself to make a worthwhile terrorist target. That decision made, I moved on to the next. Now the emptiness of the room and the circularity of her progress towards me lent some weight to the possibility that the attractive, dishevelled lady in the green leather suit and silk blouse with two buttons undone was on a different mission entirely, one I thought I could handle. It occurred to me that there was another dimension to her behavior with the attache case, that she must know the effect on a stranger in a London hotel of asking him to guard a case, and that she was testing me.

I nodded and stayed where I was.

She returned too quickly for someone who had had to use a pay phone in a London hotel lobby, and threw herself into the armchair, giving me a harrassed smile. Then she jumped up and fumbled some more for change, eventually putting together enough coins to buy herself a small bottle of mineral water from the lady at the bar. She sat down, poured herself a glass, sipped, pushed back her hair, jerked her open blouse this way and that across her breasts, moved her case closer to her feet, smiled at me, sipped again, all the time watching me with her sideways air. Then she said in her thick accent, "You are English?"

"No," I said. "I am Canadian."

"I hate the English."

Once more my brain was in motion. If I had replied 'yes', what would she have done? But some instinct on her part, prompted perhaps by my button-down collar, still not common in England, had made her guess accurately.

She nodded four or five times. "I hate the English," she said, as if to make sure I had heard.

It was a demand for me to enquire why, but I resisted it. The first thing I wanted to confirm was that she would not be put off by politeness or indifference. If she pursued the subject then I could be pretty sure it was me who she was interested in, not the English. The most likely possibility at this stage was that she was about to pick me up. I was wary, of course, but once I had gathered my wits I could find little risk in seeing how she went about it. There was a slight chance that she was mad, that she would suddenly leap up and scream that I had attacked her; she looked distraught, but, I judged, not out of control.

There was a limit to how far I would let her go, not out of any fear for myself, but out of consideration for her. I have been in the situation before of having an attractive woman in a strange place come on to me—who hasn't, and why does it never happen in Toronto?—and if you are at a resort hotel or on a cruise ship, sheer decency requires that you let her know quickly if she is wasting her time, that your wife is standing behind her. You can enjoy the opening encounter, but there is a point at which her investment in you will become an embarrassment when she finds out she has been wasting her time, an embarrassment that could turn to anger. On a cruise ship she might retaliate by telling the other passengers that you … well, whatever.

If she is a professional, then it is that much more important, for her sake, to break off quickly so that she can scout a more likely prospect and not lose too much work time.

We hadn't reached that point yet. For the few minutes that she had been there, and for a few more yet, I had a right to appear puzzled. I had listened politely but given her no encouragement. And she was attractive. I wondered how much she charged, if that was the case. She had certainly worked out an original technique. I kept in mind that she might yet be a lady in distress.

I glanced across the room as she rooted in her bag, conscious that the middle-aged couple from Leeds were watching, and I smiled slightly at them, sort of indicating that what they were thinking was probably true, but I was in control of the situation. They looked away immediately. I could almost see the woman's lips move. ("Don't get involved, Henry.")

"He invite me here," the dishevelled lady said. "Invite me. Here. I pay for hotel, everything, he say. I pay all money." She lit a cigarette and put it out immediately. If this was an act, she was performing brilliantly. Perhaps it was true.

"Then he say, is cancelled," she continued. "But I have no money! No matter. Is cancelled."

"Who," I asked, "is he?"

"Big man with factory. He come to Prague, tell me, come to London. I give you job. Then he cancel."

"It happens," I said.

But she was not interested in conversation. "Filthy English." She added a few words in her own language. "I have no money. Nothing."

"Back to Prague?" I asked.

She leaned forward and put her hand on my knee. "You English?" she asked again, and squeezed hard as if searching for the answer there. She shook her head in answer to her own question. "You stay here?" she asked.

Here it comes, I thought. I said I did.

"You have room by yourself?" She leaned forward and I got a whiff of perfume, dark and heavy.

"Yes I have my own room."

Suddenly she burrowed in her purse again and brought out a wallet. "Look," she said. "Filthy English. All my money. Gone. I have nothing to eat today. Yesterday, one omelette. One. That is all."

I judged she was leaving her options open. She was a professional, pretending to be an amateur who was obliged through circumstances to offer herself for the price of a bed, in which case she would be asking for money in the morning. Or she really was a lady in distress. Then why didn't she go to the embassy, or to the police? No, getting into my room was just step one. I had no intention of leaving the lounge with her, of course, but it was too soon yet to say so. As far as possible, I wanted to get the whole of her plan.

"Can I buy you a meal?" I asked, pretending that her last remark was the whole point of the encounter. It seemed a fair price to pay for the story I would get out of it.

She went into a flurry of shrugs and nods to convey that she was embarrassed, but she was also hungry. "I will have omelette," she said. "All the other food here is … dirt, English."

I walked over to the bar and gave the woman the order, adding two cups of coffee. I looked over to tip the wink to the couple from up north to let them know I wasn't being suckered, but they had gone.

While we waited for the omelette and I waited for her next move, she gave me an expanded but even more garbled version of her predicament. All I could get out of it was that a glass manufacturer on a visit to Prague had employed her as an interpreter, and subsequently asked her to come to England and work for him as a translator. She had paid her own fare from Prague, and he had assured her she would be taken care of when she arrived. But when she got to London there was no one to meet her, no message, and her calls to the factory in Birmingham had gone unanswered.

It was a good story, even possible, but I didn't believe a word of it, mainly because I had been to Prague when it was under the old regime, and the interpreters for our party were all excellent linguists. This lady could barely make herself understood. She was now overplaying her part ludicrously.

"What are you going to do tonight?" I asked, as if I hadn't heard her question about my room. According to my rules, I should not have asked her this. It was time to leave, while I could still pretend ignorance of her real purpose, and she could look for someone else. But I wanted to let her know that in enquiring about my room, at least, she was wasting her time.

I could not penetrate the look she gave me, but I guessed that she was calculating the lack of progress that my question implied. Then she smiled. She kicked off her shoes, curled her feet under her and smiled with an unmistakable openness. "I make you afraid," she said.

This was irritating. "Of what?"

"Perhaps you don't like me. Perhaps some English woman has cheated you. You have no money?"

So there it was. I was still holding open the possibility of a Czech lady in distress, but now she brought all the sexual hints together in her smile.

It was time for me to go to the lavatory and not return, a slightly mean trick but I should not have let things get this far. And then she said, "You think I am prostitute? I am not prostitute. I have no money." She began to cry quietly. "I did not ask to sleep with you. Oh, God, no."

"Then what did you mean?" I asked.

"I thought, you have a room with two beds, I could have the other one, just for tonight."

"How do you know what kind of room I have?"

"This is tourist hotel. All rooms have two beds. Sleep with you! Oh, God, what is happening to me?" She pulled herself together and stood up. "Now I go." She stood up and looked bleakly around the room.

"Where to?" I asked.

"Somewhere. It is not cold." She looked at her watch. "If I have money, I could get single room, like you. I don't want your bed, Englishman. Keep your bed."

She almost had me, but a sudden sideways shift of her eyes, the same gesture she had used when she circled the room, held me back. I had just been about to give her the fifty pounds she needed for a room but that little gesture made me see it all. She was not a tart, of course. This was the end of the con. This was exactly the feeling in me she had been working towards, and I felt so cheered by seeing through it that I wanted the encounter to end on a slightly better note for her than it was doing. I thought of a gesture which would allow her to leave with the impression that I had not had the faintest idea what she was up to, that she had been defeated by my stupidity. I dug for my wallet. "Here," I said. I offered her ten pounds. "For breakfast."

She looked hard at me, perhaps considering a gesture of her own. But ten pounds is ten pounds. "I have to take it," she said almost to herself. "I have no money. Goodbye, Englishman."

It had taken her an hour, and she had earned ten pounds. Worth it to me, but hardly to her, I thought.

The lobby was empty as I walked through to get the elevator, and so, too, was my room when I got to it, stripped bare—my clothes, the travellers cheques from under my mattress, even my alarm clock.

The police, when I began to tell them where I had been while my room was robbed, were very interested in the Czech lady, even supplying me with details about her appearance that I hadn't noticed. "But she was with me the whole time," I protested. "She had no time to come up here. She had nothing to do with it."

"Coincidence?" the sergeant asked. "Did you see anyone else about in the lounge or in the lobby, sir? A couple maybe, middle-aged, re-spectable-looking?"

"They left about an hour before I did."

"Plenty of time," he said. "Half an hour would be enough. They're very good, those two. Those three, I should say. Don't forget to get a refund on your travellers cheques. If you call in at the station, we'll give you a document to get you home. If you don't mind my saying so, sir, it's as well to be careful when you're travelling alone. We do our best but we can't protect all you Americans from … adventuresses." He smiled. "There's too many of you and not enough of us. And she's not always Czech. Sometimes she's French. Once she was a Russian. Goodnight, then, sir."

An Irish Jig

It had been raining on and off all day, but this was Ireland and they were prepared for it. They had no intention of letting a bit of Irish mist interfere with their holiday.

They arrived at the hotel in plenty of time to take the small nap their age required, and to make plans for the evening. "There's a place called Bewley's which advertises light suppers," Mrs. Grantham said. "It's on our way. If the rain's stopped we could walk there and be at the theater in plenty of time." They had been lucky enough to get tickets for a new play by Brian Friel at the Abbey Theatre. They had seen two of his earlier plays and enjoyed them very much.

When they were rested, the sky was clear and they had a lovely walk to Bewley's, across the green, past the Shelbourne Hotel, which they promised themselves to stay in one day.

"This what you'd hoped?" Mr. Grantham, asked.

"It's nice, but it isn't an Irish experience, is it?"

He didn't have to ask her what she meant. What she was seeking was the moment that couldn't happen anywhere else, the defining moment that, recalled later at home, would bring back with it the whole holiday. In Corsica it had been the discovery of ratafia, a wine she had thought belonged to the eighteenth century. In Italy the experience had been sharing a table at dinner in their hotel by Lake Como with an elderly Englishman on a pilgrimage, revisiting the Italian farm family who had hidden him in 1944 from the retreating Germans. "Pure Eric Newby," Mrs. Grantham had said. In France, when they crossed from Italy, it had been the discovery of how easy it was suddenly to speak and understand the language after two weeks of pointing and grinning in Tuscany, although their French had never got them far before. In England they experienced the pleasure of overhearing a farm worker in a pub speaking an unintelligible Gloucestershire dialect (he pronounced Ebrington as 'Yubberton') when they had thought that the B.B.C. had long ago homogenized the country's speech.

But nothing Irish had happened yet, nothing which she could coat in amber to show back home as a parable of their Irish experience. So far, Ireland seemed a slightly wetter version of England: at its worst the food was only slightly worse than the food in Scotland, and the best food—the chowder for example that they had been served in Donegal, and the Irish stew they had eaten in Galway, was better than the bourguignonne they had eaten in any of the places recommended by the Good Food Guide in England. A laborer walking along a country road raised his cap to them as they sat on a wall, eating apples, which was a nice anachronism but not enough to stand for the whole Irish experience. "Maybe Brian Friel will do it," Mr. Grantham said.

The light supper was excellent: fish cakes followed by an apple tart. The play, though, was not the holiday entertainment they had hoped for but a dramatization of an incident in the ongoing civil struggles. They left at the first intermission.

"Grim," Mr. Grantham said. "Still we've seen the Abbey Theatre."

Although the streets were wet, the rain had stopped, and they decided to walk back to the hotel to see what Irish television had to offer. The sky stayed clear and starry until they reached their hotel.

The hotel consisted of two large houses, back to back on parallel streets, joined by an inner courtyard fashioned out of the two gardens. The path across the courtyard was covered with a corrugated plastic roof but not enclosed, and the yard was bricked in by walls six feet high. At night, they had been told, only the front door was open, and so they had to walk round to the next street, through the other house, across the courtyard and along the corridor to get to their room.

Mr. Grantham fiddled with the lock for a long time until his wife took the key from him and jiggled it herself before giving up. "You'll have to go back to the desk and tell them to come and unstick this lock," she said. "Don't hang about. I'll wait here."

When Mr. Grantham returned, he was accompanied by the night manager, a youth still in his teens, who took his turn at jiggling the key. "It's not responding," he said, looking at them for help.

"Call the landlord," Mrs. Grantham said.

"He's in Sligo at his holiday cottage. I'll get my arse in a sling if I phone him there."

"Then call a locksmith."

"This time of night! He'll want fifty pounds!"

"At least. So you'd better call Sligo and get the okay."

"Sure I had. There's nothing else for it, is there? Would you wait in the lounge while I call, then?"

"We'll stay here," Mr. Grantham said.

Half an hour later the locksmith let them in the room. "The inside bolt was on," the locksmith said as he withdrew his probe. "The one that's supposed to keep out burglars."

The four of them stood by the door, looking around. Mrs. Grantham said, "I didn't close the curtains like that." She crossed the room and took her suitcase from the closet and opened it. "I've been robbed," she said. She peered into a wallet that she had stored in the case. "All my English money has gone, and the Canadian, too."

"Ah, no," the manager said. "You've mislaid it, surely."

Mr. Grantham opened his own case. "Mine's gone, too. Just the money. They've left the traveler's cheques and the passports. You'd better call the police."

When the garda arrived, he noted everything down, saying about the failure to take the passports, "It'll be just kids, then." He walked to the window and looked out. "They came over the wall, on to the covering over the walkway, up the drainpipe and in. Easy. I could have done it meself, once." He patted his stomach and looked up at the closed window. "Did you leave that unlocked, sir?"

Mrs. Grantham said, "I left it open a bit because it was so warm."

"So he came through the window, closed it after him, then left through the door. Right?"

Mrs. Grantham said, "I only left it open about six inches."

"Be a little fella, then."

The locksmith said, "How did he lock the door after him as well as close the window?"

"That we have to sort out," the garda said. "What we have here is a real Locked Room Mystery. I know all about them."

Mrs. Grantham crossed the room and sat on the window seat. "Perhaps if he closed the window first, then shut the door hard behind him, the bolt would have sort of slid across. What do you think, Constable?" She looked at her husband. "I'm enjoying this." She took a peppermint from her purse and sucked on it while the garda thought.

"I think I've got it," he said. "I saw it done in Toronto when I was visiting the brother. By a book writer. A demonstration. What he did was tie a piece of thread round the knob of the bolt, and pass the thread through the keyhole. Then he closed the door—it was very loose, like this one—and pulled on the thread to jerk the bolt along. He didn't tie the thread, d'ye see, just wrapped it around the stem of the knob three or four times, enough to take the strain. Then, when he'd slid the bolt across, he could yank it a little bit harder and so undo the thread. Yes, that's the way of it. Perfect."

"And unbelievable," Mr. Grantham said. "You saw the locksmith free up the bolt. There was so much old paint on that bolt, you'd need a hammer to move it."

"Oh, now, George, it's a lovely solution. Don't spoil it. Now, officer, we'll have to make a claim for our money from the insurance company. We'll need your corroboration."

"I'll send you a copy of my report, missus. Might take me a month or so. We're very busy with all the holiday traffic."

"Where do we start?"

"You'll need to make a statement down at the station in the morning. It's too late now."

"We're leaving on the eight o'clock ferry from Dun Laughaire," she said.

"You could write when you get back to Canada. My sergeant would take it up eventually."

"What are the odds, do you think, of our seeing our money again?" Mr. Grantham asked.

"Well it's not a lot you've lost, is it, sir? It won't interfere with your holiday, I shouldn't think." He smiled. "And it'll make a good tale when you get back, surely." He put away his notebook. "I'll say goodnight, then. There's a man on our night shift fancies himself as a bit of a book writer, though I don't know that he's ever been encouraged. He might be interested in this."

The night manager waited for the door to close. "The owner told me there'll be no charge for the room," he said. "He's very upset it should happen to a guest of ours."

They reassured him they were not distraught, shaking his hand as he backed out the door.

Mr. Grantham said, "With a hundred off for the room I think we should write off the rest to experience."

"No need for that. Bolt that door, and grab that poker." She pointed to the set of fire irons in the hearth. Then she slipped off the window seat and opened the lid. "Out you come," she said.

A scruffy underfed boy, perhaps twelve years old, poked his head above the edge of the box, looked warily at Mr. Grantham's poker, uncoiled himself and slid out on to the floor, where he stayed crouched.

"Don't think of running," Mr. Grantham said, waving the poker. "You have me and two sets of locks and bolts to get through. You'd never make it."

"How did ye know I was in there, missus?" The boy straightened himself up.

"It was the only answer. I eliminated the Impossible, including the garda's silly idea about the bolt, and I was left with the Improbable: that you were still here. Besides, I saw you lift the lid a bit when we first came in. Now, 400 pounds, please."

The boy reached into his sock and pulled out a flat wad of banknotes. He tried for a smile. "You'll be making a profit now, will ye not? With the free room, and the claim you can make to the insurance?"

"It's everybody's lucky night," she said. "Including yours. In a minute we will turn our backs and you will make a run for it, through the back door."

"Yous're nivver goin' to let us go!"

"Yes. Before you go, though, I want to know why you closed the window again. If you'd left it open you might have got away while we were trying the door."

"It jammed. After I got in it started to rain, d'ye see, and the curtain was blowin' in so, and someone from outside could see in. I had to have a light on. So I closed the window and drew the curtains, and then I couldn't lift the bloody thing up when I heard you at the door."

"Why did you bolt the door?"

"In case. I didn't expect you for another hour; that'd be normal for gents on holiday, wouldn't it? But I didn't want to be disturbed by the maid or whatever, so I slotted the bolt, just in case."

"All right, then. Off you go."

The boy wiped his nose with the back of his hand and pointed to the money in her hand. "Could you spare me a little something to be going on with? I haven't got a copper. I'll nivver say a word."

She laughed and gave him a twenty pound note.

"You're a dascent skin, missus, so you are."

When the boy had gone, Mr. Grantham asked, "Why?"

"Do you want to spend tomorrow morning filling in forms in a police station? Miss our ferry? Wait heaven knows how long for the next ferry? Arrive late and pick our way across Wales in the dark? Anyway we're quids in, as the English say."

"But you didn't have to tip the little bastard."

"I didn't have to, no. I just thought he'd earned it."

It took Mr. Grantham a few seconds, but then he got it. "Ah, right," he said. "That's Ireland taken care of. Right?"

The Lady of Shalott

(For Gilly Emery)

"Now what?" Annie Salter asked. By pressing the side of her face hard against the bedroom window she could squint down the street to the front yard of the house where a sign had appeared while they were asleep. "Joe Wallace's house is up for sale. You spoken to him lately? Where's he going?"

"I've talked to him twice this year so far," Staff Superintendent Charlie Salter of the Metropolitan Toronto Police, still in bed, replied. "What is it now, October? The last time I spoke to him was in August. I think. Maybe July. No, August. Yes, August. He called to me from across the street, I remember. Hullo, Charlie, he called. What's up? Nothing much, I called back. What's up with you, Joe? Same old stuff, he said. I would have responded to this but by now I was past his house and I would have had to shout, so I just waved and walked on."

"What are you talking about?"

"I just want to give you an exact, word by word account of what has lately passed between me and Joe so you won't keep asking me if I'm sure he didn't mention moving. He didn't, I'm sure. What I have just reported is exactly what he said." Salter, waking earlier and earlier as he moved into oldish age, was pleased this morning to find himself still in bed at seven, still with some sleep left in him, perhaps. It felt luxurious. "Come back to bed," he said.

This wasn't a serious invitation, just a shorthand way of saying he had slept well enough to feel younger by several years than he usually did, and the sunlight was making Annie's nightgown diaphanous.

"I wonder where he's going." Annie crammed her cheekbone harder against the glass to try to see a bit more of Wallace's yard. "He's not much older than you."

"He's significantly older than me, by at least four years, and looks it, too, so where he's going doesn't signify a trend that includes me. The Preakness maybe." The Preakness was a retirement home where the elders of Toronto's Anglo tribe went to die, playing bridge while they waited.

"He still plays tennis. Mary Tomalkin says he spends a lot of his time at that club on Price Street."

"Where else does he put in his days?"

"Mary says he's been in semi-retirement for about seven years. He belongs to a fishing club up near Huntsville, spends the winters in Bonita Springs in Florida, and most of the rest of the time he plays tennis."

"He's got that cottage in England, too, in Gloucestershire, where he spends a couple of months a year, remember. He told *me* that."

"So where's he going now?"

"I doubt if he's going out of town. Probably to a condo. Probably he's just tired of people looking at him from behind their curtains."

"What about his friend?"

"Which friend would that be? He must have more than one."

"His *friend*."

"Oh, *that* one. Have you seen her lately?"

"Not for a couple of months, at least."

"Maybe that's why he's selling up. Maybe she's tired of the surveillance, too."

"The what."

"The neighbours, logging every movement."

"Don't be silly. She only comes weekends. Mary says she sometimes answers the door in her bathrobe."

"That's pretty blatant. Personally I think she's Joe's cover. He's gay, didn't I tell you?"

"I think he's probably just simplifying his life. He only uses the house for about four months a year and he's probably figuring that the market is about to peak, so he's cashing in."

"That's it. You've solved it. The Mystery of Joe Wallace."

"How much will he get?"

"A hundred and fifty. The place has only got two rooms."

"You're joking. It's exquisite. Half a million more like it."

"It's goddam *tiny*, I know that," Salter said, jerked out of his playfull mood by Annie's outrageous estimate.

Wallace's house had originally been a labourer's cottage, put up in 1860 with the stone left over from building a Catholic seminary. It was virtually a doll's house, an indulgence of a doting builder for his unmarried daughter. Left to himself, the builder had allowed his fancy to romp. The stone exterior was embellished with a pointed front door with iron studs, and with diagonally-paned leaded windows. The wide drive, really the other half of the double lot that went with the cottage, was cobbled, ending behind the cottage in a coach house nearly as big as the cottage, crowned with a small steeple and a weather vane.

Inside there had originally been two bedrooms and a bathroom upstairs, and a kitchen, dining room and living room downstairs, all very small. Wallace had called in a renovator when he moved in, twenty years before, who had removed all the interior walls except those around the bathroom, thus creating two good-sized spaces, one up and one down. Here Wallace lived, alone except on most weekends. He was a good neighbour, giving two parties a year for his immediate neighbours, a brunch with wine and quiche and chili on the Sunday before Christmas, and a similar party with cold meats and salad in the garden if possible on the first Sunday in June, both hosted with his friend.

"Who in hell would pay half a million for two rooms? Because that's all it is. Nice rooms, but only two of them."

Annie said, "Maybe it's a tear-down. The house is on a double lot."

"A what?"

"A tear-down. It's a term I heard a real estate agent use for Mrs. Gorecki's house."

"A tear-down? Jesus Christ. Mrs. Gorecki lived in her house for fifty years. Her kids were born in that house. A tear-down. Is it collapsing, or something?"

"It was well-cared for, but anyone buying it would have to spend a fortune to modernise it, and they would probably decide to tear it down and start again. In this neighbourhood, on this street, the money is in the lot. You could tear down most of these houses and build new ones for the cost of renovating them."

"Why? Why would you have to modernise old Mrs. Gorecki's house? It's what it is, for anyone who likes old houses. It's dry, warm, made of solid brick and the foundations haven't shifted." Salter was awake now, the sun gone behind a cloud. He slid out of bed and creaked his way to the bathroom. "You think this is a tear-down?" he called to Annie, before he turned on the shower.

"No. We're semi-detached and we don't have a driveway."

"You've thought about this, haven't you? Are we planning to move?"

"Not as long as one son and his girl-friend live in our basement, and the other son and his infant child live in the attic. Don't panic."

But it was a reminder that the two of them felt life differently. Annie liked change and thought about how to make it happen. Salter liked things to stay as they were and did his best to appear immoveable. Annie claimed to be only preparing for the inevitable, while Salter preferred not to have to think about his life at all, waking up only for major anniversaries.

2

Old Sally lived by scavenging the waste food put out by restaurants along Yonge Street, north of Dundas. She was one of half-a-dozen regulars in the area and the pickings were good enough for them all. Sally's only other need was for Fine Old Canadian Sherry, of which she drank a bottle a night. For this she required seven dollars which she begged for, pushing her shopping cart at the pedestrians on Yonge Street, black claw outstretched, targetting the women who looked at her with something like compassion. Sometimes, when times were hard, she pushed her cart over to Jarvis Street where one of the coffee shops would give her a cup of coffee and a donut, if she didn't try to sit down, and where the prostitutes could be generous with their change.

When she had her sherry money, she called in to the wine shop on Church Street where the assistant bagged her bottle as he saw her coming through the door and hustled her out as quickly as he could. From there she shuffled off to where she would rest for the night. In summer her favourite place was the back porch of one of the downtown churches where they knew her and tolerated her as long as she arrived late and left early in the morning. In winter, when the temperature dropped below freezing, often to twenty degrees below, she sometimes found an unoccupied hot air grating to sleep on, and on the worst nights allowed the patrol to take her to a shelter. Her real preference was for a nest that she could return to, sometimes for most of the winter, like she had found this year, a shed in the yard of a derelict house below Queen Street, a place out of the wind, a sometime gardening shed with a tiny rusty woodstove where she could make a bit of a fire from the scraps of lumber she had gleaned during the day, and where she could wrap herself up for the night.

The house to which the garden belonged sheltered another pair of derelicts, Molly and Buster. They sometimes came down the garden to beg a mouthful of wine from Sally, but otherwise they left her alone. Now, in October, Sally had been in the hut for a week. The days were ending earlier, and soon the Daylight Saving Time would be gone, but the hut's filthy but intact single window let in enough light from the street lamp for her to see by. Once Buster had come to the hut drunk and nasty to demand money, knowing, he said, that she had plenty, but she was stronger than Buster and beat him off with the hatchet she kept to protect herself from night crawlers.

The activists appeared two days later, two neighbours, or rather, two women the Salters had never seen in their lives who lived three blocks away. "We want to make everyone aware that their environment is being destroyed," one of them said, more or less as Annie opened the door. "Did you know?"

She was a very tall woman in her late fifties with a large voice who spoke from beyond the normal conversational distance, her head moving from side to side as if she was addressing a peripheral audience. Her companion was smaller but equally thin. She kept her eyes on her companion's face until she had finished, then came in nodding hard, with "There goes the neighbourhood."

Annie backed away a little and Salter appeared from the kitchen. "What's up?"

Annie made a gesture linking the two women with Salter, and the tall woman repeated her message, the small woman chiming in at the end.

Now Salter tried to ease himself away to let Annie deal with it, but she held his sleeve, saying to the women, "You're talking about the house that's up for sale?"

"What else?"

Salter, immediately irritated by the if-you-aren't-immediately-with-us-you're-probably-one-of-them attitude, asked, "Is that bad?"

"Have you seen the price they're asking?"

"I hope it's a potful. I might want to sell this one day."

"You wouldn't get that kind of price for this," the tall woman said, Salter adding silently for her, 'pile of crap'. "The reason they can ask what they're asking is that they've got the double lot which means they can sell it to a developer who can build something twice the size and destroy your streetscape."

"And there goes the neighbourhood," the little woman chanted.

Salter said, "There's no 'they'. There's just him."

"Who?"

"Him. Joe Wallace."

"Is he a friend of yours?"

Annie spoke up. "He's a good neighbour, or has been. Who bought it?"

"A developer."

Salter said, "What kind of developer would that be? Don't developers need more room than that. All he's got is a small double lot."

"Enough room to build a monstrous great castle and destroy the streetscape. We're collecting signatures to prevent him from tearing it down until we have had our input."

Salter said, "But if that's why he's bought it, or she has, just to tear it down, I mean, then you can't stop him, can you? I mean who's going to compensate him or her or them for what they've already paid. Call it them. If they can't take it down it'll be worth a couple of hundred thousand less, as I understand it."

"That's not sufficient reason to destroy the quality of your life, surely." The woman stepped back a pace so as to address a larger crowd.

Annie said, "I'm cooking a frittata. Are you going to every house on the street?"

"We've just started. Yes."

"Then why don't you call in again on the way back."

The tall woman began to speak. Annie said, "Look, I have to go. Call back, would you?" She ran back to the kitchen, leaving Salter to shrug and slowly close the door on the two women, who were making no move to go away.

They talked all through supper. Salter initially still irritated at the confrontational attitude of the women, as Annie took him house by house through the history of the street since they moved in, about twenty-five years before. They counted thirteen houses, some in good shape some not, that had been torn down. Annie came to Salter's Achilles heel.

"Thirteen houses gone, replaced by expensive garages with chauffeurs' quarters above, built mainly to accommodate pairs of cars and creating a streetscape of garage doors. Like the back alley of millionaires' row, you said, a mews."

Salter bowed his head, conceding that on this point he was with the women.

Annie continued. "And every new garage cuts out one more parking space on the street so that the owners of houses without driveways—us—are finding it harder and harder to park, even with a permit. Angus had to drive three blocks away the other day to find a place to stay overnight, and even then he had to be out of there by eight a.m. And when Mike comes up from Detroit, there's nowhere, literally, where he can park for a couple of days. It's become illegal to have visitors."

"There are twice as many cars now as there were when we moved on the street."

"We've gone up market. There are no more mailmen like old Mr Simkins left on the street."

"Christ, yes. There were, then, weren't there? So our new neighbours have money. You can't preserve the street in aspic to stop them spending it. The next thing will be a movement to make every house a heritage home."

"That's probably already started. The thing is, it shouldn't be too easy to buy up a couple of nice houses, tear them down, and put up a redbrick version of the Chateau Laurier, should it?"

"Now you've gone too far. I think I'd enjoy that."

"Did you see her come back?" Buster asked.

"I haven't seen her for a couple of days. But her cart's outside the shed door. She usually takes all her shit in with her at night and loads up in the morning."

"Is it there today? This morning?"

"It was there when I woke up."

"This *morning*, I said, you stupid bitch."

"And I told you, I was asleep this morning. Prickface."

"Passed out, you mean."

"Like you. Now I need a drink. Got any money?"

"Where the fuck would I have money you don't know about? I been trying to tell you. We've got to get over to Starbucks. Get the spot against the wall with the blanket. Look fucking pathetic. Orphans in the fucking storm. You got our sign?"

"I can't sit outside Starbucks without a drink in me."

"Now we're back to where we started. Right. I'll ask Sally."

"She won't give you anything."

"She'd fucking better. She's *gotta* share. We're all on the street together. Old bitch."

The two women returned with a sheet full of signatures and Annie added hers but declined the invitation to join the group that would stand ready to go down to city hall to oppose any application for a building variance. "I work," she said. "You couldn't rely on me."

Salter didn't sign. His employers, he said, discouraged the police from getting involved in local protests. "I can't even stand for parliament," he said.

"Mary, Mary. Wake up, for Chrissake. We've got to get out of here. C'mon. Get your shit together, we've got to go."

"She give you a bad time? Old Sally?"

"Worse than that. Christ. Now, bring that sign so no one can tell we were here. Everybody knows our sign."

"Where are we going?"

"Over to Starbucks. We'll sit there for half an hour and you have one of your fits and I'll yell for help. Won't take long."

"They'll split us up." Mary gaped and began to cry. "I don't want to be on my own again."

"Don't start fucking crying. I'll be in the next room. Promise. I'll find you in the morning. Just get it in to your head, if anyone asks, we usually spend the night over the grating beside the Women's College Hospital. And yesterday we sat outside the coffee shop on Victoria Street all day."

"Did you smash her up, Buster? Old Sally."

"It's worse than that. Now c'mon for Chrissake. Let's get away from here."

3

The two women, now identified as Betty Micklewhite, the tall thin one, and Nancy Koo, the short one, were back in Salter's living room. The house, they had learned, had been sold to a developer.

"Do you know what he's going to do with it?" Salter asked.

"Tear it down, of course. Tear it down. What do you think?"

"I mean, *after* he's torn it down. What's he going to put *up*?"

"A monstrosity, probably."

"How do you know? Have you seen the plans? Has anyone?"

"It's the only way he could get his money back."

"By building a monstrosity? Good market for monstrosities, is there?"

"By building something out of proportion."

Salter started to speak, and Annie tried to interrupt him, but he won. "You know," he said. "I sort of sympathise with you. I like the street the way it is. And I can't say that many of the changes we've had are good ones. I've been counting: since we've lived here we've lost seven kind of nice houses and seen seven not so nice ones take their place. Townhouses. And we've had six other major renovations that actually improved on the old buildings. Of the seven that are not so nice, the neighbours tried to stop three of them but the Committee of Adjustment allowed them all. I don't give you much chance."

"That committee has no regard for aesthetic or human values. If the application is for something that won't interfere with the cash value of a neighbour's house, they allow it. Money and the law, that's all they base their standards on." She was addressing the corner of the room, near the ceiling. "But Councillor Feschuk is on our side and she says if we speak as a body it might impress the Committee. The developer has got to apply for a permit, and we'll be ready to oppose it."

"Permit for what?"

"Any non-conforming variance. An extra bathroom, say. That's not allowed. Or an extra sink."

"Why? Why aren't they allowed?"

"The zoning dates back to when the chief worry was that people would convert their basements into separate apartments, making it a sort of rooming-house district. So if you renovate, whatever you do you have to get permission for an extra bathroom."

"But the reason this developer might want to put in an extra bathroom is the opposite of what the by-law was protecting the area from. This guy will want to go up-market, bathrooms for everyone in the family, rather than turn the place into a rooming house. Right?"

"Whatever he wants to do, we're going to oppose it just to air the question of what right residents have to protect the neighbourhood."

"You think they'll listen to you?"

Annie said, "Charlie, they don't like citizens' groups, especially near an election."

Salter said, "*We* just put in another bathroom. Sort of. In the basement. Without a permit. One of our sons lives down there, with his girl-friend. I wouldn't want to draw attention to it. The spirit of that old zoning by-law might get invoked."

The silence thickened for several minutes. Then Betty Micklewhite said, "That's not the kind of thing we're interested in now. Anyway it's a fait accompli, and you usually get away with that." She stood up. "We'll let you know of developments," she said to Annie. "I mean permit developments."

The door closed behind them.

Annie said, "I think I will go down with them if I can. I'd like to see how it works."

Salter said, "I'll tell you how it works. When this item comes up, they'll ask if anyone wants to speak for or against it. All of you will speak, one by one, about how your—what's the word? streetscape?—is being destroyed by builders with no sense of the history, the architectural qualities of the street, stuff like that, making you all sound like a lot of aesthetes who chose to live here because it looked like a painting by what's that guy? Kurelek. Then the developer's lawyer will stand up with a lot of pictures of all the grotty houses on the street and argue that all you really care about is having the right to interfere in other people's plans. She will have done a survey of the street and show that maybe forty-five per cent of the residents are delighted with the increase in property values on the street in the last decade, and now regard their houses as their chief retirement provision, and they don't want anyone stopped until a developer has made them a decent offer. There are at least six old people who are counting on selling their houses for a reasonable profit which too much interference from the council might cut back."

"The Curnows paid seventeen thousand for their house. It's worth six hundred thousand now. That a reasonable profit?"

"Ask anyone on Bay Street what seventeen thousand wisely invested say thirty years ago should be worth now."

"Anyway, the Curnows are not a little old widow. He's an academic with an indexed pension and a rich wife, and he supports our petition."

"Sure. He can afford to indulge himself in his old age. They don't even have any kids. He's a liberal."

"So am I, I hope."

"You can afford it, too."

"But now you're all for progress, are you, Charlie? Now you want to raze the street and put in high-rise. Make some money?"

"Don't be silly, and when you get down in front of that committee at City Hall, keep your cool there, too. Of course I'm not a liberal. I'm a conservative, I was told the other day. I want to preserve the best. I want this street to stay the way it is, and the people, too. I don't want anyone to move, or die, until I do."

"Have you been thinking about this a lot lately?"

"Moving or dying? Both. I was talking to Marinelli at work. He lives on Dupont, near where it meets Avenue Road, and he wants to sell his house which he bought very cheap, like Curnow, and buy a condo on the lakeshore now his kids are married. He's got a little sailboat. But there's a movement to have his area declared a historic district and that'll cut the price in half, he thinks. Marinelli is up on all the arguments."

"So which side are you on?"

"I told you. I like it here, and I've got a rich wife, too."

"Duncan. William Duncan, same as it was the last time you asked me. Everyone calls me Buster."

The officer gestured towards the figure on the hospital trolley.

"That's Mary, my sister."

"You bullshitting me, Buster?"

"She's been my sister for fifty years, in the orphanage and out of it. We got split up a few times to be sent to foster homes and such, but I always found her again. Now what?"

"Soon as the doctor clears her, we'll take you to a shelter, both of you."

"They'll split us up there, too."

"That right?"

"You can live common-law, but not as brother and sister, not in a shelter. Can't we stay here for the night? It's nice and warm here. Leave Mary in the corridor here. She won't be in the way. I can doss off in this chair."

"Haven't you heard? You need a reservation to get in to the emergency ward now. The shelter's warm, too, and you'll get something to eat there."

"I know all about shelters. Give me a couple of bucks for tomorrow morning so we don't have to start off hungry. Just a toonie."

"Don't you have any shame, Buster? Here, here's my change. Must be a couple of bucks there. Don't spend it all at once."

"What the hell are you doing giving money to those two?"

"Hullo, George. I thought a bum who's got the nerve to ask a cop for a handout deserves two bucks or a kick in the ass, so I gave him two bucks. Next time I'll kick his ass."

"Let's leave them spend it now. Somebody sent for the mission wagon to take them over there."

"Didn't you realise that we have a three-family dwelling here? There's Angus's family above us and Seth's below stairs. Certainly non-conforming, if not illegal. It would be in Leaside."

"But we're a family, Charlie."

"So were the Joads. Thank God we snuck that basement washroom in during the last renovation. The way things are going it might be a shade risky to do it now."

"We've renovated three times and we haven't changed the streetscape at all."

"That's because we have exquisite taste. But if you start meddling with the by-laws we might wind up being inspected and find ourselves with a notice to change it all back to the way it was twenty-five years ago."

"Are you serious?"

"I'm just wondering what I would do if I were on the other side and felt like getting nasty, especially if it looked as if your gang was going to defeat my application. Report your non-conforming use to City Hall? It probably wouldn't be hard to find one wrinkly old neighbour who is counting on selling his house for a potful and gets upset when you guys win and the developers lose interest. You know how the blue rinse crowd on Hagan Boulevard were up in arms when we wanted to introduce speed bumps twenty years ago to protect our kids a bit. They objected to having to slow down just because a lot of parents were out working when they should have been home, minding their children and training them to keep off the street. In their day, they said—well, you remember. As I recall there were about ten of them signed the protest."

"We won, though."

"Protecting your neighbourhood was a lot more fashionable then than it is now. In this case, it would only take one of them to write to City Hall about the swarm of people living illegally whose cars are filling up the street."

"You're being ridiculous, Charlie."

"I hope so. I hope I am."

"You hear that, Mary? We're going to the Mission shelter. Now don't start to fucking cry. I'll make sure they know who we are, and I'll find out what room you're in. And don't forget, where did we spend last night? Right. Anything else, you don't remember. If they keep on, ask them for a drink, show them why you don't remember."

4

"You know what he said, Charlie? You know what that bastard of a councillor said?"

"Let's hear what *you* said first. How many of you were there?"

"Six of us."

"Did you all make a speech?"

"We all spoke, yes. I spoke last."

"What did you say?"

"Well, the others had talked about the new building being clearly designed for two or three-car occupancy—I thought those were good words. Not a house, or a family, but some kind of collective of rich people owning Mercedes's and filling the street with their cars."

"We're already doing that."

"Yeah, but worse."

"What about Joe Wallace's house? Do they plan to take down the front fence and make a parking space in front?"

"Actually, they plan to park in behind."

"So nothing much will change except that a cottage will be replaced by a two-story house."

"With an attic, and a kind of sun deck. No, you're right. Truth is, I rather liked the sound of it. Joe's cottage is kind of ugly."

"So what did you say?"

"I took the high ground. I said that I had examined the plan very carefully and considered the effect that the new house would have on the street—they are even preserving the big maple in front—and felt obliged to say in all honesty that I could not object to *this* particular house, but … I paused here, Charlie, then went into your point. I wanted to use the opportunity to ask that the city planning department or whoever is responsible for these things hire Jane Jacobs or somebody to study the effect of this kind of change, and how to manage it. I said that in the past, under out-dated by-laws, some of the old houses had been built too close together, denying their neighbours access to light; nevertheless the way those houses were built defined the norm so that afterwards, wherever houses do have some land around them, grass where our kids used to play, they are being torn down and in one case replaced by three row townhouses, and in most cases replaced by something built to the lot line. The point to be made, I said, was that under the present by-laws the street, the district, is changing from a family-oriented street to a mews—your word, I had to explain that one. Ironically, I said, the very things that attract newcomers to the street—the safety, the families, the presence of old people, the trees—

"People getting born, people dying …"

"All right. That's what I was saying. The street presently is a community of people, but soon it will be a community of cars."

"What happened? They all clap? Except your five friends who were pissed off I bet to hear you've changed sides on Joe Wallace's house."

"One of the councillors on the committee asked if I wasn't really trying to protect property values. The asshole was so obsessed with what *he* would be arguing for in my place that he didn't have the sense to realise that I was arguing for the opposite. I think. But he gave me my second wind. I said he obviously hadn't been listening, that property values were not the problem, and he sneered. You ever see someone really sneer? People mostly give up sneering after adolescence except in sitcoms. I said we were as much concerned about the quality of life on our street as the people on the Bridle Path were—somehow the Bridle Path got into the discussion earlier—and he sneered again and said those houses were worth three million each, so you couldn't allow infill there because it would destroy the values. Surely we could see the difference. I said he was an ignorant boor who was sitting on his brains and the chairman told me to sit down."

"So you tried. But all you did was make an enemy of that councillor."

"And he of me. I haven't finished trying. His *attitude*. Christ! I'm going to make a real bloody nuisance of myself, just like those two women."

"So what are you going to do?"

"Every time a house goes up for sale, we'll watch who buys it, and find out their plans. At the same time, work to get zoning restrictions that will make it hard for developers to do what they like."

"Lotsa luck."

"Why would someone kill an old baglady?"

The two detectives looked down at the bundle of rags on the floor of the hut.

"Who called it in?"

"One of the patrol cars. They were led to her by another street person who was looking for somewhere to spend the night. She knew that old Sally used this hut and hoped to bunk in with her for the night."

"Old Sally? You know her?"

"That's what this other old gal called her. *She* knew her, although I bet half the bagladies in Toronto are known as Old Sally."

"Did she kill her?"

"This old bat's as weak as a kitten. Besides, she came to us."

"To allay suspicion?"

"You've been reading again, Bernie. This isn't Minette Walters. What we've got here is an old derelict chopped up by someone with the strength to lift an axe, not the one who came to us. But here comes the whole circus. Let's see if we can hand this over to the CID and get out of here. God, what a stink."

5

"There it goes," Annie said, from the window.

Salter said, "What? There what goes?"

"The fence is up, and three large pieces of mechanical equipment are now lined up to dismantle the house. Two men are on the roof, lifting tiles. There goes Betty."

"Betty. The tall thin one, right? What's she doing?"

"Talking to the foreman. Now he's showing her the permit."

"What's her next move? She going to lie down in front of the bulldozer?"

"I'll let you know. I'm going to join them."

"What!"

"I'd like to find out what kind of control I have over my environment, and what I ought to have. I can't think it through on my own, so I'm joining the committee to see whose arguments fill my head. Including the developer's."

"What, exactly, are you going to do?"

"First of all, I'm going to help them canvass neighbourhood opinion. And go back with them to city hall to find out what the options are."

"Lotsa luck."

"Don't keep saying that."

When Salter arrived for work, the frosted glass door between his office and the inner office of his boss, Deputy Chief of Police Mackenzie, was closed, but the light showed that the deputy chief was already in his office. Salter hung up his raincoat and moved to greet his boss and then, with his hand on the door-knob, responded to some atavistic self-preservational instinct and considered. For two years now he had been Mackenzie's assistant, his office manager, but also and mainly his confidant. Mackenzie knew all the rules about the running of a police force but when confronted by an unfamiliar situation he became uncertain of himself. The day he got a call from the store on Bloor Street, saying they were holding the wife of a very senior officer for shoplifting, and she had pleaded with them to call Mackenzie first, was typical. Mackenzie hadn't the faintest idea what to do, seeing some way down the road a personal involvement that would earn him the enmity of his colleague, simply for knowing about it. Salter, at the time only one year away from retirement and indifferent to anyone's enmity, offered to take the problem off Mackenzie's hands and got a cruiser to switch on its flasher and take him to the store, where he negotiated a quiet resolution of the problem. The store wanted to ban her, at least, but Salter got them to agree not to go that far if she would agree to check in with the management whenever she was in the store, and before she left. At the same time he got the woman to agree to tell her husband, and gave her his card so that her husband would know who it was who took the call when Mackenzie was supposedly out of his office, so that only the woman and Salter knew the story. He got a phone call for that from the officer, a grunted "Thanks," a pause, and "It won't happen again." That was all, but he was fairly sure that the man would be glad when Salter was gone and his family linen no longer at risk, which Mackenzie had realised would happen.

On two or three such occasions Salter's help or advice had been basic to the solution, but consistent with Mackenzie's need for certainty before he acted was his subsequent need to rearrange the story so that it was he, or at most "We" who had come up with the solution. Sometimes he would rearrange it in such watertight fashion that he would retell it to Salter, later. Sometimes the theft of Salter's advice and help was so blatant that Salter wondered if Mackenzie in the retelling was winding him up, but after the third or fourth time he realised that once Mackenzie had taken Salter's advice, it was his own.

Over the two years, the relationship between the two men had softened from the formality of its beginnings, so that Mackenzie after a year of "Salter!" now regularly called him Charlie unless anyone like the Chief of Police was listening. Now Salter paused, his hand around the door-knob, as if it was his first day with the deputy, and knocked.

It was a good instinct. "Come in," Mackenzie commanded, just as if they did this all the time.

Salter opened the door and stepped inside.

"Close the door, Salter," the deputy ordered, in his new loud voice.

Salter did so, and waited, staring at his boss. All of Mackenzie's professional life—and Salter had observed him for the last twenty years of it—ever since he was a staff inspector on the morality squad, Mackenzie had worn the same three-button blue suits, white shirts, blue ties with various insignificant patterns, and black shoes. Now he was wearing a medium grey suit, a cream shirt, an Italian-looking tie and brown brogues. He looked, Salter thought, like a deputy chief of police on a cruise ship, dressed for the formal night.

"A big day?" Salter asked, adding, almost immediately, "sir," because there was that about Mackenzie that suggested Salter should be wary.

"Sit down, Charlie," the deputy said, relaxing Salter slightly. The "Salter" was only for the benefit of anyone in the outer office. The closed door restored the normal world. "Look all right?" Mackenzie passed a hand over his facade.

Salter took the chair in front of Mackenzie's desk. "You look great, sir. But what's the occasion?"

"I've decided to apply for the job."

"The chief?"

"What else?"

"I thought you weren't interested."

"I've been approached."

"Who by?"

"Two or three were in to see me."

"Of ours?"

"Of course. Who else? These guys told me that one of the ways the committee is going to get the information they need to make up their mind is by surveying the force, the unit commanders at least. They have one simple question: Is there anyone on the force you think would make a good chief? These guys want to be able to say me."

"But why the ..." Salter wanted to say "the costume" but couldn't find an unloaded term quickly enough and settled for "the new tailor?"

"Same tailor, Charlie. I always go to the Bay, get the best. But these guys said that I ought to project a more energetic image. They said blue suits are for yesterday's chiefs. I think you should listen to good advice, so my wife and I went downtown and here I am. What do you really think? I feel as though I'm going to a wedding." Mackenzie looked a little shy.

"Dynamite," Salter said. "Better a wedding than a funeral. Those guys are right," he added quickly. "Trudeau used to wear sandals when he was Attorney General and it didn't do him any harm."

"Never mind Trudeau. I never voted for him. Point is, do I look livelier? Eh?"

"A man for the times," Salter assured him.

"What about the hair?" Mackenzie revolved his head to remind Salter of his rear view. "Do I need a haircut? It's getting kinda thin, too. Might make me seem too old."

"Who's your hairdresser?"

"Barber over on the Danforth."

"Greek?"

"I think so. Plays classical music all the time. I've been going to him for thirty years. Why?"

"It's kind of military-looking. Cut a bit close for a guy with a tie like that."

"That's how I like it."

"How much does he charge?"

"Eight bucks. I give him two bucks tip."

"Find one closer to downtown, someone who charges at least twenty bucks. Skip the next cut first, though."

"Grow it *long*, you mean?"

"Longer."

"I don't want to look like a goddam *swinger*. Besides, there's a couple of the old guard councillors on the Commission."

"There's a stage in between before it reaches your collar."

"Should I get it tinted? A little hair piece over the bald spot?"

"No."

"I'm just kidding."

"Yeah, sure. No, just try and bring it down closer to your ears, then get a very light trim."

"Right. Could you find me a good barber, Charlie? Now, about the door."

"We're keeping it closed?"

"I want people to have to knock, so that'll have to include you. Makes me look more in control."

"You don't think a closed door policy clashes with the new image you're after?"

"You think so?"

"It does to me."

"Okay. Leave the door open. But if anyone's around, I'll still call you Salter."

"I'll be sure to answer."

"What? Oh, yeah, right. What about my shoes? I've never had shoes like this before. They're not golfing shoes, are they?"

"The golfing shoes you mean had those leather flaps with tassels that covered the laces. I don't think even golfers wear them any more. No, the shoes are good." Salter just prevented himself from calling them 'swell'. "When do these people make up their minds?"

"That's the trouble. Three weeks is all I've got to impress them. I can't grow curly hair in three weeks."

"Just don't get it cut. Do you know who else is applying?"

"Two outsiders and Haskell, I've heard," Mackenzie said, naming another deputy chief. "That's why I'm letting my name go forward. The union has let it be known they want an insider this time. I think I can take Haskell if it comes down to it. If not, I'll resign."

"But ..."

"I've thought it through, Charlie. The odds are on my side."

"But why would you have to resign if Haskell gets the job?"

"We go back a long way. He knows what I think of him."

"He does?"

"I told him often enough. He's an asshole. Even if I hadn't told him, I couldn't work for him. Now, these committee guys will come to you, too, Charlie."

"Okay." Salter said nothing. A minor tease; a minor cruelty, but Mackenzie owed him.

"I mean," Mackenzie said, forced to ask, "Do I have your support?"

"Don't ever doubt it. I'll start working on my speech right now."

Mackenzie coloured slightly and grinned. "Lay it on thick, Charlie."

6

"Move some of this earth to the front edge," the foreman said. "I want to build the road so they can dump in the hole and keep backing away from the edge. See?"

"No, I don't see. You telling *me* to keep backing from the edge, or them? The front edge of what? The lake?"

"The *site*. Look, it's marked out. I'll pace it off for you." The foreman walked away from the bulldozer and stopped by a surveyor's stake. "This is the left marker." He paced off fifty feet and touched the second stake with his boot. "This is the right marker. The front edge lies between those two."

"Gotcha."

"So move the stuff they've already dumped and fill in behind this line. Do the centre first to give the trucks somewhere to turn. Jesus Christ, what's that!"

"What?"

"*That.*"

"Looks like a glove. The thing is, people, construction cowboys, do-it-yourselfers, dump all kinds of garbage and shit in these sites at night to save driving out to the other dumps. You oughta put a nightwatchman on."

The foreman moved warily forward towards the object, then stopped and waved frantically at the bulldozer operator to cut his engine. "That's a *hand*, for Christ's sake. A goddamn hand. You got a cell phone? Dial 911. God Almighty—a hand."

"Sir, they think they know where the hand came from."

"That would be good to know. It's going to be in the news tonight. The bulldozer guy couldn't keep his goddam mouth shut." The deputy chief leaned forward. "Who is it?"

Salter said, "Two of our men were led to the body of a derelict, an old woman, last Thursday night. It was logged as a possible homicide. One hand had been chopped off."

"Go on."

"That's it. Seems someone might have cut off her hand for a ring or some such that they couldn't get off."

"Let's say so, eh? How come it took so long for these two officers to speak up."

"They've both been off duty since the hand turned up."

"Did nobody else know about the body?"

"The C.I.D. guys. They just heard about it. Actually they've been looking for the hand ever since, around the site where the body was found."

"Where was that?"

"A derelict house on Sackville in Cabbagetown."

"In the meantime we've had two bulldozers and twenty men with shovels turning over the landfill site looking for the rest of the body, all the time it's been lying in the morgue. Right?"

"More or less." Salter watched the anger rise to the surface of Mackenzie's face, then something else start to break through, like the bubbles rising through the skin of a saucepan of porridge. Mackenzie had found something funny. It took him some time to frame the thought.

"Which hand was it the digger found?"

Now Salter guessed what Mackenzie had found. "I don't know," he said, helpfully.

"Maybe the left hand which didn't know what the right hand was doing?" Mackenzie's face creased into lines, then almost immediately resumed its usual take-no-prisoners expression, then immediately softened slightly as the signal that he was thinking again. "You know, Salter, I was beginning to wonder if we'd find a lot of body parts, one by one."

Salter stayed attentive-looking. Mackenzie still looked thoughtful, and in that mode he did not need to be interrupted, or even prompted. The role for the listener was to look interested, and nod to keep Mackenzie's wheels turning. After an unusually long silence, Salter risked, "Really, sir? Why?"

Silently, Mackenzie arranged his ideas. Raising a hand slightly to show he was soon going to speak again. "Couple of things," he said. "We've had one mutilation this year, remember. That head left on the GO-train, the rest of the woman cut up and left in a deep-freeze locker. The guy apparently was going to dispose of it a piece at a time, starting with the head, but he got off the train and forgot his parcel. It may have started something."

"You think these things come in threes?"

"I'm not talking about superstition here. I'm talking about copycat stuff. Weirdos get ideas from reading about them, and you can get videos now of people doing stuff that I never knew about when I first got married. Sex stuff, I mean. I knew all about perverts, of course, and learnt a lot more on the force pretty quick, but I didn't know what ordinary people were doing, and I don't think they were doing it then. You know what I mean? Point is, Salter, you see a video of someone, some couple, doing weird stuff, you might get ideas you would never have had."

"If nobody could read, nobody would fall in love," Salter said.

"What? What? Oh, yeah. Who said that?"

"Yogi Berra or Shakespeare," Salter said. "I heard it from my wife."

"Yeah, right. But that gets me on to something else. Books. Crime stories. You read them, Salter? Thrillers. like?"

"No."

"Never?"

"No."

"You should try one. Some of them are quite well written. Anyway, my point is that most of the best-sellers lately involve cutting up bodies. Good-bye Agatha Christie. The women are all into carve-ups now. What I'm saying is that if there's anything in what we've been talking about then we can expect that out there some weirdos are going to get ideas."

"The jury's out on that one, sir."

"What are you talking about?"

"There's been a lot of argument about the influence of books on people, especially in the area of sex. Kids know the details so early now that the argument is that they're bound to want to try it themselves. I don't know. I think it's not likely, though, that normal adults would want to cut off someone's head just because they read about it. I don't know."

"Then why are they reading about it?"

"Maybe it's a kind of pornography."

"Sounds like that proves my point."

Salter resisted the temptation to debate the point further. He was fairly sure of what he thought and had been into the arguments thoroughly with Annie, but he heard in Mackenzie, ten years his junior, a lack of sophistication, an innocence, not of life, but of argument, so that he felt like a Jesuit instructing an adolescent, and he wanted to avoid any more discussion. "I don't know," he said.

Mackenzie changed the subject. "This hand," he said. "This hand has been cut off to get at the rings, maybe?

"That was an idea we had, yes."

"Any of the fingers missing on the hand?"

"You've got the picture on your desk, sir."

"Right, right. Doesn't look like it. So what's the theory now? Hold on, here's the autopsy report. 'The flesh at the wrist indented and bruised consistent with having worn a bracelet.' See? A bracelet. That's why all the fingers were on it. Right? Okay. We should tell them they can stop digging, I guess. But somebody mutilated a body, right? Do they have any ideas?"

"I think they are covering the neighbourhood, sir. Shall I ask them to report directly to you?"

"No, no. Let me know if any more body parts show up, though." He grinned briefly.

Annie said, "What's happening about that old woman that was found with her hand cut off? Do the police know where to look for whoever did it?"

"No."

"Where did she live?"

Salter told her.

"That's her home? A shed, with a tin stove?"

"There's a lot of them out there."

"Aren't there enough shelters?"

"What I hear is there are never enough shelters."

7

"Come in for a minute, Charlie. Never mind the door. They've found another hand."

"Jesus. Where?"

"Same place, thank Christ. The landfill site. They wouldn't have found it if I'd sent the order out earlier to stop digging, which I should've. But now, finally, they've taken a good look at these hands instead of *deducing* and apparently they have nothing to do with the body our men found. I say, Thank Christ, because if we had three different places where these body parts were turning up I'd say we would have a serial mutilator. This way we can treat it as a coincidence. Now all we need is a body without any hands, and a hand for the baglady. I've told them to sift that landfill site very carefully, and I've doubled the team looking for anyone who saw the baglady the night she was killed."

Salter said, "Do the hands give you any idea of the body you're looking for? They are a pair, are they?"

"The pathologist said they came from the same woman." He picked up a report from his desk. "Nails clipped short, but a bit of soil underneath; none of that ingrained dirt you get in someone who hasn't washed for a month; skin rough and used to work but no callouses or cuts or anything major. Some kind of working woman, probably in her fifties. Not the baglady, that's for sure." He leaned forewad. "You know what I just thought, Charlie? Could this be the anti-Olympics gang, you know those people who don't want the Games?"

"Why would…"

Mackenzie interrupted him, excited. "Anything to slow down the construction. It's well known that area may be the site of some of the events. Some of these protesters will do anything to make a point."

Mackenzie was alluding to the fact that everyone was on tenterhooks, waiting to find out if Toronto was to be chosen as the site for the Olympic Games. 'Everyone' meant everyone who mattered: the mayor, the premier of Ontario, and the MPs who represented Toronto federally, as well as all the hotels and restaurants and the escort services. But there were a lot of people who didn't matter who were less keen, people who had a variety of reasons why the Olympics should be held in Beijing, or Paris, or anywhere but Toronto. These people said that spending several billion dollars on a Roman circus when there were sixty thousand homeless people in Toronto was wrong. The hand-on-heart response of the Olympic boosters, that many of the buildings required for an Olympics would be available after the Games to shelter the homeless sounded like telling the hungry that there would be left-overs from the banquet.

Another argument raised by these malcontents was that nearly every city that had hosted the games had been left with a huge debt that took years to pay off. Montreal was still labouring under such a burden after twenty years.

Finally, the Games came under attack from those who jeered at the proliferation of events so far removed from the ancient Greek contests. Once you included synchronised smiling as the malcontents called it, and ballroom dancing, who should say what should not be allowed? Why not Indian club twirling, or line dancing, or bocci?

Once upon a time in Toronto there was an organisation known as the Celebrities Club. In a spirit of unmalicious mockery there began in a beer parlour next door to the Club a regular Friday night gathering of people who called themselves The Nonentities Club, membership of which was open to all except members of the Celebrities Club. Now, in the same spirit, an organisation called the Real Olympics Committee was created. Real Olympics proposed an alternative competition, an attempt to catch the spirit of the original Games. Each nation, they ruled, could send twelve athletes to the Real Games, and those twelve athletes would be welcome to compete in any and all of the events. And that was the only rule.

The Real Olympics organisors pointed out that the problem of find-ing twelve athletes who could run, jump, swim and play basketball, tennis and soccer, would be fascinating, especially if (they hadn't de-cided this yet) six of the athletes had to be women. It would surely be impossible to predict the overall outcome, and even the result of indi-vidual events. The Netherlands, renowned for its tall athletic women, could well win more gold medals than China, and Fiji, by sticking to heavyweight wrestling and weight-lifting, more than the U.S.

The proposal was so sensible that it was made hay of by all the newspapers, who assigned to it their apprentice editorialists to practice their wit on.

Thus no one was taking any notice of the malcontents; money was easily found and work begun on Toronto's oldest eyesore, the Lakefront, to make it suitable in time for the Olympic Committee to inspect it as the major site for Toronto's bid. Landfill sites were marked out which would extend the shore out into Lake Ontario, and to these sites, construction companies with clean fill had been bringing their loads.

Salter said, "I wouldn't go public on this idea, sir, not yet. What you're saying is that a group of protesters might have killed someone just to use the parts to slow down construction of the buildings needed for the Games. I don't think that will go down well."

Mackenzie, seeing the idea clearly now, retreated. "I was just speculating, Charlie. Nothing in it. What do you think of my raincoat. Got it yesterday."

"Nice."

"It's Swiss."

Annie said, "We met today with Elizabeth Verners. You know, the woman who writes books about how neighbourhoods ought to work."

"And?"

"She agrees with you, you can't freeze the neighbourhood, dip it in aspic, but she says you can define the components of a street or a neighbourhood so as to show what makes it a good place to live, and thus to show that a particular projected change will probably bring about a deterioration. They've got Collier Street declared a heritage street."

"That right? Sounds like you've acquired the lingo."

"I'm practising. The trick is to get comfortable with this language so as to impress the Municipal Board with the coherence of your view and perhaps win because the developer doesn't have a coherent view. Also to get the press on your side."

"You sound comfortable with the jargon. All right."

"Not so much of the 'jargon' and 'lingo', Charlie. I'm not amusing myself. I'm getting caught up in it. We *ought* to have some say in the way the world looks, starting with the street, if we've lived in it as long as we have."

"Sure."

"I went up to the sixteenth floor of the apartment block over on

Compton Boulevard, the one that overlooks the street. The demolition of Joe Wallace's house has left a hole that looks like something a dentist should work on."

"Just waiting for a nice tooth on a bridge, one that will match the others?"

"Maybe a gold tooth? One with a diamond in it?"

"You officially joined the crusade?

"I'm going round with Betty Micklewhite. It's something I do. I've never even helped out with the street party on Labour Day."

"Don't forget, when you are looking for people to go door-to-door, I'm not allowed to help out at any level."

"No fear of forgetting that, Charlie."

"Who lives in the apartment block? And why should they care?"

"Our street is part of their world, don't you see? But Betty Micklewhite has got a real ally up there. Some time ago she got involved in one of their tenants' complaints."

"I thought you said she lives on Denton?"

"She does, but the apartment tenants got her to help them draft a petition …"

Salter interrupted, "This had nothing to do with her, though. She's just the neighbourhood agititator, is she? Like the village letter-writer in India."

"She's well known in the world of citizens' groups, if that's what you mean. You know it was women like her who sounded the alarm on the Spadina Expressway. You want me to go on?"

"Sure. I just don't want you to go off half-cocked."

"I'll remember my position as your wife, don't worry. Now, in the course of helping them out she was befriended by one of the tenants, a young single man, just in a neighbourly way, and when he heard about our problem he called Betty and offered to help. So she took me up to his apartment to show me the view. It was a bit strange. He certainly worships the ground Betty walks on."

"The tall thin one?"

"Yes. He thinks she's wonderful. His apartment is a bit creepy. The whole place is decorated with pictures, collages, I suppose, cut out from magazines and pasted on the walls, all the walls including the bathroom. Collages and plants; he's got dozens of plants, literally, it's a jungle up there. Hardly any furniture. Other people's lives, eh, Charlie? Anyway, he's prepared to do anything for the cause, including getting up a petition of his own among the tenants in the block."

"Oh, come on. A dot is changing its shape sixteen floors below and they're going to protest?"

"Its a bit far out, I agree, but this fellow is determined to help out. Talking about tear-downs, I drove down Sackville Street this afternoon, past the house where that old baglady was found. Now that it's a topic, you start to notice how many street-people there are. I wrote out a cheque."

"Who?"

"The Open Door people. The ones who find shelters for the homeless."

"You want half from me?" They kept separate bank accounts.

"No. Send them your own money. Oh, no. You can't get involved, right?"

"Has anyone been reported missing?" Salter asked.

The search at the landfill site had continued, the mechanical shovel piling up the fill that had been brought in during the last week on to an adjoining undeveloped site so the searchers could sift it more thoroughly, gingerly turning over the earth with shovels.

Mackenzie said, "No, but people like these derelicts hardly exist, do they? I mean *missing*. That's how they live. They've already gone missing once. You know."

"The hands look as if they come from someone respectable, someone who lived among folks who would miss her if she disappeared."

"Yeah. I'll tell Marinelli."

"No sign of the other hand, the other missing one? From the derelict?"

"Not yet. And I figure if we do find a hand, we might find another torso. You know?"

Salter looked polite while Mackenzie ordered his thoughts.

"I mean, if it is some kind of weirdo, going around maiming people after he's killed them … ?"

"There's certainly something weird about the hands that turned up on the landfill site."

Mackenzie grunted. "I just had a thought, talking to my wife. Maybe it isn't a weirdo but someone very rational trying to pull off a clever bit of misidentification to conceal the identity of the victim. My wife was telling me, there's this story about a corpse being found—you don't read these murder mysteries, right?"

"No."

"Yeah, well, my wife was telling me about this one, someone murdered someone and cut off their hands and head so they couldn't be identified, then put them in a rowboat and shoved them out to sea."

"Why?"

"So they wouldn't be able to identify the torso. No prints, no teeth, see?"

"No, I meant why did they push the body out to sea? In a boat. Where was this, anyway?"

"I don't know. England, probably. I'll ask her, and about why the body had to be pushed out to sea. But it might be similar here, don't you think?"

"It's a possibility."

"Give Marinelli a call, tell him to tell those diggers to watch out for a head."

"Where are the hands now?"

"Marinelli's got them on ice."

"If you're right, then we might be able to establish the chopper, mightn' we? I mean it ought to be possible to get some prints off them, and work around them to find out who did it. You could let the media know we expect to establish a complete identification from the forensic evidence of the hands. Have Marinelli give a full description of them, even take a picture."

Mackenzie grinned. "I'm ahead of you, Charlie. I've called a press conference for ten o'clock this morning in the lobby. And I'm taking personal charge of the case."

"Is that necessary? Marinelli can handle it."

"Necessary for what? Don't forget, a little public exposure might not hurt me in the next couple of weeks."

8

The two detectives went from shanty to shanty and tent to tent in the village of the homeless that had sprung up on the lakeshore. The settlement was being temporarily tolerated until the province and the city could find a response to the problem of the homeless. The city lacked enough shelters, and razing the camp and sending its tenants on to the street would dramatise the problem. The camp was unsightly, it occupied soil so badly contaminated with industrial waste it was dangerous, and it was in the way of the development planned for the 2008 Olympics, if Toronto was blessed with being host. Certainly it would have to go before the Olympic committee arrived to make their first assessment of Toronto's suitability. The humanitarian considerations were great; even greater was the problem of the bad publicity that would be gained by trying to get rid of the squatters without offering them a decent alternative. One or two human interest stories had already appeared as the tenants of the shacks picked up the rumour that the authorities planned to evict them, and they formed a small committee and called the media themselves. It made a good story, with some lively television pictures, and the immediate result was a stand-off, with the authorities on all sides insisting that "No evictions are planned at this point in time."

Here the two detectives searched for someone who might have known old Sally.

"Youse are looking for a corpse, youse guys, right, to go with the hands you found."

"What hands?" The standard response when caught out.

The man jerked his thumb towards the lake. "The hands you found in the dumpsite along the spit."

These two detectives had a single task, to find out who mutilated old Sally. They had a hatchet, surely with fingerprints; there would be blood still on the clothes of the butcher. What they needed was somewhere to look. They were here because they had asked themselves where the hatchet wielder would head for to try to lose himself. Away from the area of the body, certainly. Possibly, then, to the most celebrated centre of population of their kind, this one. The detectives were not concerned with the other pair of hands.

"You people been here long?" Detective Constable Gynt asked one man who was warming himself over a fire of wood scraps in a tin drum.

"All summer. Fucking holiday camp it was until it got cold. They're thinking of making me mayor." He grinned horribly, his mouth a cavern of decaying teeth and half masticated food.

"What's your name?" Gynt asked him.

"Cyril. What's yours." He waggled his bottom at the policeman invitingly.

Gynt said, "Anybody new arrived lately? In the last couple of days?"

Cyril shook his head. Then, "Wait a minute. Ask Cogger. Dirty old fucker in the shed over there." He pointed to a shack of corrugated iron. "He showed the reporters around yesterday."

Gynt's partner, Detective Constable Konig, standing a few paces away, said, "I'll bring him over."

He returned in a few minutes trying to keep Cogger, who was walking close behind him, from getting too close, as he lurched along in broken boots, grinning.

"What's up, Inspector?" he asked Gynt.

Gynt told him what they were looking for.

"There's three that I know of," Cogger said. "One Irish fella who found a place to sleep in the shelter that those volunteers put up last week."

Cyril interrupted. "Some of the contractors dump their scrap lumber with us, to burn. Last week some volunteers begged a few sheets of plywood to put up a bit of a roof for the ones without cover."

"Where are these three?" Gynt asked.

"What's the reward for helping police with their enquiries?" Cogger asked, turning his back and stage-gesturing with hand bent for a bribe.

"A kick up the ass if you don't," Konig, standing slightly outside the circle, barked. "Now where are these three?"

Gynt, who had been mildly entertained by Cogger's clowning, raised his eyebrows.

"They should bring in a fire truck, put a match to this place, then hose it down," Konig said.

Three or four homeless citizens who had come close to listen, now shuffled away from the threat, like dogs anticipating a kick. Gynt said, "Take us to the Irishman first."

Cogger led them across a patch of scrub to the plywood shelter where a very thin man in his forties with long black curly hair was drinking from a paper cup of coffee, and eating a donut. He looked at Gynt with one eye over the rim of his cup.

"When did you get here?" Gynt asked.

"As soon as I heard about it. Yesterday."

"Where were you before that?"

"For the last three days I've been in the mission on Bathurst."

"Why did you leave?"

"You're only allowed three days, which is better than most, But then you have to move out for a day before you can come back. It's a dascent enough kip but it's a bit tiring, running back and forth."

"You know a person, homeless, called old Sally?"

"Which one is this? I've known two or t'ree old Sallys in me time."

"Lately she stayed on Sackville Street. In a hut in the back yard of an empty house."

He shook his head. "I never cross University Avenue myself. I just came over now to inspect this …" he waved his hand at the tent city … "but I won't be staying. You can't trust the people on the east side. All my mates live west of Spadina."

"Let's find the other pair," Konig said.

Gynt nodded and turned to Cogger. "Where are they?"

"If you mean the pair across the way, they took off when they saw you coming. They'll be down the road a ways now."

"When? When did they take off?"

"About five minutes."

The pair hobbled as quickly as they could, carrying sleeping rolls they had not had time to tie up, and a bag each. Mary's shopping bag was leaking clothes; Buster had a filthy parka stuffed into an old sports bag which he was carrying by the zipper.

"Move yerself for Chrissake," Buster urged. "We've got to get over the lakeshore road. Once we're over to Eastern Avenue we can lose ourselves. We'll go to that corner shop that had a fire, the shed behind."

"I can't go any faster. Don't make me run, Buster. Why can't we go home?"

"They'll be waiting for us, that's why. We've got to give it a couple of days. It's *me* they'll do for. Not you."

"Tell 'em. Tell 'em, what you found, Oh, Buster, I'm pooped. Let 'em come. Fuck 'em."

"Come *on*, you stupid bitch. Oh, shit."

The two policemen had caught up with them on the edge of the Lakeshore Boulevard. Mary and Buster stopped, waiting for the hand on the collar. Mary's knees gave way and she folded down and sprawled forward. Buster dragged her up to a sitting position.

"She all right?" Gynt asked.

"Top of the fucking world. Look at her. All right? Asshole."

Konig took a half step towards him; Gynt held his colleague away. Mary wiped the mixture of snot and drool and tears off her face with her sleeve and looked up at Gynt. "What do you want with us?" she asked.

Gynt took a flyer. "You were in an abandoned house on Sackville three days ago. There's a shed in back, used by a homeless person known as old Sally." He waited.

"Mister ..." Mary began.

"Shut up," Buster said. "I'll tell what happened." He turned to Gynt. "I didn't kill her."

"Nor did I ..."

"I told you, Mary, shut up. I found her after she was killed, so we took off."

"What did you do with her hand?"

"Her *what?*"

"The hand you chopped off to get at her rings or whatever."

"Oh, Christ, no," Mary shouted, struggling from behind Buster's restraining arm. "Oh, Jesus, no, not that. Me and Buster are human beings, mister. Buster's a bit rough sometimes, but only with me. He's not into cutting up bodies. Jesus, no. He just went down to the shed to see if he could bum a drink off old Sally and ..."

Buster hit her, sending her staggering back. "Will you fucking-well shut up!" He turned back to Gynt. "I went down to the shed like she says to see if Sally had brought any wine back at the end of the day. She was lying on the floor covered in blood and the hatchet was there beside her. I never touched her, or anything about her. I ran back to the house and me and Mary took off. End of story. Period."

"Are you a pair? Married or common-law. Or just buddies?"

"We are a pair, yes, but not any of those. She's my sister. You want the whole heart-breaking story like them reporters, starting with the foster home, or the home run by the church? Which one was it reamed out Mary's arse with a broom handle when she was constipated? No? You don't want to hear about that, right? Well, she's my sister. Some times we go separate ways, after an argument."

"And he's punched me out."

"Shut up. Mostly we're together, looking out for each other as much as we can. What's this got to do with old Sally? I didn't kill her. Mary didn't kill her. Neither of us touched her."

"If it turns out you're lying you two won't see too much of each other for a while."

"The autor' … the autoris … the autorities usually try to keep us apart. Whenever they decide to look after us they start by separating us, or they used to. Maybe things have changed. The same people are in charge, though, the Prime Minister, the Premier, the mayor, the Pope. I expect they'll separate us."

"I didn't mean a shelter, I meant …"

"I know what you meant. So arrest us. Get on with it. You might need leg-irons for her. She can be fierce." He pointed to the fragile bag of bones his sister had become, slumped against a light standard, hardly listening. "Hurry up. I need a piss."

"Get in the back of the car. Take your stuff."

Konig said, "Let's send for a wagon."

Buster grinned. "Afraid I'll piss on the floor of your nice car? I won't. She might, though. I've had to tell her about that, before."

"Okay, okay. But if it will settle you down, no one killed old Sally. She died of natural causes."

"Then what was all the blood?"

"I told you. Someone chopped her hand off."

"Jesus." Now Buster's face lost its colour. Gynt pushed him into the car and slammed the door on the pair.

Konig said, "I think he may not be lying."

Gynt said, "I think you may be right."

"Then why are we taking them in?"

"Because they might know something we don't, even if they don't know it. Know what I mean?"

"All I know is the little bastard might piss on the floor."

"It's a hazard, Lionel, yeah. Goes with the territory."

9

Mary and Buster washed their hands and had their fingerprints taken, and were told to wait while the prints were checked. "You want some coffee?" Gynt asked.

"I want a steak and fries and a piece of pie. So does she."

"I'll get you a Danish."

"Like a fucking hospital," Buster said. "Sit here all fucking day waiting for someone to come near you. Likely they've forgot us."

Finally Gynt got the news he was waiting for and expecting and he joined Buster and Mary in the interviewing room. "We have no reason to hold you any longer," he said. "Your finger-prints are not on the hatchet, there's no sign of any blood on your clothes."

"There wouldn't be. I never went near her once I saw the blood. I should sue for false arrest."

"You can leave now, if you want. But I'd like you to help us if you can. Did you know old Sally well?"

Mary, who had been dozing, opened her eyes. "We knew she was there, is all. I found her a bit disgusting myself. Every once in a while me and Buster go to a shelter just to get a shower-bath, after we've got some clean clothes from the mission, but she never did. You think we look scruffy? He does, I know." She jerked a thumb at Konig. "Old Sally was a dirty old toe-rag, that's what she was. They said she was mental, but I don't see why she couldn't wash once in a while."

"Did you ever see any rings on her hands?"

Mary and Buster exchanged glances, but only enquiringly. Mary shook her head, answering for both of them. "As far as I can remember. I never looked at her hands if I could help it. She used to wear those woollen mitts, summer and winter, the ones with the fingers cut off."

Buster said, "She might've. I seem to remember her fingers were all puffy. They might have swollen up and covered any rings she had." He turned to Mary. "You remember Gran had the same thing? She couldn't get her wedding ring off." He turned back to Gynt. "Our mother dumped us on our Gran and fucked off. That would have been all right because Mum was a useless bitch, according to Gran. Then Gran died and we got put into a home."

"Think about this, you say Sally never took a wash?"

"Not to our knowledge."

"So you never saw her without her mitts, maybe no one did."

May said, "You got any more coffee. And another Danish?"

Konig nodded to Gynt and went off to the coffee shop. They filled in the time until his return trying to remember any street people they could remember near the house lately. The fresh coffee arrived—"they're out of Danish," Koonig said. "Then get us a donut," Mary said and Gynt nodded to send him back to the shop.

"Your friend is a cheap bastard," Mary said.

"It's not that," Gynt said. "He just doesn't like you. Now, where were we?"

Mary said, "I bin thinking. You could try the church basement." She explained. Every Saturday night some volunteers took over a downtown church basement and fed stew and pie and coffee to whoever turned up. "It's the best grub we get," Mary said. "Old Sally used to turn up regularly."

"You think if we went down there on Saturday someone might know about her?"

"You don't have to wait until Saturday. The woman who runs it took a bit of an interest in Sally, not that Sally gave a fuck for her or anyone else, but the woman sat with her sometimes and tried to talk to her while she was eating. If anyone could tell you about Sally's hands, she could."

"Lapis lazuli," Leslie Duncan said.

They were sitting in her office in the front of the house on Berkeley Street, Gynt and Konig.

"Could you describe it?" Konig got out his notebook.

"It was a piece of lapis about the size of the nail on my index finger, set around with tiny pearls, the whole thing bound in gold."

"What colour was it?"

"Lapis-coloured." Duncan grinned. "About the same colour as your tie. Did she lose it? I would have said she would have had to cut it off."

"It's possible that someone might have got it off her in that way," Gynt said.

As the possibilities flitted across Duncan's face, she said, "Is she dead? Did someone kill her for her ring?"

"She's dead, but no one killed her. It's a nasty business, but she died of natural causes."

Duncan said, "Starvation, alchoholism, exposure—the usual natural causes for a few hundred people every winter in the richest city in Canada, one of the richest countries in the world."

Konig began to suck in his breath preparatory to taking up arms, but Gynt cut him off. "Yeah?" he said. "A bit of an exaggeration, but we're used to it. The real figure is three or four. This is our turf, ma'am. We do what we can to save the ones we notice, like you do. Now I know where to find you, I'll bring them to you. Just on Saturdays, that is."

"Most of them already know about us. How nasty a business is it? Robbing a body? That kind of nasty?"

Konig said. "Cutting off a hand."

Gynt stared at Koonig until the constable looked away. Gynt looked back at Duncan whose face had gone still.

"Yes, that's nasty," she said. "Don't worry, I'm not going to faint. Look for someone with the strength to do it. A lot of these people are as weak as kittens."

"They used a hatchet," Konig said noisily.

Now Duncan flinched, the detail, the picture, forcing itself upon her. "Is that so," she said, articulating the words slowly as the images formed.

"You know anything about her?" Gynt asked. "Was she a total loser, or did she have any, whatdoyoucallem—mates, pals?"

"She was too far gone to relate to anything outside her head. She could manage her existence—I wouldn't call it a life. She operated among a few fixed points. She knew where she lived, or slept, rather, and she knew how to scavenge food, and beg for enough for her sherry, and she knew to come to our basement on Saturday night. She probably knew where to go to get the soup the mobile volunteers give out at night. The rest of the time she was a baglady, collecting rubbish and storing it. I met someone who claimed they knew her before she lost it; they said she used to be a clerk in the works department in City Hall, lived with her mother. Then she got unreliable and they moved her to sorting mail, which she was okay at, they thought, until she started to take the mail home to keep it safe overnight. Then she started hoarding it at home. The found her wandering the street one night looking for her mother who had died a few months before. At home they found a room full of the department's mail, all neatly sorted and tied in bundles. Apparently there's a brother, or was, a big deal heart surgeon here in town, and he tried to get her committed, but she disappeared and he washed his hands of her, as they say."

"You know the whole story."

"It may all be bullshit, though. All the characters in our basement have a story, a lot of them invented a long time ago. I used to talk to Sally a lot, when she was eating, trying to make myself a link with reality for her. Actually, I kind of took to her."

"Did she tell you about herself?"

"She told me to fuck off." Duncan grinned.

"That's it?"

"Every Saturday night. I'd wait until she had her dinner in front of her, then I'd sit down opposite her and say hullo and she'd say fuck off. That was it."

"You spend every Saturday night feeding these bums?" Konig asked.

"Just until nine. Then my husband comes by to take me to Pronto for dinner."

"Yeah? I've never seen you there."

Duncan laughed. "There's hope for you after all, officer."

"Now what?" Konig asked, when they were outside. "Patronising bitch," he added. "I've never been to fucking Pronto in my life. That's the one where they park your car, isn't it?"

"I think she knew that," Gynt said. "Now we go over to Church Street and find a pawnbroker with a lapis lazuli ring he just bought."

"No, no, I wouldn't buy anything off a derelict." The wispy moustache and beard surrounded his protesting mouth, making a hairy "O". "You should know better than to ask me. Where would such a person get it, I would ask myself. Legitimately, I mean. Oh, no."

"Whoever was trying to sell it might have had the idea that it was worth a lot of money. Would it be?"

"Not necessarily. Depends. I'd have to see it."

"A couple of hundred at least? Twenty? A thousand. What league are we in?"

"The hundreds."

"Okay here's a possibility. This street-person might have found it or stole it, but when he came to someone like you they wouldn't touch it, but he finds someone a bit respectable-looking, someone who runs the coffee-shop next door, say, and *this* guy brought it to you. Or might yet. You never know. So keep your eyes open, will you?"

"Can I have a description?"

Gynt handed it over the counter. "Copy it, would you?"

Konig said, "We don't know the colour."

The pawnbroker blinked, opened a case of rings, picked one out and showed it on his palm. "That's lapis. That's the colour. My birth-stone."

"How much is this worth?"

"Four hundred and fifty. Say four hundred."

"Can I borrow it for a couple of days?"

The pawnbroker jumped as if prodded. "Take it away, you mean? Out of the shop? Oh, I suppose it's safe enough with you. Let's value it properly then—I was giving you a special price—seven fifty, in case you get robbed. The insurance value. Okay?"

10

Patiently they visited all the pawnbrokers in the area, keeping them-selves entertained by also asking each one what the ring was worth. They received estimates from fifty to a thousand, depending if the pawnbroker thought the ring might be for sale.

"There's no link between those two derelicts and the hands that turned up on the landfill site," Salter said to Annie. "And no other body parts have appeared. But these are early days."

"Are they still looking?"

"They've just about given up. The contractors want the landfill site reopened, because the alternative site is twenty miles north. Mackenzie's holding them off until he gets an idea."

"Has he considered the possibility that the hands were brought to the dump site?"

"Well they didn't grow there."

"What I mean is, you've been thinking, everybody's been thinking, that someone walked up to the site one night and disposed of a pair of hands he'd chopped off a body, somewhere else. But maybe whoever it was threw the hands into a dumpster and the dumpster brought them to the site."

"Give Mackenzie credit, he thought that right at the beginning, but then he got this notion of a serial mutilator and that took precedence, so he's been looking for a torso."

"The body will turn up somewhere else, won't it?"

"They usually do."

"How would you go about finding out where the dumpster that brought the hands came from?"

Salter, interested now, thought for a moment or two, then said, "We may have screwed up already."

"How?"

"We were looking for a torso. We should have been sifting that site by hand, like archeologists, establishing where it came from. I can see the story now: 'Police destroy evidence they were searching for' followed by how the first rule of homicide cases is to preserve the integrity of the site, but we churned it into rubble. What we have to do is sift through that pit, establish a context, look at the other garbage, see if we can find the construction job the hands came from."

"You've just finished saying that you've destroyed the context."

"Right, but I'd better get to Mackenzie before he says something to the media. He's very conscious of wanting to look good right now."

"I went down to the Open Door today."

"Remind me."

"The homeless place."

"And?"

"That's it. I had a chat with the director. When he'd finished, I felt as though I'd heard about conditions in Dickens' London. Does nothing ever change?"

"No sweat, Charlie. Marinelli already thought of that. I called in to the dump site on my way to work this morning and he was talking to the cat operator. We're going to round up the truckers to see where they got the stuff they brought in around that time. Apparently it has to be booked in, every load, so we should get all the possibilities. Might be looking at a dozen investigations, though."

"They seem to be taping off the lot," Annie said. She was standing at the bedroom window watching the activity down the street. "Two cruisers and one of those so-called plain clothes' cars. If you guys really want to be anonymous, Charlie, why don't you buy the kinds of cars people actually drive?"

"We get these cheap, wholesale." Salter rolled out of bed and joined her at the window. "Well, well, well. Who'd have thought it."

"What's going on?"

"Some of the fill they dug out of Joe Wallace's basement found its way to the site on Cherry Street. Remember, they're looking for the rest of the body in all the places where the recent loads of fill came from."

"Here?"

"This is one place. Reminds me, we haven't seen Joe Wallace's girl-friend around lately, have we?"

"Don't be grotesque. Mackenzie thinks there might be a body here?"

"There's a body somewhere." Salter moved off to the bathroom.

"The digger has started up again."

Salter came back to the window and watched for a few moments. "A shovelfull at a time. This is happening at nine or ten other sites. One man on a digger and two others watching to see what he turns up."

"Don't they have any idea whose hands they might be?"

"Not a street-person, they think, and not a whatdoyoucallit—a lady. Lousy manicure job, used to work, you know."

"That rules out Joe Wallace's girl-friend."

"Coincidentally, we do have the baglady whose one hand was chopped off, but the hands we've found don't fit. So we have a pair of hands and a one-handed baglady. The deputy thinks they may be connected. He's inclined towards a serial mutilator—at least a second mutilator who got the idea from the first. Someone picking up the idea from reading about it."

"How long will they dig?"

"Long enough to know they've taken out all the loose soil. Make sure there's no head."

"No what?"

"Mackenzie's wife's idea is that whoever cut off her hands did so, like in the books, to stop us identifying her. So they probably cut off her head, too."

"How long? A couple of days?"

"Say three. They have to check that no appliances have been taken to a metal dump. You could fit a head into a washing machine."

"Pity."

"Why?"

"I was hoping you would hold things up for a couple of weeks. Give us more time. This is nice, this breathing spell."

"Us? Who is us?"

"The S.O.S. committee. Save Our Street."

"You?"

"Would that be embarrassing for you? Me being on it?"

"I don't know. I'm glad you told me. But don't start calling me a pig. This is nothing to do with us. We're just interested in corpses."

"Don't get up tight. You're nearly retired, anyway."

"I went through this with my first wife, remember? Gerry. Joined the protest movement in the sixties. While she was waving a placard outside the American Embassy I was trying to keep her mob under control."

"Not really. Not the same place."

"Yes, but not the same time."

"The things is, your wives are politically mature, or they become so by marrying you and learning about fascist pigs." She laughed.

"Fuck off. She never talked like that. There wasn't that much at stake, no kids at least, and we agreed to disagree and she moved on. As far as this scene is concerned, all I've done is overheard you and a bunch of other women on the one hand, and listened to Mackenzie on the other. The two don't seem connected except …" he pointed out the window "… by this coincidence. But what *are* you up to?"

Annie was silent, watching the street. She said suddenly, "That wife-murderer the police let go last week. What happened?"

"*Suspected* wife murderer. We didn't have enough evidence."

"Why did you arrest him?"

"Because he did it."

"So what makes you suspect someone if you don't have the evidence?"

"Possibility. Motive. Hunch. You just think he did it. It's okay to speculate, you know. And then sometimes you become positive, because your guts are doing the thinking and they are sometimes a lot more reliable than your head. So you take the next step, hoping to find the evidence, but you don't, and the prosecutor won't go ahead."

"You don't just choose a suspect and try to make the evidence fit?"

"The English phrase is 'fit him up'. No, you generally think he did it."

"There was that Indian in Winnipeg the police charged, didn't they, before they found out he was in jail the night he was supposed to be doing the killing."

"Everyone remembers that one, and brings it up all the time. He confessed, remember."

"But you do start with just a feeling sometimes."

"You have to start somewhere."

"Oh, look. Isn't that your deputy chief? There, in the street. My God, what's happened to his head?"

Salter, after a long hard look, said, "He's shaved it. He's trying to change his image. More dynamic. He wants the chief's job."

"He looks like a bouncer in a night club. What's he doing here?"

"Being seen. The media will be here any minute. We've never had him here, to the house, have we? He doesn't know where I live."

"I don't think so."

"Then stay away from the window. Keep out of sight until he leaves. Here, lie down."

11

Gynt was alone when the pawnbroker's call came through. He drove over to Church Street and parked half a block away from the store on the other side of the street. He walked along until he was opposite the pawnbroker's door and could see, in the back of the store, the shape of the owner talking to a customer. He crossed the street and entered the store.

"There's no market for lapis," the pawnbroker said, his eye on Gynt. "I could give you twenty for it just in case someone comes in and takes a fancy to it. But I might have it in the store for years."

"Twenty?" The man was tall and thin, with a fringe of beard, in his fifties, in a dark brown corduroy suit, his pant cuffs crumpling over the tops of his desert boots. Underneath his jacket he was wearing a black turtleneck sweater. "I had it estimated at Grice's in the next block. He estimated three hundred."

"Did he offer you that?"

"No, that was his valuation. He was overstocked at the moment."

"I'd value it at three hundred, too. But if you want me to *buy* it, the price is twenty."

Gynt moved close, an interested outsider, trying to get a peek at the item under discussion. It was the ring, as described by Leslie Duncan.

"A word, friend?" He showed his card.

The man smiled, frowned, then dropped the ring on the counter as if to disown it. "What's the problem?"

Gynt picked up the ring. "Thanks, Mr. Silverwood," he said, and took the man by the elbow to lead him out of the store.

The man looked at the pawnbroker then back at the detective. "Is something wrong with the ring? I bought it off a guy."

Gynt guided him to his car. "Get in," he said. When they were settled, he took out his notebook. "Now. Name?"

"What's wrong? What are you looking for?"

"Right now, your name."

"Dennis Forman."

"Where do you live?"

Forman gave his address. "Am I under arrest?"

"Don't be silly, Dennis. What do you do?"

"I'm a writer."

"That right? A proper one? A book writer?"

"More or less, yes."

"Would my wife have read any of your books? She's the reader in the family."

"I doubt it. I have a fairly specialised audience."

"Tell me one of your titles. I'll ask her."

"They're very hard to find. But why are we here, now?"

"What?"

"What do you want from me?"

"Me? Oh, yeah. Where'd this come from, Dennis?" He showed the ring on the palm of his hand.

"I picked it up somewhere. I'm not sure."

"Don't piss about. A week ago this ring was on the finger of an old baglady who is now dead. So where'd you get it?"

"I don't know anything about that. I never saw or spoke to any baglady. I bought the ring off a guy in a coffee shop on Jarvis."

"Bought it, eh? Now you remember. Not picked it up."

"Look, it's quite natural for anyone not to want to get involved with you people, so my first reaction was defensive."

"Naturally. That's very quick, Dennis. What's your second reaction? Where did you really get it? Think, now. If my partner were here he'd be shouting at you by now."

"As I said, I bought it off a man in a coffee shop."

"Which coffee shop?"

"I could take you there."

"Good. We'll go there in a minute. What was this guy's name?"

"Ah, come on, get real, officer. When you buy a hot ring you don't demand the provenance."

"Jesus, I can tell you're a writer, Dennis. No provenance, eh? What did he look like?"

"He was about my height. Dark-haired, heavy walrus moustache."

"That's a good description. Should be easy to spot. Did he seem like a rough character?"

"Did he kill her? This baglady?"

"I don't know what he did yet, but no one killed the baglady. She died of natural causes. But this is her ring and we'd like to meet your friend with the moustache. What did you give him for it? You know what it is?"

"Lapis lazuli."

"Right, I forgot. That's the sort of thing you would know. What did you give him for it?"

"Fifty dollars."

"You must have thought you were taking him."

"I knew I was taking a chance."

"You were, indeed. He might have killed someone for it. How come a guy like you is fencing? What time were you in the coffee shop? Before or after midnight?"

"After."

"Why? What's a book-writer doing in a Jarvis Street coffee shop after midnight."

"I was doing research."

"That explains it. Real down and dirty, eh? What were the other customers like? Lotsa local colour?"

"Cab-drivers and prostitutes, mainly. And cops."

"Which kind were you looking for? I took a writer around the area once. I checked out a break-and-enter in his house and we got chatting and I offered to show him my world. He was very keen, but it turned out to be a disappointment for him. One point I parked outside a biker's clubhouse on Queen Street—you know, the kind with a brick wall in front so you can't ram them. Well, three of the inhabitants came out on the sidewalk and tried to frighten us, stare at us, make us go away. But I knew them and they knew me, and I started to tell this writer about each of them, what they'd done that we knew about, names, records, but he just said he wanted to go home. He was frightened. You couldn't blame him. Animals some of those people. So what time were you in this coffee shop. Around one?"

"More like two."

"Two o'clock in the morning in a coffee shop on Jarvis street and a guy comes in and tries to sell you a ring. No, he *does* sell you a ring. Didn't any of the cops you mentioned watch? I could find them, help with the ID."

"They had probably gone by that point."

"That's why he came in, see? That would be it. So you gave him fifty, and he skeddaddled. Notice anything else about him? Or anyone else in the shop? Did the waitress look at him?"

"There were just a couple of other street people. I remember them because they seemed like husband and wife, and I'd made a mental note of them. But they were just after a free coffee, they didn't stay."

Gynt said, "Still, this could be my lucky day. These two. Middle-aged? About five feet tall?"

"You know them?"

"We've been introduced. Let's go for a ride."

"That the coffee shop? Let's go in."

At the counter, Gynt established his identity. "We're looking for a man ... You describe him, Dennis."

"About my height." Forman raised his hand level with this head to make sure the counterhand, a Chinese woman in her late thirties, understood. "Dark-haired with a big moustache." Forman drew a moustache on his own face with a finger.

The woman turned and fiddled with the coffee-maker. "I don't see no one like that," she said. "Not come in today." She pushed a hank of hair under her cap and moved along the counter to serve someone.

"You've frightened her," Gynt said. "Let's move on. I can come back later."

As they were leaving, a hoop-shaped old man by the door said, "I've seen the guy. He stays around here somewhere." He strained to move his body into a position so he could see them. "He's in and out."

"You know where he lives?"

The old man gestured at the window. "Out there."

"You know his name?"

"Joey. Or Eddie."

"Thanks."

"What about a dollar for the information?"

"Give the man a loonie," Gynt said to Forman. "I'm not allowed to."

They left the coffee shop, drove two blocks and turned along Dundas until they came to Sackville. Gynt pulled up outside the derelict house. "Wait there," he said to Forman and disappeared inside the house. He emerged after a few minutes with Buster and Mary, and signalled Forman to approach. "These two?" he asked.

"Yes. Yes. You were in the coffee shop on Jarvis two nights ago, weren't you?"

"I already asked them that. They go there every night around that time."

"There's two women work nights who've always got a donut and a cup of coffee for us," Buster said.

"Describe the guy," Gynt said.

Foreman did so, this time adding details.

"Ticker," Buster said. "Ticker. I don't know his other name."

"You know where he is?"

"In the neighbourhood. Not far away."

"If you see him, tell one of the cops on the street, would you? Tell him to call me." He produced a card.

"Hey, hey. Look at this, Mary. A card." He looked up at Gynt. "If I keeled over and they found this on me would they think you was me?"

"You're too short," Gynt said. "They'd be suspicious that you'd done for me."

"Him?" Mary jeered. "Him? Do for you? That's a good'un."

"Shut up," Buster said, punching her hard away from them, "Or I'll do for *you*."

"You fucker." She came at him with hands bent like grappling hooks.

Gynt grabbed Buster by the collar and threw him across the sidewalk, against the fence, then turned to prevent Molly from getting at him. "Count fifty, Mary," he said. "Give me time to get out of here. Then kill him."

But it was over already. Buster leaned against the fence grinning and Mary slid down until she was sitting on the edge of the curb. "Give us a coupla bucks," she pleaded.

Gynt threw her a loonie and got in the car. "You need a ride?" he asked Forman, through the window.

"To a subway station?"

"Get in."

12

The call came the next day. Ticker, the patrolman reported, was four yards away. The description was perfect.

"Stay with him," Gynt said. "Don't touch him unless he looks like disappearing."

"He looks pretty stationary. There. He's stopped outside The Gap."

"I'll be right over."

"Ticker," Gynt said, a few minutes later. "I've got a couple of men watching us just in case you try to run away. I want you to walk quietly across the road and into the police station in the subway stop. Okay? A little chat. Don't panic. Don't try and run. That's the boy. Off we go. I'm right behind you."

In the station house Gynt said, "Hands is what we want to know about, Ticker. One hand specifically. Where is it?"

"I don't know what you're talking about. What hand?"

"The hand that had the ring on it. The blue ring. The one you cut off the body."

"Jesus. I never cut off no finger."

"*Hand*, Ticker."

"Nor no hand. Jesus. You must want Murphy."

"You had the ring, Ticker."

"I got it off Murphy."

"He gave it to you?"

"I took it off him, in a fight. He owed me. When I saw the ring, I took it off him. There was never no hand or finger. Jesus."

"Where can we find Murphy? Where was he when you took the ring off him?"

"In Allen Gardens, but he sleeps in a car, a wreck on Lupin Street off Parliament."

"Would he be there now?"

"Could be."

"Let's visit him."

They had to wait for two hours until Murphy shuffled home, a sack of rubbish he had scavenged from garbage cans on his back.

"I found old Sally like that. Dead. I didn't kill her."

"But you did cut her hand off."

"Someone else would've, if I didn't. It looked like a good ring."

"Where's the hand?"

Murphy led them to a corner of the yard where he dug into a patch of soft soil. About a foot down he came to the hand, with one finger missing. Gynt, who had been anticipating the sight, quickly opened the plastic evidence bag and turned away as Murphy dropped the hand in. "I didn't kill her," he said.

"Nobody did. But you can't go around cutting off people's hands just because they've got something you want …" He dialled and called for a squad car. "I'm bringing in a couple of guys," he said.

"Me? Why me?" Ticker asked.

Gynt turned to Murphy. "Did you tell him where you got the ring?"

"Sure I told him."

"But it's your fingerprints on the fucking hatchet," Ticker said, furious.

"You're still some kind of accessory," Gynt said.

"To what? Accessory to what? What have I done?"

"Oh, Christ knows. Get in the car, both of you. COME ON, FOR CHRIST'S SAKE!"

"No doubt is there?"

Gynt was talking to the head of the hospital unit that prepared cadavers for teaching purposes. Before the technician could reply, he added, "Could we move to somewhere else. Like among the living."

"Gets to you, does it? I thought you dealt with corpses all the time."

"Would you believe that I've only seen two corpses in thirteen years on homicide?" He glanced warily around the room, then pointed to a jar. "What was his problem?"

"Syphilis."

"Yeah. Pre-penicillin, I guess. Let's go into your office, at least."

They left the jar-lined room and Gynt breathed in deeply, searching for a purer air. "So that's her hand?" he said.

"It fits old Sally perfectly."

"Now what? Use her for science?"

The technician shook his head. "Sally has too much identity now. We prefer anonymous cadavers. We'll send her off in the next batch."

"Bury her?"

"Cremate. We have a multiple ceremony periodically with a non-denominational service. We just ask God to take them back and look after them." The technician spoke quietly, meaning it.

Gynt said, after a respectful pause, "You don't have a spare cadaver, do you? One without any hands. See, we've got another pair of hands we can't identify."

"Careless lot, aren't you." The technician smiled. "It'll turn up."

Annie said, "We are going in front of the Municipal Board next week. Would you come along if you can get away? If you have time?"

"I'll make time. Sure I will. But what can I do? I'm no expert. It's not even my street."

They were talking in the young man's apartment, sixteen floors up, looking down at the hole that had been Joe Wallace's house.

"I know. It's good of you to come. We need bodies. The idea is if a lot of neighbours turn up the media might take more notice and we'd get some publicity. It works at city council committee hearings. The size of the crowd is an index to how important the issue is, and if you get a TV camera, then the councillors like to be seen, too. People power. It helps the politicians make up their minds which side they are on. But don't lose any work time. What do you do?"

"I'm a customs clerk."

"Don't worry if you can't make it, then."

"Of course I'll make it. I'd do anything to help Mrs. Micklewhite." This was a passionate outburst, and Annie waited for some explanation. "She's been fantastically good to me, personally. When the landlord jacked up my rent she organised all the tenants, showed us how to protest."

"She doesn't live in the block, does she? I thought …"

"That's the point. There was nothing in it for her. She just heard of the situation and came over to see if she could help. She knew all the right things to do. From that we struck up a good friendship. Sounds strange to you, perhaps, a person of my age being friends with a fifty-five year old woman, but we are. We often have coffee together if we bump into each other near Timothy's. She's amazing. And it's not all one-sided. I look after her cat when she's away, and I'm available when she wants something moved or lifted. If I were handier with electricity and stuff I could do more. So there's your answer. When Mrs Micklewhite got involved with that tear-down, I got involved, too."

Salter looked up from the paper. "They found the hand they were looking for."

"Where?"

"Buried in someone's yard."

"What's the story?"

"Don't get upset. Someone found her, old Sally as she's known as, dead in her hut, and went for a valuable-looking ring."

"What do you mean—'went for'? Oh no, don't tell me. How did they get caught?"

"They tried to sell her ring, and one of our people was tipped off and he followed the trail back to a character named Murphy, who's admitted taking the ring."

"Not to killing her, though."

"No. We're charging him with defiling a body, or some such."

"What about the other two hands that turned up? I see the construction down the street has started up again. Did they find the body the hands belonged to?"

"No, but they decided they had searched most of the sites pretty carefully including Joe Wallace's house. All the contractors have been pressing to be allowed to resume. They want to get their jobs covered in before the snow flies. Once the guy down the street has got a shell up he can cover it in plastic and put in a temporary heater to finish the inside."

"There's still the Municipal Board hearing to go."

"Are you really involved?"

"I don't know what I think yet, so I'm staying with it until I do. I'm pretty sure already that in a situation like ours, the neighbours ought to have some say in a project that affects their lives, the way it will change the street and how it looks."

"You will keep me out of it, though, won't you."

13

"There's only four days left before they have to decide," Mackenzie said. "I haven't heard a thing yet. You still think I've got a shot at it?"

In the last week Mackenzie had abandoned all pretence that he was interested in anything other than the chief's job.

Salter said, for the fifth or sixth time, "The odds are in your favour. If they choose an inside man." He had learned from a neighbour who was in the business of head hunting executives just what probably lay behind the interviews the commission had conducted to see what the senior heads felt. They were not, said his source, looking for opinions about the interviewee's colleagues, but using that as an excuse to get a look at the interviewee's own suitability for the job. From this and a few other hints, Salter had come to the conclusion, or rather reinforced his private conviction, that Mackenzie had no chance, that he was already employed to the limit of his capability.

"They have to choose an inside man, don't they? They'll have the union on their backs."

"That could cut both ways," Salter said. "Having the union on your side, I mean."

Mackenzie said, "How's this case of the missing torso? Do you know?"

Salter understood that Mackenzie was casting around for anything that might make him look good in the media.

"Officer Gynt got a call from the hospital morgue before you came in this morning. They may have something on it."

"They've got a torso?"

"No, but someone thinks they might have recognised the hands."

"Recognised the hands? Recognised the hands? How? They're just hands, aren't they?" Mackenzie was ready to be angry at anything.

"I told Gynt if he has any news to bring it here first."

At eleven-thirty Gynt appeared, accompanying a woman in her forties, a woman who looked familiar because she had the striking looks of a fashion model, every fashion model.

"Sir, this is Rosalind Filer. She came forward this morning … would you take over, Mrs. Filer?

The woman stepped up to the desk and drew from a large brown envelope a pencil drawing of a pair of hands. At the same time Gynt, indulging the theatrical, took from a similar envelope a photograph of the hands found at the dump.

Mackenzie looked from drawing to photograph and back again. He shrugged. "They look alike, sure, but so would a lot of others. They could both be my wife's."

Mrs. Filer shook her head. "I saw the hands in the morgue." She drew her finger along the edge of the drawing. "I saw the photograph this morning on Dr. Soame's desk, but I wasn't sure until I looked again."

"How can you be so sure?"

"When you draw something, you look at it much harder than you normally look at things around you. When you draw hands, you own them. They become yours. Those are my hands." She began to get ready to leave, the interview over as far as she was concerned.

"Where did you see them?"

"In the morgue. I work there a lot, drawing anatomy, heads mostly."

"Jesus."

"When I drew those hands they weren't, well, … here." She took out another drawing from the envelope, this time of a sketch of a middled-aged woman, with curly fair hair to her shoulders, hair in which there one or two flowers appeared to be entangled, whether real or artificial was not clear. Her hands were crossed over her naked stomach. She appeared to be sleeping. "I called her The Lady of Shalott. That's who she reminded me of."

Mackenzie waited for more.

"It's a poem," Salter said.

"More important, it's a painting by someone I'm interested in," Mrs. Filer said. "John Waterhouse. He painted her like that, but with clothes on, of course."

"When did you see her? And draw these pictures?"

"About ten days ago."

"She was just like this?"

"Yes. I think one of the medical students arranged the pose before I drew her. But her hands were so distinguished I had to do those on their own."

"Were they attached then?"

"Yes."

"Then what happened?" This to Gynt.

Gynt said the record showed that she was cremated. "Dr. Soames would like a word with you."

"Call him."

They waited while Mackenzie was connected, and listened to his replies. "How many people would have had access?" he asked finally. "I see. Someone will be down right away. Don't let anyone go home." He put down the telephone, and started to speak, then looked at Mrs. Filer. "You already know the worst, I guess. Somebody in that morgue cut her hands off, it seems. It's what they do there. She arrived marked for the anatomy students. Apparently she lived by herself. When she died she left a note saying she wished to be returned to the elements, or some such. This was interpreted as wanting to leave her body to science until a friend who had been away turned up and said she meant cremated and her ashes scattered in the garden. Her friend said being cut up was the last thing she would have wanted. This friend made a fuss and the woman was cremated, and no one noticed any—er—discrepancy at the time. Normally these cremations take place in batches, but having nearly made one mistake they didn't want to make another, so they cremated her right away. Gynt, that your name?—get on down there and start the investigation. Tell Marinelli what you're up to. Poor, crazy, lady."

"The world still wants to know about the hands, sir."

"But all this Lady in the Lake stuff?"

"Just say someone in the morgue finally identified her."

"Right. But hold on to it for a few days. There's no rush. I don't think I want any credit for this."

"You know what?" Salter said. "That guy you met in the apartment block across the street. The one helping those women …"

Annie cut in. "He did it, didn't he?"

"How the hell did you know?"

"I just guessed. Just as you spoke. Did he kill her?"

"All he did was throw the hands into Joe Wallace's basement. He thought they would find them next day, but no one noticed them until they got to the dump site."

"Where did he get the …?"

"Idea? From the story of that baglady in the newspaper. Mackenzie was right about that."

"I was going to say, the hands."

"Pal of his in the morgue. Your friend had been telling his pal about how he'd like to halt the excavation to help his friend, Mrs. Micklewhite, and his pal came up with this idea. Apparently this pal is the last one to deal with bodies that are being cremated, so he's the only one who might get away with it. If it hadn't been for the artist we'd never have known where to look." Salter explained who the artist was. "How did you know?" he asked Annie.

"The lad just seemed strange from the start so I realise now I have been trying to 'fit him up' for it all along. He seemed a little unbalanced."

Salter nodded at the window. "The frame is up for the new house. Everybody happy with it?"

"There's nothing to object to."

"Are you still campaigning for neighbourhood preservation?"

"Oh, sure. But I've got interested in other things. I went down to that camp on Cherry Street you told me about, and I gave the Open Door Centre the cheque, delivered it by hand so I could get another look at the inside. I talked to the director again. I came away feeling a little selfish. This neighbourhood preservation is fine, but it's very me-ish, isn't it? I mean even the women—who I admire, by the way, you don't see too many husbands tramping the streets collecting signatures—they aren't up in arms about anybody else's neighbourhood. In the end, it's our street that matters. What about the people who don't have a neighbourhood, or a street, all sixty thousand of them, wandering the city, night after night."

"What's on your mind?"

"I want to think about them, that's all. Just think about them."

"You can tell me what you're thinking. I'll be home."

"You've finally retired, haven't you?"

"How do you know *that?*"

"A gut feeling. When?"

"Today. Two weeks notice. Mackenzie didn't get the job. Nor did Haskell. It went to an outsider. So Mackenzie didn't have to resign, but he's going to be depressing to live with."

"Let's have a holiday."

"What about Seth and Angus, and significant others?"

"I think they'd enjoy having a holiday, too."

"With us?"

"From us. Just for a couple of weeks."

An Eric Wright Checklist

Charlie Salter Novels:

The Night the Gods Smiled. London: Collins, 1983; New York: Scribner, 1983.

Smoke Detector. London: Collins, 1984; New York: Scribner, 1985.

Death in the Old Country. London: Collins, 1985; New York: Scribner, 1985.

A Single Death. London: Collins, 1986; New York: Scribner, 1986 (as *The Man Who Changed His Name*).

A Body Surrounded by Water. London: Collins, 1987; New York: Scribner, 1988.

A Question of Murder. London: Collins, 1988; New York: Scribner, 1988.

A Sensitive Case. London: Collins, 1990; New York: Scribner, 1990.

Final Cut. London: HarperCollins, 1991; New York: Scribner, 1991.

A Fine Italian Hand. London: HarperCollins, 1992; New York: Scribner, 1992.

Death by Degrees. London: HarperCollins, 1993; New York: Scribner, 1993.

The Last Hand. Toronto: Dundarn, 2001; New York: St. Martin's Minotaur, 2002.

Mel Pickett Novels:

Buried in Stone. London: HarperCollins, 1995; New York: Scribner, 1996.

Death of a Hired Man. New York: Thomas Dunne Books, 2001.

Lucy Trimble Novels:

Death of a Sunday Writer.   London: HarperCollins, 1996; Woodstock: Foul Play, 2001.
Death on the Rocks.   New York: St. Martin's, 1999; Toronto: Dundurn, 2001.

Other Books:

Moodie's Tale (A Comic Novel).   Toronto: Key Porter, 1994.
Always Give a Penny to a Blind Man (A Memoir).   Toronto: Key Porter, 1999.
The Kidnapping of Rosie Dawn (A Joe Barley Mystery).   Santa Barbara: J. Daniel/Perseverance Press, 2000.
A Killing Climate: The Collected Short Mysteries.   Norfolk: Crippen & Landru, 2003.

Short Stories:

"The Cure," *Fingerprints*, ed. Beverley Beetham-Endersby, 1984.
"Jackpot," as "Looking for an Honest Man," *Cold Blood*, ed. Peter Sellers, 1987.
"Hephaestus," *Cold Blood II* ed. Peter Sellers, 1989.
"Kaput," *Mistletoe Mysteries*, ed. Charlotte MacLeod, 1989.
"Twins," *A Suit of Diamonds*, ed. Elizabeth Walter, 1990.
"Two in the Bush," *Christmas Stalkings*, ed. Charlotte MacLeod, 1991.
"The Lady From Prague," *Cold Blood IV*, ed. Peter Sellers, 1992.
"Licensed Guide," *Criminal Shorts*, ed. Howard Engel and Eric Wright, 1992.
"The Duke," *2nd Culprit*, ed. Liza Cody and Michael Z. Lewin, 1993.
"Duty Free," *Cold Blood V*, ed. Peter Sellers, 1994.
"The Boatman," as "Start With a Tree," *Paper Guitar*, ed. Karen Muhallen, 1995.
"Bedbugs," *Das Magazin* (Zurich), April 26, 1996.
"One of a Kind," *The Ottawa Citizen*, July 5, 1998.

"An Irish Jig," *The Globe and Mail,* December 22, 2001.

"Caves of Ice," *Ellery Queen's Mystery Magazine,* March 2002.

"The Lady of Shalott (A Charlie Salter novella)," *A Killing Climate,* 2003.

"Lodgings for the Night," separate pamphlet to accompany the limited edition of *A Killing Climate,* 2003.

A Killing Climate

A Killing Climate: The Collected Mystery Stories by Eric Wright is set in Baskerville and Baskerville Old Style, and printed on 60 pound Glatfelter Supple Opaque acid-free paper. The cover and dust jacket painting is by Barbara Mitchell and the design is by Deborah Miller. The first edition was printed in two forms – trade softcover and two hundred twenty-five copies sewn in cloth, signed and numbered by the author. Each of the clothbound copies includes a separate pamphlet, *Lodgings for the Night* by Eric Wright. The book was printed and bound by Thomson-Shore, Inc, Dexter, Michigan.

A Killing Climate was published in August 2003 by Crippen & Landru Publishers, Inc.,Norfolk, Virginia.

CRIPPEN & LANDRU, PUBLISHERS
P. O. Box 9315
Norfolk, VA 23505
E-mail: info@crippenlandru.com; toll-free 877 622-6656
Web: www.crippenlandru.com

Crippen & Landru publishes first edition short-story collections by important detective and mystery writers. The following books are currently (August 2003) in print; see our website for full details:

The McCone Files by Marcia Muller. 1995. Trade softcover, $17.00.

Diagnosis: Impossible, The Problems of Dr. Sam Hawthorne by Edward D. Hoch. 1996. Trade softcover, $15.00.

Who Killed Father Christmas? And Other Unseasonable Demises by Patricia Moyes. 1996. Signed unnumbered cloth overrun copies, $30.00. Trade softcover, $16.00.

My Mother, The Detective: The Complete "Mom" Short Stories, by James Yaffe. 1997. Trade softcover, $15.00.

In Kensington Gardens Once . . . by H.R.F. Keating. 1997. Trade softcover, $12.00.

Do Not Exceed the Stated Dose by Peter Lovesey. 1998. Trade softcover, $16.00.

Renowned Be Thy Grave; Or, The Murderous Miss Mooney by P.M. Carlson. 1998. Trade softcover, $16.00.

Carpenter and Quincannon, Professional Detective Services by Bill Pronzini. 1998. Trade softcover, $16.00.

All Creatures Dark and Dangerous by Doug Allyn. 1999. Trade softcover, $16.00.

Famous Blue Raincoat: Mystery Stories by Ed Gorman. 1999. Signed unnumbered cloth overrun copies, $30.00. Trade softcover, $17.00.

The Tragedy of Errors and Others by Ellery Queen. 1999. Trade softcover, $16.00.

McCone and Friends by Marcia Muller. 2000. Trade softcover, $16.00.

Challenge the Widow Maker and Other Stories of People in Peril by Clark Howard. 2000. Trade softcover, $16.00.

The Velvet Touch: Nick Velvet Stories by Edward D. Hoch. 2000. Trade softcover, $16.00.

Fortune's World by Michael Collins. 2000. Trade softcover, $16.00.

Long Live the Dead: Tales from Black Mask by Hugh B. Cave. 2000. Trade softcover, $16.00.

Tales Out of School: Mystery Stories by Carolyn Wheat. 2000. Trade softcover, $16.00.

Stakeout on Page Street and Other DKA Files by Joe Gores. 2000. Trade softcover, $16.00.

Strangers in Town: Three Newly Discovered Mysteries by Ross Macdonald, edited by Tom Nolan. 2001. Trade softcover, $15.00.

The Celestial Buffet and Other Morsels of Murder by Susan Dunlap. 2001. Trade softcover, $16.00.

Kisses of Death: A Nathan Heller Casebook by Max Allan Collins. 2001. Trade softcover, $17.00.

The Old Spies Club and Other Intrigues of Rand by Edward D. Hoch. 2001. Signed unnumbered cloth overrun copies, $32.00. Trade softcover, $17.00.

Adam and Eve on a Raft: Mystery Stories by Ron Goulart. 2001. Signed, numbered clothbound, $42.00. Trade softcover, $17.00.

The Sedgemoor Strangler and Other Stories of Crime by Peter Lovesey. 2001. Trade softcover, $17.00.

The Reluctant Detective and Other Stories by Michael Z. Lewin. 2001. Signed, numbered clothbound, $42.00. Trade softcover, $17.00.

The Lost Cases of Ed London by Lawrence Block. 2001. Published only in signed, numbered clothbound, $42.00.

Nine Sons: Collected Mysteries by Wendy Hornsby. 2002. Trade softcover, $16.00.

The Newtonian Egg and Other Cases of Rolf le Roux by Peter Godfrey. 2002. [A "Crippen & Landru Lost Classic"]. Trade softcover, $15.00.

The Curious Conspiracy and Other Crimes by Michael Gilbert. 2002. Signed, numbered clothbound, $42.00. Trade softcover, $17.00.

Murder, Mystery and Malone by Craig Rice, edited by Jeffrey Marks. 2002. [A "Crippen & Landru Lost Classic"]. Cloth, $27.00. Trade softcover, $17.00.

The Sleuth of Baghdad by Charles B. Child. 2002. [A "Crippen & Landru Lost Classic"]. Cloth, $27.00. Trade softcover, $17.00.

The 13 Culprits by Georges Simenon, translated by Peter Schulman. 2002. Unnumbered cloth overrun copies, $30.00. Trade softcover, $16.00.

Hildegarde Withers: Uncollected Riddles by Stuart Palmer. 2002. [A "Crippen & Landru Lost Classic"]. Cloth, $29.00. Trade softcover, $19.00.

The Dark Snow and Other Stories by Brendan DuBois. 2002. Signed, numbered clothbound, $42.00. Trade softcover, $17.00.

The Spotted Cat and Other Stories from Inspector Cockrill's Casebook by Christianna Brand, edited by Tony Medawar. 2002. [A "Crippen & Landru Lost Classic"]. Cloth, $29.00. Trade softcover. $19.00.

Jo Gar's Casebook by Raoul Whitfield, edited by Keith Alan Deutsch, [Published with Black Mask Press]. 2002. Trade softcover, $20.00.

Come Into My Parlor: Tales From Detective Fiction Weekly by Hugh B. Cave. 2002. Signed, numbered clothbound, $42.00. Trade softcover, $17.00.

The Iron Angel and Other Tales of the Gypsy Sleuth by Edward D. Hoch. 2003. Signed, numbered clothbound, $42.00. Trade softcover, $17.00.

Marksman and Other Stories by William Campbell Gault, edited by Bill Pronzini. 2003. [A "Crippen & Landru Lost Classic"]. Trade softcover. $19.00.

Cuddy – Plus One by Jeremiah Healy. 2003. Signed, numbered clothbound, $43.00. Trade softcover, $18.00.

Karmesin, The World's Greatest Criminal – or Most Outrageous Liar by Gerald Kersh, edited by Paul Duncan. 2003. [A "Crippen & Landru Lost Classic"]. Cloth, $27.00. Trade softcover, $17.00.

Problems Solved by Bill Pronzini and Barry N. Malzberg. 2003. Signed, numbered clothbound, $42.00. Trade softcover, $16.00.

The Complete Curious Mr. Tarrant by C. Daly King. 2003. [A "Crippen & Landru Lost Classic"]. Cloth, $29.00. Trade softcover, $19.00.

A Killing Climate: The Collected Mystery Stories by Eric Wright. 2003. Signed, numbered clothbound, $42.00. Trade softcover, $17.00.

The Pleasant Assassin and Other Cases of Dr. Basil Willing by Helen McCloy. [A "Crippen & Landru Lost Classic"]. Cloth, $27.00. Trade softcover, $17.00.

Lucky Dip and Other Stories by Liza Cody. Signed, numbered clothbound, $42.00. Trade softcover, $17.00.

Forthcoming Short-Story Collections

Kill the Umpire: The Calls of Ed Gorgon by Jon L. Breen.

Murder – All Kinds by William L. DeAndrea. "Lost Classics" series.

Suitable for Hanging by Margaret Maron.

The Avenging Chance: Roger Sheringham's Casebook by Anthony Berkeley, edited by Tony Medawar and Arthur Robinson. "Lost Classics" series.

Murders and Other Confusions: The Chronicles of Susana, Lady Appleton, Sixteenth-Century Gentlewoman, Herbalist, and Sleuth by Kathy Lynn Emerson.

The Adventure of the Murdered Moths and Other Radio Mysteries by Ellery Queen.

Sleuth's Alchemy by Gladys Mitchell, edited by Nicholas Fuller. "Lost Classics" series.

Banner Deadlines by Joseph Commings, edited by Robert Adey. "Lost Classics Series."

Tough As Nails by Frederick Nebel, edited by Rob Preston. Published with Black Mask Press.

The Couple Next Door: Collected Short Mysteries by Margaret Millar, edited by Tom Nolan. "Lost Classics Series."

The Mankiller of Poojeegai and Other Mysteries by Walter Satterthwait.

14 Slayers by Paul Cain, edited by Max Allan Collins and Lynn Myers. Published with Black Mask Press.

Hoch's Ladies by Edward D. Hoch.

Murder! 'Orrible Murder! by Amy Myers.

A Pocketful of Noses: Stories of One Ganelon or Another by James Powell.

Murder – Ancient and Modern by Edward Marston.

More Things Impossible: The Second Casebook of Dr. Sam Hawthorne by Edward D. Hoch.

You'll Die Laughing by Norbert Davis, edited by Bill Pronzini. Published with Black Mask Press.

Dr. Poggioli: Criminologist by T. S. Stribling, edited by Arthur Vidro. "Lost Classics" series.

Slot-Machine Kelly, Early Private Eye Stories by Michael Collins.

The Evidence of the Sword: Mysteries by Rafael Sabatini, edited by Jesse Knight. "Lost Classics" series.

The Confessions of Owen Keane by Terence Faherty.

Who Was Guilty?: Three Dime Novels by Phillip S. Warne, edited by Marlena Bremseth. "Lost Classics" series.

The Grandfather Rastin Mysteries by Lloyd Biggle, Jr. "Lost Classics" series.

Francis Quarles: Detective by Julian Symons, edited by John Cooper. "Lost Classics" series.

SUBSCRIPTIONS

Crippen & Landru offers discounts to individuals and institutions who place Subscriptions for all its forthcoming publications, either the Regular Series or the Lost Classics or (preferably) both. Collectors can thereby guarantee receiving limited editions, and readers won't miss any favorite stories. Standing Order Subscribers receive a specially commissioned story in a deluxe edition as a gift at the end of the year. Please write or e-mail (info@crippenlandru.com) for more details.